PRAISE FOR JULIE SHIGEKUNI

"Artfully evocative... The lesson one takes from [Shigekuni's book] is time-honored in every culture."

— *THE NEW YORK TIMES*

"This is an intense and introspective book. Shigekuni's well-crafted first novel succeeds in engaging the reader in its exploration of a universal theme."

— *SAN FRANCISCO CHRONICLE*

"A family saga on an intimate scale... Shigekuni evokes with skill and sensitivity the many colorations of unhappiness that tinge these interwoven lives."

— *BOSTON GLOBE*

"An accomplished novelist, Shigekuni tells a powerful story of the strength of family and the creation of identity... A first novel that betokens a promising career indeed."

— *ATLANTA JOURNAL-CONSTITUTION*

"Julie Shigekuni explores both the stories that connect us and the silences that keep us apart. This graceful and compassionate novel reminds us how we can never fully know the people in our lives, including (and maybe even especially) ourselves."

— GAYLE BRANDEIS, AUTHOR OF *DELTA GIRLS*

"With delicate detail and cold-blooded precision, Julie Shigekuni tells this story of shattered family emotions that is at once disturbing and beautiful."

— DAVID WONG LOUIE, AUTHOR OF *THE BARBARIANS ARE COMING*

The Unnamed Press
P.O. Box 411272
Los Angeles, CA 90041

Published in North America by The Unnamed Press.

1 3 5 7 9 10 8 6 4 2

ISBN: 978-1- 939419-98- 9

Library of Congress Control Number: 2016917169

This book is distributed by Publishers Group West

Cover design & typeset by Jaya Nicely

IN
PLAIN
VIEW

A NOVEL

JULIE SHIGEKUNI

The Unnamed Press
Los Angeles, CA

FOR VALERIE
ROMEO & NAUGHTY CHULA

I don't understand how a woman can leave the house without fixing herself up a little—if only out of politeness. And then, you never know, maybe that's the day she has a date with destiny. And it's best to be as pretty as possible for destiny.

—COCO CHANEL

PROLOGUE
IN PLAIN VIEW

Early that morning she woke to the sound of her father's stockinged feet brushing against the tatami mats as he hurried down the hall that led away from her mother's room next door to where she slept. With her eyes closed she'd listened, visualizing his large hands as they collected his even larger-sized shoes from the cabinet. The streetlamp outside her window was the only source of light when the sliding door opened, then shut, indicating his departure. Later, with the sun cresting the sky and the familiar sound of the television announcing the return of her happy life, she joined her mother for breakfast. As usual, her mother served tea with the morning meal, which she sipped while her mother tended to her futon. From the other side of the wall, she could hear the thump the dusting stick made, which she knew meant Tuesday, the day the futon needed to air. Once the futon had been stored, her mother smiled at her from the doorframe, and she followed her to the main sitting room to pray.

The small shrine held a beautiful and perfect miniature world, its black lacquered doors opening to a shining gold Buddha who sat peacefully against the back wall. As her mother prayed, she watched the steam rising off the bowl of rice placed before the Buddha. She'd eaten the same rice with fish for dinner the night before, and again for breakfast with egg and pickled vegetables.

Nothing out of the ordinary had happened, nothing to signal danger. Her mother had lifted the gate latch, then turned back to secure it before taking her hand. She'd worn her winter gloves, which her mother had brought out again after having stored them away, because the cold weather had returned. A frost covered parts of the footpath, creating patterns of ice for them to sidestep. Her mother had used the word "disgrace" to describe the fallen petals that dotted the walkway, making it slippery. The plum blossoms had been ruined, but in their place the closed pink buds of cherry blossoms had started to show. The ancient trees stood along the still-deserted path, just as they had for hundreds of years. Her mother had told her about the history of the park. She was fond of the trees and had once been lucky enough to unfurl the tight bud of a cherry blossom between her fingers.

As they walked, light filtered down through gray, almost silvery clouds. Hanging low along the horizon, the half-moon seemed to be playing a game. It hid behind the branches of the fruit trees before reappearing. They had just entered the park grounds and passed the child's favorite stone statue of a dog when a small white van stopped and the driver got out. Her mother pulled her hand close to her body and held it there momentarily, then released it with a slight tug. "*Matte.*" She cautioned the child to wait where she stood before walking ahead to greet the driver.

The side of the van hid the driver so that only his head and the bottoms of his pant legs were exposed. The incongruity of this fractured image reminded her of a wooden picture puzzle her father had given her. The puzzle man came with several expressions and clothing items, and each segment could be changed to suit your mood. But in this case the man's face had been turned away and the van door had obstructed the torso and the upper part of the legs.

The weatherworn face of a neighbor soon replaced the puzzle image. It was Ichinose-san, calling out to her, his steps quickening as he approached.

"Why are you trembling?" he asked, squeezing her gloved fingers together in his strong hands. "You mustn't stand here by yourself."

Grasping her forearm, he ushered her along the path she'd walked with her mother, leaving her at the police kiosk at the entrance to the park.

The desk workers stopped what they were doing and looked up when the tall man entered. As he made his way through the crowd the child mouthed the word "stranger." She hadn't comprehended at first that it was her father, noting only a well-dressed man, taller by a head than anyone standing around him, his thick black hair pushed to one side. He did not look familiar, but she recognized the iris-blue-tinted shirt her mother had taken from its paper wrapping and placed in a stack with the others inside his black lacquered dresser. Each drawer held a different clothing item, which she recalled from top to bottom as she waited for him to find her behind the waist-high counter.

He repeated the word her mother had used, but this time in the form of a question: *"Matte?"*

His expression changed from expectant to worried as she searched for something more to offer him. She knew what he was asking for, and she wished she could satisfy him with an answer that would lead them both to her mother. She'd stood waiting, as she'd been instructed to do, her hands clasped in front of her as they still were. "A man stopped to ask directions."

"What did he look like?"

The picture puzzle image appeared again, and she tried to banish it from her mind. She'd seen close-cropped hair that seemed to signify a man, but she was no longer certain even of that. The door to the van had opened, and through the rectangular window she'd seen a navy sport coat and, at the bottom, sticking out beneath the door, a pair of shiny brown shoes.

Concern etched itself into her father's face and she pitied him. How could her mother have just disappeared? More important, why had she let go of her mother's hand? Why had her mother not wanted her to go along? For her father's sake, she thought through the scenario until her head began to throb: maybe she'd gotten it wrong. Her mother would have resisted. Her mother would never have allowed herself to be separated from her. How could she, being right there, not have perceived a struggle?

But the answer was simply that there had been no struggle. The van had sped off as she'd waited, alone under the boughs of the fruit trees, transfixed by the sight of the half-moon hovering over the high wall.

She'd waited, believing only later how lucky she'd been to have her childhood intact, that vanished period of innocence and trust. She'd spend years afterward judging the motivations of the adults around her, unable to find among them a reasonable substitute for the care she'd received from her mother.

Of course the story would change as she reconstructed what had happened. Events she'd once assumed to be factual might really have just been remnants of an imperfect memory. But the feeling that encapsulated her childhood didn't change; the first nearly five years of her life had been sealed inside her. Those years during which she had lived in the constant presence of her mother had endowed her with fortitude and the insistence that meaning lay beneath the fabric of her existence, even when at times it should have been obvious that there wasn't any.

PART ONE

|

A DEATH IN
LOS ANGELES

|

The long shadows of morning had just barely given way to full-on sunlight, and already the pavement that lined the shops along East First Street had soaked up the summer heat. Blotting sweat from her chin on to the strap of her sundress, Daidai cursed at the shopping totes that pulled at her arms like children, slowing her pace. Ordinarily, she was not one to be thrown off by a couple of bags of groceries. She was tall, thin though not wispy, and prided herself in being able-bodied, but Hiroshi's persistent and extraordinary demands the night before had taken their toll.

She'd looked forward to spending time in Little Tokyo as a way to lighten her mood, but so far she'd enjoyed nothing about the day. Marukai had been out of several ingredients she'd needed, the checkout lines long and slow moving like the traffic into downtown. Now her sinuses stung from the sulfurous tang of hibachi grills, and she raised an elbow to wipe back the hair that had stuck to her cheek. A pretty child smiled as she passed, pulled along by her well-heeled mother, who quickened her gait and cast Daidai a nasty sideways glance. *At least I don't need to get laid,* she thought, arching her brows at the tightness in the woman's hips and remembering Hiroshi going at it as if there were no tomorrow, while she—both of them probably—prayed for release. Did traces of the night before show in the way she walked? Remembering the child, she averted her gaze and shifted the groceries from one arm to the other.

She didn't want to be late for her lunch date with Louise, but she stopped anyway when the door to the confectionary swung open, beckoning her inside with its string of bells. What better place than Fugetsu-do to get out of one's head? How could anyone resist those old wood-and-glass display cases lined with colorful, handcrafted *omanju*? Setting her bags down, she could already see Hiroshi rubbing his hands together in anticipation of the taste he knew from growing up. Her husband loved the dark adzuki bean fillings and, like her mother, looked down on her for her preference of plain mochi. Her stomach barely tolerated the starchiness of the thickened rice, forget the bean paste loaded with sugar, but she was pleased to see Hiroshi's favorites. *Yomogi, habutai, dorayaki*—they were all there. The store clerk yanked paper off the fat roll with one hand and used the other to snip from the mechanical spindle a length of red string, which he wrapped expertly once, twice around the white confection box as Daidai looked on, intoxicated by the sweet, thickened air. She'd asked for one piece of *chofu* to go, and she ate it as she walked, believing that perhaps the problem with the day might merely have been hunger. The fertility specialist had found no abnormalities, so nothing was wrong. But how then to account for Hiroshi's going on and on? He'd always required a certain amount of roughness before he'd yield to her, but lately it had become increasingly difficult to bring him to climax, because before she could mount him he needed to bear down on her, and her assurances that she could take any amount that he had to give had grown thin. He loved her. She knew it. But she knew he felt humiliated all the same.

"Let me help you." The voice came from behind her.

"Excuse me?" Daidai turned against the bustling foot traffic in time to see a small man stutter-stepping backward. Her hand shot out reflexively to steady him, and feeling the strained sinews of his forearm beneath her fingertips, she began immediately with apologies. His slight stature only made matters worse. She was a tree waving its useless branches in the wind as he struggled to regain his balance, the skittering sound of rice hitting the pavement sounding like rain.

The stranger removed the rice sack from her shoulder with exaggerated care and turned it upside down on the sidewalk. Was he Japanese? His stoop-shouldered, scrawny frame bore no connection to his face, which was lit with bizarre self-satisfaction.

Amid the stink that felt so distinctively downtown—brine from the sea contaminated by all the filth hosed from the sidewalk into the gutter—passersby began kicking at the spilled rice. Soon, some thin-boned, elderly person would probably slip and fall and she'd have a lawsuit to add to her burdens. But as if to respond to her concern, the peculiar little man pulled from his back pocket a neatly folded advertisement printed all in Japanese and began sweeping rice grains over the curb. Daidai watched with fascination. "Carry this way," he said, returning to her side and lifting the heavy sack to his chest.

Daidai held out her arms, but the bag was not proffered back in her direction. Instead, the man turned away with her rice, signaling for her to follow, which she might have done had a familiar figure not appeared just then. Gizo, Louise's little brother, held an arm out to slow the vehicles on both sides of the busy street so that he could jaywalk, the capped sleeve of his shirt stretched across the taut muscles of his biceps.

"Hey-hey!"

Clearing the curb with his self-assured, athletic stride, Gizo pulled her in for a side hug, his thick hair draping moisture across her cheek. Turning to face him, she noted the line of perspiration streaking his forehead and the cool dampness of his skin. He had the post-workout look of someone freshly showered, but beneath the clean scent of his shampoo, she recognized a familiar musty odor, a fishy tang she associated fondly with the inside of the Hashimotos' house that caused her to lean in before pulling away. Behind him, the sack of rice, its trademark red peony blossoming wrong side up from the ground, offered no explanation for what had just happened.

"I haven't seen you all summer. You gonna at least say hi?"

"Hi, Gizo." She smiled, her cheeks going hot.

"That's better."

Gizo threaded the grocery bags through one arm and with the other lifted the rice sack, managing not to let even one grain escape through the rip while she stood by admiring. Reminded of her mother's claim that rice left behind in your bowl signaled bad luck, she took Gizo's showing up as a good sign and let him lead her the long way back across the street. The detour meant she'd definitely be late for lunch, but she felt buoyed. The heat of the day and weight of the bags had worn her down, and the approving nods of shop owners as they passed set things right again.

Inside Akai Electric, an attractive teenaged salesgirl smiled at Gizo from behind the counter, the position usually occupied by Louise and Gizo's father, Danji. Gizo saluted her as he strode down the housewares aisle with Daidai in tow, her eye catching on an assortment of steamers, strainers, teakettles, and, in particular, an industrial-sized rice cooker that she supposed might come in handy given all the rice she'd just bought.

At the rear of the shop, Gizo held the service door open for her to pass through. It took a minute for her eyes to adjust to the dim lighting. She'd been in the back only once before, brought in by Louise, who'd nudged the heavy bag with her shoulder as she passed and let Daidai try punching the speed bags, purchased by their father to teach Gizo to fight.

After disappearing into a storage closet, Gizo reappeared with tape and scissors, flicked a light switch, and gestured Daidai to his side.

"Didn't that used to be out in front?" Seeing the old, hand-painted AKAI ELECTRIC sign above the door that led to the alley, Daidai was stirred by a memory of tracing a finger over the Japanese lettering.

"City ordinance made us take it down a long time ago." Gizo smiled, pointing out the two thin chains from which the sign had once swayed above the sidewalk.

Across the wall separating the shop from the warehouse, rows of wooden shelves held stock that seemed less random than the contents of the store they would replenish. The worktable where Gizo had placed the sack of rice also held a MacBook and a bank of small black two-way radios. A row of lockers leaned, though without risk of falling, slightly away from the far wall and toward two black couches, and the irregular-shaped glass coffee table top carefully balanced on two old wooden crates somehow explicated the intentional decor of the room.

"You like it?" Gizo asked.

Daidai turned, made self-conscious by the realization that Gizo had been watching her. "It's kind of great."

"Pretty professional, huh?"

"What's it for?"

"I have a little side business—keeps Dad's store afloat so he has a place. I do security for some tourists, mostly Japanese businessmen, when they come to L.A. You know, executive parties, drivers, that sort of thing.

"You need to be careful," he added, looking up. Having set the rice sack down on the makeshift worktable, he began cutting strips of athletic tape.

"What are you talking about?" Her gaze shifted from Gizo's smooth, sun-darkened skin to the perfect razor slice in the rice sack, the image juxtaposed in her thoughts with the side part in the stranger's slick black hair.

"I don't want to see you get hurt," Gizo said, casting suspicion on the intentions of the stranger who'd commanded her attention on the street. Having pulled out a chair, he tapped her arm at the elbow to sit.

She preferred to stand, but at Gizo's urging she sat. Had the stranger been following her? She watched as Gizo lined strips of tape neatly across the table's edge, the precision of his work seeming to say that the task at hand was connected somehow to his purpose in life. His fingers were square-tipped and callused, with an unhealed gash that ran the length of his index finger to the joint of his thumb, suggesting he knew something she didn't know.

"How'd you get that?" she asked, signaling to him with her chin, suddenly cowed by doubt.

"That?" He flexed his thumb. "It's nothing."

The rice sack repaired, he stuck a strip of leftover tape to Daidai's forearm in a gesture he found riotously funny. Buckled over with laughter, he playfully ducked under her hand when she attempted to smack his shoulder. In an instant, he'd turned from serious into the annoying boy he'd been as a child. Only he was quicker now.

"Ouch!" Daidai rubbed at the hairless stripe left behind by the tape.

"It's what you get."

"What are you talking about?" she demanded, folding her arms across her chest.

"Heard you left the museum."

The pang in her chest moved up to her head, and she met his eyes, wondering how much he knew. "What? I'm not allowed to take some time off?"

"Everything okay?"

"Yes." Trying to smile, she felt her cheeks flush again and figured she may as well just answer him outright. He probably knew anyway, since people were always talking. "Hiroshi and I are trying to have a baby."

"Really?" he gasped. "You gonna be a stay-at-home mommy?"

She shrugged. Why was he mocking her?

"Thought you were a career woman."

"What are you talking about?" Daidai flinched at his use of an anachronism to describe her.

"Take it easy, Daidai." He brushed his fingers over the reddened splotch on her forearm in a way that would have made Hiroshi uneasy, and she pulled away. "No one gets to have it all. I understand that."

"I never said I had it all."

"Really?" He looked surprised. "I thought everything about you said that."

Daidai drew a breath in and held it. Was that really how he saw her? Gizo cocked his head, the same gesture Hiroshi sometimes used to ask if she was for real. Slowly, so as to make her intention clear, she reached for him, grabbed a quarter-inch piece of arm flesh between her thumb and forefinger, and twisted, watching his face for signs of pain as she increased the pressure. She held on, waiting for him to pull away, reading the energy between them in the shape of his eyes, before shifting her gaze to the gash that ran the length of his index finger and the room with all its appurtenances and odd angles. Her grip released only when the doorknob turned and the sales clerk they'd passed behind the front counter stuck her head in to ask about an order.

"Who's the new help?" Daidai said, acknowledging a different kind of tension in the air when the door shut.

"That would be the delightful Patty Shinoda, Ralph's daughter."

Gizo examined the darkened mark on his arm as Daidai looked on, wondering who Ralph was. "I'm late to meet Louise for lunch," she announced, dismissing him.

"Almost done here," Gizo said. After standing the scissors in an old coffee tin and hanging the tape roll on a nail, he reached for the shopping bags, having transformed back into his chivalrous, adult self. "Where to?"

Daidai set the pace, walking a half step ahead to let him know she was still offended by his misguided perception of her, daring him to repeat the error in his judgment of her. Others might think of her as the light-skinned, freckled, unknowable stranger, but he knew better.

Fortunately, the hot midday air would not hold on to anger, and she could feel his attention at her back as she walked. By the time they arrived at the storefront restaurant, she didn't know why she'd been so irritable. And as if to show regret for his behavior, he handed the rice sack and groceries over with exaggerated care, emphasizing his devotion with a slight bow.

"I love you, too," she said, aching at the distance she felt from this boy she'd grown up with.

Tilting her chin up to just past where it felt comfortable, he looked her in the eye somberly before letting go, the heat from his fingers still palpable along her cheek when he turned to leave.

Daidai sat at a four-top with the taped-up rice sack in the chair next to her, startled out of her reverie when Louise tapped her shoulder from behind. Leaning in for a hug, she spoke in a whisper, as if to deliver a secret. "All that white rice isn't good for you."

"It's for a party," Daidai whispered back.

"You look nice." Louise assessed her outfit the way her doctor had evaluated her health, Louise's eyes calling Daidai's attention back into her body.

"Thank you." Daidai smiled, having spent more time than usual in front of the mirror that morning hoping Louise would notice. "You look nice, too."

Louise looked sharp, cool in a restaurant that felt oppressively close with only fans to blow the air around. Her flawlessly manicured, soft hands and skin tone beamed good health and goodwill, and her eyes reflected back an image of Daidai that felt safe and familiar. Louise had that gift of lighting up whatever object caught her attention. Combined with persistence and intense curiosity, it made her a good lawyer. Still, Daidai wondered how anyone, let alone her best friend, could get to be their age with no personal life to speak of. Who knew what lay beneath her flawless exterior, because everyday questions led to defensiveness, as if threatening to expose what her routine lacked.

Like Louise, Daidai avoided conversations that focused on her, though on this afternoon she'd come to lunch with an important matter to discuss. Earlier in the year, Hiroshi had been promoted to program director, news that had come as a shock since he'd been a faculty member in the university's Asian American Studies department for only six years. The appointment would begin that fall, and along with the title came the honor of hosting the beginning-of-the-year graduate student reception. Daidai watched Louise run down the ingredients list with concentration that marked her as an expert. "Fresh, seasonal. Smart nod to the discerning palate. Good!"

"Do you think so?" Daidai raised a nail to her lip and bit down, needing Louise's praise.

"Of course!" Louise reached across the table and squeezed Daidai's arm, her touch bringing on a wave of feeling.

"I've missed you" was all Daidai could think to say, not wanting to tip Louise off to her forlorn state.

"Do you want me to come to this party?"

"Please."

"I'll have to see." Louise took out her calendar, marked as Daidai's used to be for months in advance, making no promises except to say that she'd try to be there. "What's wrong?" she asked, looking concerned.

"Nothing," Daidai said, dejected, feeling the obviousness of what was wrong. A year ago, her work at the museum had consumed her. She wouldn't even have made it home in time to greet the guests.

"I just don't understand how one poorly reviewed installation could be enough to make you quit."

"I'm on leave, remember? I didn't quit, and my putting my career on hold was the fertility doctor's idea." Daidai stared across the table with a look meant to remind Louise that they'd been over this before. "It is what it is."

"Bored?"

"Not at all," Daidai lied, resenting the insinuation that Louise had been right, that she'd made the wrong choice about how to spend her time.

The peeling back of her life, though brief, frustrated them both.

After lunch, when the door leading back to the street swung open, the pleasantness of the air caught Daidai off guard. Expecting a rush of heat, she felt instead the drop in temperature, the aftereffect of a rain shower that had blown unexpectedly through downtown. The weight of the rice sack and grocery bags ceased to bother her; the carbon emissions polluting the underground garage, rather than noxious, smelled satisfyingly familiar. She'd parked in that garage, mostly in the same spot, practically every day for six years, and was grateful not to have been stripped of her privilege.

Sliding her plastic card into the metered gate, Daidai noted that the permit, paid for by the museum, had exactly one month left on it. The next time she and Louise had lunch she'd be forced to park on the street.

2

It seemed unfortunate though predictable that two weeks into September the heat had edged back up. Instead of temperate late-summer weather, the day of the party arrived even hotter than had been forecasted, stressing the cooling unit until its usual hum became a bleating roar. Daidai had spent the morning with WD-40 and a screwdriver, coaxing it back into quietude, and then a good part of the afternoon cursing it, along with the oven that couldn't contain its heat, which she regretted not having considered when she let Hiroshi convince her to go with premade hors d'oeuvres à la Whole Foods. Louise had shown up with a bag of cherries fresh from the fruit stand in one arm and one of peaches in the other, which Daidai and she had pitted and skinned and spooned into the tart shells Louise had rolled out and baked the night before. Offsetting Daidai's anxiety over the heat, the tarts beamed good cheer, set primly in a row across the high counter alongside bowls of raspberries, apples, and plums for fruit saketinis.

With the guests due to arrive, Louise took over the last-minute preparations and sent Daidai into the bedroom to change out of her sweat-stained, fruit-glaze-spattered T-shirt. That morning she'd lain out a Picasso-blue patterned sundress alongside a chiffon blouse and pale melon skirt, unable to choose between the two. Now, faced with the decision, one appeared drab, the other self-effacing. Back in the closet, her eye caught on her orange-sherbet sundress buried in the back. Simple but short. Sexy—maybe too short? She'd tried for six years to affect the right look at the museum and should have paid more attention to her legs. Daidai looked at herself in the full-length door mirror, at her freckles dancing across her heat-stained cheekbones. She placed the more conservative outfits back on hangers and, after mouthing an apology to her high-minded mother, shut the door to the walk-in closet behind her. Hiroshi had purchased some nice-smelling French perfume as an anniversary gift, which she spritzed into the air, and practiced a smile, which appeared spontaneously later that evening when she spotted her husband motioning to her from across the room.

Hiroshi planted his hand firmly on the small of her back in a gesture she read as proprietary, a remonstrance for her choice of an immodest outfit. Leaning in, she clamped her teeth around the flap of his earlobe, just hard enough to shift his attention inward. She'd worked too hard to be criticized. Taking a deep breath, she let her thoughts move from the work she'd done to prepare for the party to the fact that it'd soon be over, and she calmed down a little. Hiroshi loved her, but he was afflicted with an unusual degree of social anxiety. They both were, and it made them perfect for each other: she consumed with worry that she might not fit in, and he put off and at the same time attracted to her for the ways she didn't.

Beginning on his right, Hiroshi introduced the new assistant professor, who sneezed several times when her cheek brushed against Daidai's, embarrassing them both in front of the rest of the group, all grad students, who waited in turn to be acknowledged. Daidai found something nice to say to each of them while keeping her distance in case her perfume should cause another fit of sneezing. For entertainment, she looked intermittently through the cutout window at Louise, who was showing off her skills as a bartender, until a woman roughly her own age, though clearly not American in her economical gestures and cadences, surprised Daidai by brushing past her outstretched hand.

"Pleased to meet you. I'm Satsuki Suzuki," she spoke into Daidai's ear. "You smell so good!" The air between them vibrated as she and Daidai pressed shoulders.

The overt gesture of affection had been enough to make the students stop their private asides and stare, but Satsuki offered no explanation. Inclining her head slightly in Daidai's direction, she looked up with a broad smile that revealed an uneven set of teeth, each pushing at the next to be the one out in front. It was the only awkward feature on her lively, intelligent face.

"Very nice to meet you." Daidai looked past the group of curious first-year onlookers, whose mass of eyes and nervous tics underscored Satsuki's singular presence in the room.

After dinner, Satsuki breezed into the kitchen followed closely behind by a tall, good-looking student she didn't bother to introduce. "Your home has a very festive spirit tonight," she said in accented but perfectly intoned English, clearing a spot for her empty drink glass, which she then set on the countertop with both hands. "I wanted to tell you how much I'm enjoying myself."

"I'm glad," Daidai said, sensing there might be something more that the woman had come to say.

"The seaweed salad was delicious. I never would have thought to add lemon."

"Thank you." Daidai smiled, indicating her readiness to converse. Perhaps more time was needed for the woman to formulate her words in English. "I made the drinks and desserts, but everything else came ready-made from Whole Foods," she said, stalling.

"A wise decision, I think." Rejecting Daidai's hesitancy, the woman turned to the person behind her. "Daidai Suzuki, meet Leonard Quan."

"Nice to meet you, Dr. Suzuki," Leonard said, showing impeccable manners.

"Very nice to meet you, Leonard." Daidai extended her hand after drying it on a kitchen towel while Satsuki looked on. "Thanks for coming to the party."

"This is too much work for one person." Satsuki glanced over her shoulder at the empty drink glasses, flatware, and plates stacked in the sink.

It *was* too much, Daidai would have agreed, were it not for Louise, whose movements in the big room she monitored from the corner of her eye. "It's fine. Go enjoy yourself." Daidai waved the two back to the party.

But rather than leave, Satsuki reached under the sink and located a pair of kitchen gloves, which she handed to Leonard. "These should fit." Satsuki wiped her elegant fingers on the dish towel Daidai had used and stood by to watch Leonard put them on before excusing herself out of the kitchen.

"You two friends?" Daidai asked, wanting to understand the exchange she'd just witnessed.

"Housemates." Leonard's thumb joints bulged uncomfortably in the yellow gloves.

Daidai pondered what she perceived to be Leonard's predicament: the financial constraints that necessitated a housemate, the awkwardness built into social functions stemming out of academia. "You don't have to help me clean up," she said, wanting to give him a break.

Leonard laughed. "I don't mind. I'm not a very social person."

"I'm not either."

With nothing more to say to each other, they turned their gaze to the cutout window to view what they'd confessed they were not. Satsuki was chatting up a group of students, and then, finding them to be inadequate conversationalists, she turned over her shoulder to interrupt Hiroshi's conversation with the new assistant professor. Above the party clatter, her gestures rang clear. *Choose me.* Flipping her hair close to Hiroshi's ear, she reached out to brush his arm with her fingertips, signaling that something he'd said had pleased her.

Once the countertop had been cleared, Daidai joined her friend behind the bar. "Who do you like?" she asked, conjuring the game they liked to play.

Louise wiped a strand of hair from her face and set her gaze on the crowd. "They're mostly very young," she said, noncommittal. "Except for the new assistant professor, and who's the older student?"

"The one our age?" Daidai laughed. "Foreign?"

"Japanese." Now it was Louise's turn to laugh.

"That would be Satsuki Suzuki." Louise's choice of whom to single out amused Daidai.

"Watch out for that one!" Louise said, just as she was interrupted by a request for another round.

Folding herself back into the party, Daidai wondered what Louise had seen and was disappointed when Louise refused her invitation of a drink once the guests had gone home. Work, she complained, saying that she needed some sleep.

Left behind with Hiroshi, Daidai kicked off her heels and sipped at a glass of mineral water while her husband assessed the newly configured program. "The new assistant professor's going to be a nice addition."

"How about the incoming grad students?"

"We'll have to see."

"I think Satsuki Suzuki has a crush on you," Daidai teased Hiroshi, wanting to gauge his response to the woman's flirtatiousness.

"Half the first-years have a crush on me," Hiroshi replied, and smiled. "And having met you, I'm sure the other half now have one on you. Isn't that how the school year always starts out?"

Daidai winced, wondering when Hiroshi had become so cavalier.

"By October they'll have moved on."

"If you say so." She shrugged, satisfied by this admission.

"I think you'd like Satsuki," Hiroshi said, and continued without waiting for a response. "Her father's an art dealer. She seems quite knowledgeable as well."

"No thanks." Daidai yawned. Hiroshi had clearly enjoyed the attention, but she didn't need to hear the remarks of another amateur art collector. Even from a distance, she'd found Satsuki's interest in the objects lying around their flat overblown.

After refilling his wife's mineral water, Hiroshi shook up the last of the saketinis, creating for himself a mixed-fruit bomb. "To our Period of Reinvention." He raised his glass in a toast, then reached across the couch and squeezed his wife's big toe, signaling an end to Daidai's stint as a hostess. "Thank you for throwing a great party."

Done with the praise, Hiroshi wanted sex. Daidai figured he'd have been as enervated from the festivities as she was, but he seemed intent on fucking, thrusting into her with frenzied abandon. Lying beneath him, her eyes open to his bizarre expressions, Daidai wondered whether he was even making love to her. He looked like someone involved in the pursuit of secret pleasures, and she tried to visualize his experience. Something new was happening. Watching the structure of his face shift beneath the creases of his cheekbones and the crinkles of his tightly shut lids, Daidai felt his movements slow. He seemed to be straining to feel inside her, or just to feel, drifting away and then needing to locate her as he shifted his position like an explorer lost somewhere inside her body.

The new students had been introduced, including one in particular who seemed intent on pleasing him. She felt him trying something out, which she rather resented, though she wondered if she judged him too harshly. What if she was the person of interest? What if it had been her all along? Lying beneath Hiroshi, whose body she knew so well, she shut her eyes and tried to relax, to feel the pleasure of his guttural bellows and the quickened pace of his breathing.

Connecting instead with the place inside herself that had lain for so long vacant, she wondered if it would ever be filled. Wasn't sex, after all, about the creation of a life?

3

When Daidai awoke the next morning she found Hiroshi next to her, his hand draped across her back while he scanned the newspaper. He was glad to feel her stirring, which meant he could start reading to her about the events that had amused him while she slept. Reaching over her when she failed to adequately respond, he handed her a coffee mug, which she set back on the nightstand, finding its contents distastefully cold.

She was only vaguely aware of when he'd traded the newspaper for student work, and the next thing she knew he was urging her up. Bounding from the bed and returning with a fresh cup of coffee, he clapped his hands with excitement. This was the Hiroshi she loved, ready and waiting for whatever came next, wanting to know whether she'd prefer a walk along the shore or a stroll through the Santa Monica promenade. They could sit outside at their favorite café or catch a matinee. Her brain hadn't yet begun to function, but his seemed not to have lost its high from the night before, and she doubted he'd accept her being too tired as an excuse.

"How about we drive out to Gardena for dinner?" he said, having apparently noted her failure to move in response to his suggestions. "We'll pick your mother up and have an early dinner."

Daidai smiled, holding her arms up and pulling him off his feet when he leaned over her, planting kisses along his hairline and on both his cheeks. Despite her qualms with him, he could be incredibly sweet. It had been her habit since her father's death the year before to visit her mother on Sundays. Hiroshi went along when he wasn't too busy prepping for the upcoming week, but he hadn't gone in months, and Daidai knew how happy it would make Mako to see him. While Mako loved her daughter, Daidai suspected she preferred spending time with her son-in-law, who fit so naturally with her idea of a good man. It was one of the things that had drawn Daidai to him.

Hiroshi went out of his way to indulge Mako, stopping at Marukai without being asked, then pushing the cart down the congested aisles with the old woman hanging on his arm, smiling at her idle chatter over the high price of Japanese imports that could be gotten only at this Marukai, not the other one downtown, which reminded him of meals his mother had made him before she passed. Daidai didn't believe in fate, but she remembered the evening she'd driven with Hiroshi to meet her parents, how afterward it had seemed her destiny that he should be part of her family. Seeing Mako's face light up now, she wondered why he'd stayed away so long.

Mako ordered tempura udon, her favorite, and insisted that Hiroshi take the shrimp off the top. To Daidai she gave a Japanese sweet potato, saying how good *satsumaimo* was for the immune system as well as digestion, and maybe fertility, too.

She praised Hiroshi lavishly for his promotion, referencing her late husband with a sigh, how pleased he would have been to see Hiroshi rising up through the ranks of academia, dispelling any vestige of doubt that Daidai might not be doing the right thing in giving up her career to plan a family, because without family there was no future, and without a future what did they have to look forward to?

It was late in the evening when they dropped Mako off. Daidai watched from the backseat as Hiroshi rushed around from the driver's side to open the passenger door, holding his elbow out to escort Mako up the driveway to the front door, and inserted her house key into the lock, knowing Mako had trouble with her eyesight at night. Seeing the interior light flash on as she reseated herself in her mother's place, Daidai nodded in approval at her husband's flawless performance.

"Do you know how much I appreciate you?" she said as he belted himself in for the drive home.

"I appreciate you, too," he said, reaching across the gearshift to kiss her.

The drive back to the Valley took twice as long as it normally did, with everyone returning home from their weekend pleasures. Worried about the toll all the activity might take on her husband, Daidai was surprised on Monday morning when Hiroshi hopped out of bed and left the apartment singing. He returned at the end of the day with flowers in hand: three burnt-orange gerberas collected in a Ball jar, tied with a purple bow, attached to which was a thank-you, addressed to her, that read, *I thought these would look good with your name.*

Clever Satsuki—though she didn't know Daidai had chosen her name randomly at the age of three. Carolyn Ann had been her given name. Her mother had decided on that one, which she'd later been told she'd rejected in full and even abbreviated versions. She would not respond to Carolyn, or to Carrie or Ann, or to Lynn or Annie. For no apparent reason, she'd answer only to Daidai. It wasn't until much later that she learned that the name she'd chosen for herself translated in Japanese to mean "bitter orange." But perhaps she'd been predisposed to liking the nickname Daidai because orange turned out to be her favorite color. And then along came vibrant Satsuki and her gift of the flowers.

"I guess she wants to be friends with you," Hiroshi teased.

"She wants to use me to get closer to you," Daidai teased back.

"Can't you just accept the gesture without prejudice, as an offer of friendship? Besides, aren't gerberas your favorite?"

Hiroshi was right about her fondness for gerberas, but these looked like the antennae of some gigantic species of insect, reaching into the air for purchase, as if they'd come looking for something, or signifying something. Daidai felt certain of that and was perturbed by Hiroshi's insistence that they and their bearer be viewed as innocent. "If Satsuki wanted to be my friend, she could have delivered the flowers to me herself. She knew where to find me."

Hiroshi shrugged, a sign Daidai construed as his tacit acceptance of what she'd said—that, of course, she'd been right. Satsuki hadn't brought the flowers to *her*, she'd brought them to *him*. Imagining the scenario one step further, Daidai saw the grad student showing up at her husband's office, half hidden behind the doorframe, flattering him with her stated desire not to interrupt, even though she'd shown up precisely to do just that.

As if to confirm that she'd imagined correctly, Hiroshi sat across the kitchen dog-faced, suggesting that of the three he might be the only innocent one: Hiroshi, steadfast and trustworthy in his affections, his brand of linearity a big part of why she'd married him. But after five years of marriage, he was no longer the person he'd been. Her groin still ached from his roughness with her two nights earlier, and the ache should have informed her new understanding of him.

But instead of feeling that she'd been wronged, she felt remorse. Her husband's passing interest in one of his students didn't justify her scrutiny, and she well realized that the problem could be hers alone. Without her own work to occupy her thoughts, she'd grown anxious. She needed to relax. Turning her attention back to the flowers, she admired them anew, each stem arching upward to show off its own personality.

For nearly a week, the burnt-orange gerberas added a splash of color to the windowsill. Daidai changed their water daily until the morning she woke to find the last blossom overturned. That same day, in the produce section of Whole Foods, while she bagged Persian cucumbers for a recipe Hiroshi wanted to try, a hand with slender fingers tipped with French-manicured nails held up a Japanese pickling cucumber for her to inspect. "These are better," the bearer of the cucumber said.

Daidai laughed at the pimply proboscis, made all the more grotesque by Satsuki's delicate fingers. "What are you doing here, Satsuki?"

"Where else do you shop?" She smiled demurely.

Daidai replayed the question twice before answering, her attention shifting from the whiteness of the woman's fingers to her impressively shiny teeth. "I tried those once," she said, still not understanding. "They're bitter."

"That's because they're for pickling!" Satsuki laughed, tossing the spiny cucumber into the batch of slender, darker green ones Daidai had been sorting through.

Satsuki gave no advanced warning before showing up the next afternoon, this time on the doorstep carrying a heavy, round stone, which she claimed to have brought with her from Japan. Where just the day before Daidai had thrown out the flowers, believing Satsuki's stint in the apartment over, now the woman had returned with a small boulder, presenting what seemed to be yet another puzzle. Even beyond that, wasn't it strange for a grad student to show up unannounced at her professor's apartment? Was there a different code of etiquette in Japan, one that prevented Satsuki from understanding this?

Daidai followed Satsuki into the kitchen, where she rolled the stone onto the countertop. "I'll need it back, but I want you to use it," she said, blotting a line of sweat from above her lip with her tongue. Out of breath, perhaps from the stairs, still she looked lovely with her eyes alight, her skin flushed and flawless, her fingers visibly trembling.

"I'm sorry, but I don't know what this is for." Daidai turned from her observation of Satsuki to the stone.

"Its weight will speed up the pickling process."

"Oh, of course." Hadn't her mother used a similar stone for pickling vegetables? Daidai recalled the exchange at Whole Foods the day before while she rummaged through the vegetable bin for the cucumbers, embarrassed to have missed her cue.

That afternoon, Satsuki demonstrated in quick, even strokes of the knife her prowess as a chef, transferring the thinly sliced cucumbers to a bowl, then mixing them with salt using her bare hands. She talked as she worked, glancing up to make eye contact when she wished to emphasize a point. The weather had turned fine in the week since the party, yet a memory of heat lingered in the kitchen.

The stated purpose of her return three days later was to check on the pickling process. Lifting the stone and the plate beneath it, she pinched a sample and declared the batch of Japanese-style pickles ready for consumption. Hiroshi arrived home from campus to the table being set for *otsukemono*, which was served over hot rice with a cup of *genmai* tea. Pleased with the meal, he ventured into the kitchen for a refill of water and returned palming the pickling stone like a football. "Where'd this come from?" he asked, apparently having not noticed that it had sat on the countertop for three days.

"I brought it with me from Japan." The question had been asked of Daidai, but Satsuki addressed Hiroshi directly.

"Sansen ishi. Ii desu neh! My mother had a similar one." Hiroshi held the stone at eye level, tossing it into the air a few times before turning down the hall to his office. "This one would make an ideal paperweight."

"You can't have it, Hiroshi," Daidai called to her husband's back. "It belongs to Satsuki. Can't you see she was using it?" Daidai surprised herself with her harsh response, but she'd felt left out of the repartee between Hiroshi and his student, and of the secret knowledge of pickling stones apparently known to everyone but her.

"It's okay, really." Satsuki reached across the table and touched Daidai's arm to keep her from following Hiroshi. "Hiroshi can borrow it. I don't need it right now."

In mid-October, halfway into the semester, Satsuki brought a gift of tea. She'd just arrived and was standing with Daidai in the foyer, explaining how she'd had the tea sent from Japan, when Hiroshi came bounding up the stairwell. Satsuki's visit had not been well timed, the purpose of Hiroshi's lunchtime appearance being sex, prescribed by the fertility specialist at six-hour intervals when Daidai was ovulating.

"Hiroshi and I are late for an appointment," Daidai lied, struggling to avert an awkward moment in case Satsuki should wonder over Hiroshi's arrival home in the middle of the day. "Could you come back tomorrow for a pot of tea?"

Satsuki clasped her hands in front of her, barely waiting for the invitation to be made before responding. "Would two o'clock be good?"

Daidai was not in the mood for sex that afternoon, nor was Hiroshi. Neither bothered to undress fully. He slid his pants down perfunctorily while she pulled her T-shirt over her head and released the clasp on her brassiere, lifting her heavy breasts to give him a good look before letting them drop. She pinched his flaccid cock, flipping it from one side to the other, deliberating on the task at hand before resigning to take him in her mouth. Alternating long strokes with light, teasing whispers, she began a private conversation with his cock, shutting him out when he writhed beneath her, issuing orders. She didn't need his help to get what she needed from him. Let him rant about being late for class. She'd take her time, make him return with an ache and a still-fluttering heart. Besides, it would be over soon enough. No use for him to go on to someone who'd waited him out before. With the crisis inevitable, she shifted herself onto him and bore down, riding him hard until his load poured into her.

The doctor had suggested twenty minutes on her back postcoitus, which she timed while cycling her legs in the air for exercise. Out of the corner of her eye she watched Hiroshi rush to tidy himself up, wondering whether he'd run into Satsuki when he returned to campus that afternoon.

True to her word, Satsuki returned the following afternoon at two straight up to prepare a pot of the very fine tea she'd brought over the day before.

"What's the occasion?" Daidai asked, waiting for the tea water to boil.

"No occasion," she said. "Just an excuse to spend more time with you."

Pouring water over a measure of leaves, Daidai breathed in the distinctly foreign, woody aroma, considering it an irony that her job at the museum had taken her all over Asia but never to Japan. "Haven't you made friends in the program?" she asked, shaking herself from her reverie.

"I don't find any of my fellow students particularly interesting," Satsuki said, after appearing to give the question some thought. "I'm far more interested in what you do. Hiroshi says you're an art curator."

Daidai smiled her assent, volunteering nothing more, wondering what had prompted Hiroshi to discuss her work with his student.

"What is your area of specialty?"

"Postwar art made by Japanese living on the West Coast. You're familiar with wartime internment, I assume?"

"Of course." Satsuki narrowed her eyes, as if homing in on an object in the distance. "This subject is very interesting to me. Were your parents imprisoned during the war?"

"No. My mother's family still lived in Japan at the time. And my father is Irish," Daidai explained. Having tried to avoid the subject of her work, she was irritated by Satsuki's probing.

"But this was Hiroshi's parents' experience?"

"Yes," Daidai said, believing she'd hit upon the underlying reason for Satsuki's interest. "Hiroshi's parents were both interned. They were children at the time. I'm interested in the generation that was born after the war. Not enough is known about the experience of people like Hiroshi. But I believe the trauma is as pervasive as lung damage caused by secondhand smoke, damage that began decades ago. It needs to be studied."

"Japan is so different." Satsuki shook her head. "We are an almost entirely homogenous society."

"What about Japan's treatment of non-Japanese?"

Satsuki shrugged. "I've never had non-Japanese friends."

This position, of never going out of one's social milieu, seemed to Daidai to sum up the life experience of so many Japanese, a primness that she'd found stultifying. "I *was* a curator—for the Asian American Art Museum downtown," Daidai clarified. "I'm not anymore."

"You were laid off, then? Or did you quit your job?"

"I left to start a family," she said, aching to change the subject.

"You're pregnant?"

"Not yet. I hope to be soon."

"I see," Satsuki said, taking up again with her imperious nodding.

"Hiroshi and I have had some trouble conceiving, so we're trying to increase our chances by following my monthly cycle." Having tried to avoid the subject of her personal life, at last Daidai relented. "I went on leave because the fertility specialist recommended slowing my schedule down. That's what I'm doing at home—trying to have a baby."

Satsuki stared back, wide-eyed and unblinking. It took her a minute to respond. "Thank you for trusting me with that information," she said, though the way she looked then, like someone who'd just been slapped, filled Daidai with regret. "I'm glad to know something of your life. I didn't want to breach your privacy by asking, but like I said, I'm curious about you."

"In that case, I'm sorry for responding so tersely," Daidai said, feeling the relief of having spoken the truth.

"Don't be sorry." Satsuki smiled. "I hope your baby will call me Auntie, since there's no possibility of a baby in my future."

"Why not?" Was it that she didn't want a baby or could she not have one? Daidai felt suddenly foolish for being so preoccupied by her own life circumstances that she'd not considered Satsuki's.

"My upbringing warned me against bringing children into the world," Satsuki said, giving nothing away.

"How so?" This new line of questioning only pointed out to Daidai that she knew nothing about Satsuki's childhood. But rather than show embarrassment, Satsuki reached across the table and patted Daidai's hand, the muscles around her mouth relaxing into a smile. "You want to know about me?"

Daidai nodded politely, but withdrew her hand, unable to explain the anxiety with which she felt suddenly stricken.

"You might already know that my father is an art dealer," Satsuki began, fixing Daidai with her gaze to gauge what she knew. "Did Hiroshi tell you?"

"You tell me." Daidai wrapped her hands around her cup of tea. Soothed by its curved shape and warmth, she tried to push her negative response to Hiroshi's mention of the art dealer father out of her mind. "I really don't know anything at all about your personal history."

"My father's family owned a framing business." Satsuki sighed before continuing, seeming to find the information tedious. "My father came from a generation of craftsmen known for their meticulous work, but he proved himself to be a maverick. He used acid-free and organic papers made from recycled materials long before ecological concerns made it trendy to do so. His given name was Ichiro, but his parents called him Ichiban, meaning 'Number One.' He was their only son."

Hearing about Satsuki's father, Daidai thought of Hiroshi, how he'd been the center of his mother's life; her death had come as a terrible blow. A year later his father had died, shortly before he'd met Daidai, the complete loss of family cementing Daidai's place in his life.

"My grandparents were of a traditional mind-set when it came to boys. In Japan, during my father's time and even now, a son occupies a position of great importance. My mother was not the wife my grandparents would have chosen."

"I don't understand," Daidai interrupted. "Why would your mother not be accepted?"

Satsuki's smile barely concealed her shock. "It isn't that difficult to understand. My mother grew up on her own from a very young age, without parents or financial resources. My parents' courtship began because she was a gifted painter, and my father recognized what her talent might mean for him. He allowed her to use his framing shop as a studio, where he set up a corner as a makeshift gallery for her to show and sell her work. In return for her use of the space, he bought the pieces he liked at a discount. When this worked out well, he began making similar arrangements with other artists, which was how he rose to prominence in the art world."

Daidai was losing patience. It was not hard to see the power benefactors held in the art world, but what did this have to do with Satsuki's statement that she would never have children?

"The painters whose work he promoted, these were all women," Satsuki continued, seeming to recognize Daidai's impatience, yet lingering on her words. "This got people talking. My father made a name for himself among buyers as a patron with exquisite taste and a fine eye for promise. It was only natural that the relationship between my parents would develop. He was a good businessman in need of an artist, and she was tired of the hardships created by anonymity and poverty. In practical terms, the need of each for what the other had to offer made them perfectly suited for marriage."

"So what about your upbringing made you decide not to have children?" Daidai asked, seeing that her question might go unanswered. "I assume it's that you don't want to have children, not that you can't."

Satsuki turned her gaze out the high window. "Children deserve more sweetness than most adults are capable of giving them," she said, indicating with crossed arms an unwillingness to be pressed further.

Unable to imagine her life without the certainty of her mother's affection, Daidai reached a hand across the table and brushed Satsuki's forearm. "I don't think everyone should have children, but I think you're very sweet," she said, thinking not of Satsuki but of her own mother and the week that had gone by since she'd seen her.

"Thank you for saying that." Satsuki opened her arms to clasp Daidai's fingertips and beamed a toothy smile across the table.

Daidai nodded. "I didn't start to think about wanting a family until recently." Though her comment had been innocuous, a strange thing happened then. Satsuki's facial muscles began to twitch and her smile quivered until it looked broken. "What's wrong?" Daidai asked, worried about a possible problem with the woman's health.

"Nothing's wrong." Satsuki quickly composed herself. "Do you really find me sweet?"

"I do," Daidai said, having stopped listening.

"I'm glad," Satsuki said, "because I enjoy your company." And from that afternoon on her frequent visits to the apartment made this clear.

4

Students tend to flee campus after their last final, but Satsuki
planned to stay in Southern California rather than return to Mito for
the winter break. It had been her idea to cook a traditional Japanese
meal, a celebration planned a month out for Friday of the week
before Christmas.

Although winter had officially arrived, the temperature on the
appointed day was downright balmy, perfect for leaving the sliding
door and windows open. On weekends a fan had been put in place to
blot out loud music and ruckus from the frat houses down the block,
but absent the rowdy boys the neighborhood had fallen unusually
quiet. Even with the vent open to circulate the air, the apartment was
laden with the rich aroma of the soup stock that had been simmering
all afternoon. Hiroshi was working on the garnishes, Daidai setting
the table, and Satsuki making a last-minute adjustment to the soup-
base seasoning when her cell phone came to life with a tune. After
glancing down at the number, she paused before answering the call.
Usually there was a *"Moshi moshi,"* followed by *"Hai!"* But Satsuki
instead moved silently onto the balcony, shutting the door behind
her for privacy, though she'd never required any before.

Perturbed that Satsuki would take a phone call just as dinner
was being served, Daidai carried on, making no mention of the
interruption to Hiroshi as she tossed the salad and he sampled the

soup stock. Worried about the noodles, which, had begun to adhere, she rinsed them—twice.

Satsuki was still talking when the balcony door slid open. "Ready for dinner?" she asked, slipping her cell phone into the front pocket of her jeans. Hiroshi was in the kitchen and Daidai in the dining room, pulling a chair out from the table. The couple turned from what they were doing just in time to see the color drain out of Satsuki's face as she crumpled to the ground. Daidai recalled a hibiscus flower she'd once seen wilt through the use of time-lapse photography. She stood dumbstruck as Hiroshi rushed to his student's rescue. Kneeling over her prone body, he turned a quizzical eye to his wife.

"What just happened?"

Satsuki opened her eyes, roused perhaps by the sound of Hiroshi's voice. She seemed confused, as if next she might yawn and stretch and attempt to restart the day. But instead her shoulders folded forward. With hair covering half her face she made an announcement: "My mother has been found dead."

Daidai glanced at her husband before her eyes settled again on Satsuki. She and Hiroshi had not spoken at all in the time Satsuki had spent on the terrace, figuring the best way to overlook Satsuki's absence in the kitchen was to ignore it. Now, when she needed to know what he was thinking in order to understand what she should think, she saw only abashed disbelief. A door to the past had opened, leaving them both to peer into a void.

"This is terrible." Daidai cleared her throat, struggling with the news. "I'm so sorry."

"Yes," Hiroshi chimed in. "Can we do anything to help?"

"She was living right here in Los Angeles," Satsuki said.

She was? This information did not jibe with what Daidai could recollect from their previous conversations. Scouring her memory, she recalled nothing about the mother leaving Japan. But Daidai's shock passed unnoticed. For several seconds the room went quiet, with the air vibrating the way it does after a flash of lightning, until Satsuki's shoulders began to tremble and a heartbreaking wail rose from her lungs. Daidai watched as Hiroshi petted her hair and tried to read the look in Satsuki's eyes as she stared up at him. Her gaze was beseeching, the way a child turns to a parent for succor, but there was something more, too—a glance directed at Daidai that she couldn't read. Turning away, Daidai recalled an aphorism her mother often used: *"Shoganai,"* she'd say, throwing up her hands. *It can't be helped.* Whether despite or because of Satsuki's peripheral awareness of her, she was seized with jealousy over the intimate exchange between her husband and his student.

It can't be helped, she told herself, forced to return to the kitchen alone to turn the heat off from under the pot that still simmered on the stove. A trail of steam rose into the air, giving off the fishy aroma of dashi and fresh ginger, and the sight of the table set with mismatched dishes and colorful garnishes filled Daidai with trepidation. Usually she was the one to take charge, but in this case she had no idea how to respond, whether to serve up dinner or pack the meal away.

It was quite late when the three gathered at the table at Satsuki's insistence. As if to show he still had an appetite, even at such a late hour, Hiroshi slurped down a bowl of noodles. "You should join him," Satsuki told Daidai, stroking her long fingers across the tabletop, perhaps responding to the eye roll cast in Hiroshi's direction. "You have to eat no matter what. My mother used to say that."

Daidai tried to eat but couldn't, and her voice felt strained and unnatural in conversation. Satsuki had directed the trio to focus on the meal set in front of them even in the wake of her mother's death. They'd assumed their positions at the table like three reference points on a compass with the needle pointing north and away. Unmoored and alone, they'd each been implicated in a story that had only just then begun to take shape. Satsuki had arrived in Los Angeles ostensibly to enter Hiroshi's academic program, but had she also come so that she could live closer to her mother? If so, she'd never mentioned her mother's proximity. As far as Daidai knew, Satsuki spent the time she wasn't in class at their apartment. But that fact seemed to exist at the surface of her life, which had now broken open, exposing a great abyss.

No way yet to see inside, but the air felt, for lack of a better way to put it, tainted.

Silence engulfed the table and they were forced to feel their way through it, each ensnarled in his or her own private thoughts: Daidai with questions she'd not yet been able to articulate, Hiroshi uncharacteristically fidgety and mute in his chair at the head of the table, and Satsuki by her silence, indicating she wasn't ready or had simply elected not to share information. In an attempt to ease the mounting tension, Daidai left the room and brought back a bottle of whiskey from which Hiroshi measured out a double shot. Satsuki refused, preferring the tea she'd brought with her in a Thermos. For herself, Daidai poured a tumbler of soda water.

"So what happened?" Daidai finally asked, leaving her husband out of the conversation, unable to bear any more tension.

Satsuki frowned. "Evidently the death is under investigation."

"Were you even in touch with your mother?" Daidai noted the perturbation in her voice. Was she still feeling excluded by Hiroshi's expression of concern for his student? Was that it?

Hiroshi's sideways glance clearly indicated that he found his wife's question inappropriate. "We're sorry for your loss," he said, letting Satsuki off the hook from responding.

"It's not easy to explain my life to you," Satsuki said.

She wasn't asking Satsuki to explain her life, was she? Was that how she'd come off? Of course Satsuki would need space to sort through the feelings engendered by the loss of her mother. Hiroshi nodded his understanding, tracing his finger along the length of his wife's thigh, his touch both an approbation of Satsuki and a willing of his wife into silence.

Removing his hand from her lap, Daidai scooted her chair back, still longing for a point of connection and fed up at her perceived missteps. "I'm sorry," she said, stacking the dinner plates so that she could retreat to the kitchen. "I don't know what's wrong with me."

"The first four years of my life were idyllic," Satsuki volunteered before Daidai could leave the room. "My life was perfect until my mother disappeared."

"What?" Setting the stacked plates back on the table, Daidai refocused her attention on Satsuki. "What do you mean *disappeared*?"

"Just that."

The mother who'd just turned up dead had disappeared? So there *was* more to it. Daidai's heart beat against her rib cage, shifting the energy in the room away from Satsuki.

"As a young child, I lived to please my mother," Satsuki went on, seeming caught up in reverie.

"But you hadn't seen her since you were a child?" Daidai asked.

"You're sweet to care about me. I'm touched by your concern," she said, but the way she shook her head ever so slightly, refusing to make eye contact, indicated that her thoughts had drifted somewhere else entirely.

Hiroshi pinched his wife's kneecap, causing the length of Daidai's thigh to shudder. "Why did you do that?" she scolded her husband, wondering how anyone got past the disappearance of her mother, especially at such a young age. Then her thoughts settled back on Satsuki. "What was your mother like? Do you remember?"

"I remember everything about her," Satsuki said. "You might find it odd for me to say that after having lived apart from her for more than twenty-five years, but it's true."

"You fainted after the call came just now," Hiroshi said, evidently still replaying what had just happened.

"You don't understand," Satsuki said, shuddering. "I'm sorry." She glanced up before casting her gaze downward again. "Of course it's not possible for you to understand."

"I want to understand," Daidai told her.

"I didn't know until quite recently that my mother was living in California. After she vanished, my father took me aside to explain that she was dead."

"Dead of what?" Daidai asked. "Didn't he look for her?"

"I don't remember much about the days after her disappearance. My grandmother took care of me while my father was away. In the spring that I turned six, Grandmother Nobu brought me to my first day of school. But my grandfather became ill that year, which meant that she needed to return home to him. As a result, I was sent to live at a boarding school.

"I worried that entire first year that my father had sent me away so he could find another wife and forget about me, but that's not what happened."

Hiroshi scooted his seat back from the table and picked up the stack of plates that Daidai had set down. Satsuki's gaze shifted from him to Daidai as if she might explain what had just happened, but Daidai waved her hand at Hiroshi, dismissing him from the conversation. "Who called you tonight?" she asked.

Satsuki looked perplexed. "A police detective, I think. I can't recall his name."

"I'm sure we can find out if we need to," Daidai volunteered, assuming that anyone could access the public records produced by a police investigation. It'd be as simple as tracking down background on a painter, research she did all the time. "Have the police been in contact with your father?"

"The person who called me said they had."

"Shouldn't you call him, then?" she asked.

"No," she said abruptly. "Why would I do that?"

"Why wouldn't you?" Daidai asked. "I'm sure your father has information, things only he can explain."

"I could never ask him," she said.

Seeing Satsuki glance at her Thermos, Daidai reached across the table to pour her a fresh cup of tea just as Hiroshi returned with red bean ice cream scooped into three bowls. "Why not?" Daidai asked, but her question went unanswered and they ate their dessert in silence.

5

Daidai was reviewing what Satsuki had told her as she brushed her teeth before bed when Hiroshi's face appeared behind hers in the bathroom mirror. Preoccupied as she'd been, she didn't notice him immediately, and then didn't understand why he stood motionless, glowering like some phantom image of her husband.

"I don't understand you." His words seemed to confirm her impression of him, the whites of his eyes a stark contrast to his dark skin tone and accentuated by the ridges of his cheekbones.

"I don't understand you either," she said. Why had he been so protective of Satsuki, or for that matter felt the need to privilege his student over his wife? She finished with her teeth, allowing his accusation of her to settle as she dried her mouth on a hand towel. Pulling her shirt over her head, exposing the breasts that had drawn him to her, she turned around to face him. "Do you want to understand me?" she asked with a half smile.

"You know I do," he said, going to her without missing a beat.

She was pleased with the way his body found hers. His eyes closed against the darkness of the bedroom, the bones of his narrow hips thrust against her pelvis as he found his rhythm. She'd needed to feel that he still belonged to her, or to know for sure that he'd gone missing. But the Hiroshi she knew was back. Without the pressure built up by sex that was goal driven and prescribed, she moved her hips and tilted her pelvis to heighten her own pleasure and pulled him deeply inside her when he climaxed.

"That was unexpected," he said, rolling away, back to his side of the bed.

"Do you still find me brilliant?" Daidai reached a hand out to run her finger down his biceps, testing his claim that his attraction to her had been rooted in her fine mind.

"I've never doubted your capacity, intellectual or otherwise."

"Good," she said. "Please don't."

"But what got into you tonight?" He turned to face her, shortening the space between them.

"Are you talking about Satsuki?" she asked, wanting to be sure.

"She deserves a little respect."

"I care about her," Daidai said, hurt by her husband's remark. "Why would I not be curious about what happened to her mother?"

"You don't understand," he said, his earnest tone causing her to bristle. "You could be opening yourself up for things you might not want to know."

"Nonsense!" She understood how a person could be hurt by what she didn't know, but never by what she did. "I think she wanted to talk."

"She probably didn't feel she could deny you the information you'd asked for," he said. "But the two of you hardly know each other."

"What are you talking about?" Did he not know that she'd come to consider Satsuki a friend?

"Japanese draw a sharp distinction between what can be shared and what must remain personal," he explained. No longer speaking as her husband, he'd become the expert, pontificating first on the subject of friendship and then on race.

"I'm Japanese, too." She turned her back to him, letting him know he'd crossed a line.

"Technically, you're half," he said.

Technically, he was correct, but in the context of their relationship his remark was as hurtful as it was wrongheaded. Daidai should have called him on it, as in who did he think he was? It was simplistic to mete out authenticity according to racial bloodlines, worse still to judge his wife as lacking wholeness. But Daidai couldn't see Hiroshi as wrong. Tangled in her sympathies, she'd memorized his family's history early on like the Pledge of Allegiance. How his paternal grandfather had lost his automotive business during the war when his family had been sent by the U.S. government to live in the Colorado desert, how financial losses had set the Suzuki family on a course of self-destruction that ended when Hiroshi's stoical, hardworking nisei father had taken his own life at the age of fifty-two.

Her work as a curator, which she clung to even more ferociously now that her career was on hold, had begun as an emanation of her love of Hiroshi, and in particular the last installation, which she still viewed as the culmination of her work at the museum: artifacts she'd collected as an homage to Hiroshi's past.

Turning back to her husband, she could see that his expression remained smug and unchanged, as if he'd forgotten how they'd raised each other up, their careers blossoming as a result of the mutual care they paid to each other's thinking and work. At least *she* still remembered. She'd spotted Hiroshi among a hundred other college freshmen in the lecture hall for their economics course. He'd been the quiet, well-groomed boy who always arrived at the same time and sat in the same seat. He'd open his black notebook, pulled from a sleeve in his backpack, to a bookmarked page. She'd thought him a serious student until she'd asked for his notes from a lecture she'd missed and found doodles and drawings that bore no relation to the subject at hand strewn across his tablet. Hiroshi was slyer and more imaginative than he looked, but that semester he'd also been grieving his father, whose death, preceded the year before by the death of his mother to illness, had affected him deeply.

Perhaps news of Satsuki's mother's death had stirred his own feelings of loss. Had that been the reason for his irrational response? What he needed was to separate his feelings of loss from Satsuki's. Daidai said as such, then asked, "Don't you think it's strange that Satsuki hadn't mentioned that her mother was living in L.A.? And now she's turned up dead. It doesn't make sense."

Hiroshi yawned. "It's a timing issue," Hiroshi said. "Nothing more."

He continued, bringing up a relationship he rarely mentioned, "As for my mother, it's not that she didn't love me. If anything she loved me too much."

"I'm afraid I don't know what you're talking about," she said, feeling their hold on each other slipping away.

"You just need to take care with Satsuki," he said in a cautionary tone.

"Is she that special to you?" Daidai asked, meaning, more precisely, did he value Satsuki's feelings over hers?

"She's a gifted scholar. I'd hate to lose her in the program."

Hiroshi tugged at the sheet, wrapping it tightly around himself while Daidai listened to his breathing lengthen into sleep. Clever man that Hiroshi was, he'd baited her, finishing the conversation the same way he ended class sessions, by leaving a nagging question unanswered. The person Daidai needed to talk to, she concluded the next morning, was Louise. Their weekly lunch dates had lapsed since she'd stopped working downtown, and she'd missed having the contact.

"Daidai!" The lilt of Louise's voice calling her name warmed her immediately. "How've you been?"

"I've missed you," Daidai said. "How are you?"

"I've missed you, too," Louise said. "Can you hold on a minute?"

Daidai could hear traces of a conversation and papers being shuffled in the background, as she visualized Louise behind her desk, surrounded by briefs and client files. "Sorry for being out of touch," she said after the interruption. "That was a pretty good party we threw."

"Yes, it was." Daidai laughed, thinking back to the fall.

"It's funny you called because I stopped by the museum just the other day," she said. "I'd heard about the new exhibit and I wanted to see it for myself."

"And?"

"Awful," she said, implying to Daidai that her leave had damaged the museum's impeccable landscape. "Paltry. Poorly lit."

Had she gone in looking for flaws? She must have known that her negative review of the new exhibit would brighten Daidai's day.

"It's been a mess around here," she said, changing the subject before Daidai could respond. "I've been meaning to call to tell you. But maybe your mother's told you?"

Daidai's heart sank, her first thought being Gizo.

"My father's in pretty bad shape. He's in the hospital."

Daidai leaned back in her chair. Louise's mother, Irene, had been Daidai's mother's first friend when she'd arrived in L.A. She'd shown Mako where to shop for Japanese food and helped her to "Americanize" just enough so she didn't stick out. So why had Mako not told her about Danji? Had she assumed Daidai already knew? "I'm so sorry," she said.

"It's okay," Louise said. "Gizo's been running the shop and living at my dad's place. Fortunately Dad's house, the shop, and the hospital are all within walking distance."

"Let me help cook," Daidai said. "I'll bring something by tonight. I've got the time."

"You're sweet," she said, shuffling papers on the other end as silence once again engulfed the line. "But I think we're okay right now. Gizo's new girlfriend's family owns a restaurant, so that helps."

Daidai remembered the girl behind the counter. Then, returning to the unexpected news about Danji, she stiffened and debated the appropriateness of asking Louise for the information she sought, but her thoughts seemed focused on Satsuki. "Would you mind searching through the death index and coroner's office for some information on a woman with the last name Suzuki? She's the mother of Hiroshi's student. She'd be in her mid-fifties. We just found out Friday."

Daidai could hear the faint rhythm of Louise's breathing, coupled with the sound her fingers made tapping at the keyboard. It took her less than a minute to pull up the information Daidai had requested: "Ritsuko Suzuki. Born in Mito, Japan, died December 17, 2010, in West Los Angeles, California, at age fifty-six." She stopped herself. "This isn't the foreign student from the party, is it? Our age, pretty?"

"Satsuki," Daidai said, but Louise didn't wait for her to continue.

"There's more," she said. "What's up with this?"

What she said next made Daidai wish she were sitting across from Louise, rather than alone in the apartment with the phone pressed to her ear. The cause of Ritsuko Suzuki's death had not been confirmed, but a preliminary report indicated a probable suicide:

fatal gunshot to the side of the head, .38-caliber pistol found next to the body.

At the time of death, Ritsuko Suzuki had lived as a cloistered nun at Holy Heart Monastery, located—of all places—in the foothills of Hollywood.

6

The spring term started the first Tuesday of the New Year, which happened to coincide with the onset of winter weather. Overnight the thermostat had dropped below 60 in the apartment, causing the heat to click on for the first time that season. Daidai woke in a fit of sneezing when a rush of stale air and dust poured in through the vent. "Bless you," Hiroshi called from his study on the other side of the wall. It was Hiroshi's habit to take a run in the mornings when he reached a stopping point in his writing or needed a break from grading. Hearing the sound of his chair being pushed back from his desk followed by his approaching footfalls, she hoped she'd been the reason for his staying back, that he'd been waiting for her to wake up.

"Good morning." She smiled up at him, wiping loose strands of hair away from her face.

"Good, I guess." He shrugged, extending a box of tissues in her direction.

"Thank you," she said, kicking off the covers to expose the length of her thigh. "Want to join me?"

"Wish I could," he said before turning away. "Gotta shower."

Daidai watched him from behind as he undressed, either not noticing or not caring that she was watching him, and she lapsed into another sneezing fit.

The fact that Hiroshi left the apartment over an hour before the start of his first class that morning didn't escape Daidai's attention. After her phone conversation with Louise, she'd located an address for the Holy Heart Monastery and had decided to stop in for a visit. She'd make a day of it and drop by the Hashimotos' shop afterward with something for Gizo to take to Danji in the hospital.

Needing something to occupy her time while she waited for the morning traffic to die down, she returned to the bedroom to pull out the trunk she stowed under the bed during the summer months and began going through her drawers, replacing the tanks and short-sleeved T-shirts with sweaters. By the time she got in the car, it was nearly eleven thirty, which would leave practically no time to look around, as she'd read online that the monastery closed down during the lunch hour. Fortunately, the freeway traffic was moving along without a hitch, the cars in front and behind on the Ventura Freeway eastbound enabling her to merge right without having to overshoot the exit to avoid being hit, which she'd had to do on several occasions when she'd driven that stretch of freeway more frequently.

It had been years since she'd driven through Coldwater Canyon, so long ago that the vegetation spilling over the hilltops had matured in her absence. The scenery seemed inured to the sudden change of weather, with the glare of sunlight glinting off the pavement and plant leaves showing not a hint of frostbite. Trying to recall the last time she'd driven that route, she decided it must have been high school, long before Hiroshi, on a summer night with a boy whose face she no longer remembered. The windy path seemed built for reflection and self-recrimination, and she thought over the year and a half she'd been trying to get pregnant. Could there be a connection between Hiroshi's and her inability to conceive and their being somehow unfit to raise a child? Though she'd always trusted Hiroshi, she suspected he might be contemplating or having an affair with Satsuki. Then again, she believed it possible that her judgment had been skewed by being alone so much without work to contemplate. What if the affair was in her head? What if it were her fantasy instead of Hiroshi's? But her marriage had been fine up to that point.

The monastery had listed the director as Sister Mary Agnes, a woman who'd lived as a cloistered nun for more than sixty years. From the scant description of communal life, Daidai conjured images of austerity and deprivation, but Holy Heart was located in a neighborhood that could be described only as posh. The expensive-looking coupe she parked alongside could not have belonged to a nun. The parking lot abutted an ivy-covered stone wall, and farther down a formidable wrought-iron gate blocked the entrance as if to indicate that the drive had been a waste of time. So close to Hollywood, it looked like a stage set with the small speaker box half buried in ivy and, next to it, the black welcoming bell. As Daidai reached for the bellpull, a middle-aged woman appeared from behind the wall and pushed the gate open. Brushing past Daidai, she reached into her expensive handbag and retrieved a sensor, to which her car responded with a flicker of the headlamps and a happy bleep, and in her wake Daidai passed inside the grounds unnoticed.

Birds of paradise and blue flowering ground cover lined the walkway. The same large, round stones that made up the wall had been sunken into the dirt, which emitted a wet, earthy smell. The trail led to a white stucco building with an arched doorway that served as an entrance. Through the screen door, she could see a small shop, which appeared untended. Knocking, she called out a hello, noting as she poked her head inside a musty sweet smell she couldn't quite place.

A single band of sunlight lit the cavelike interior, which prevented her from seeing the black-habited nun in the room's darkness.

"Sorry if I scared you," Daidai said, having scared herself, supposing she should have listened for a response to her greeting before entering uninvited.

But rather than appear startled, the woman spoke without even looking up. "I'm afraid we're closed for the lunch hour. Didn't you read the sign?"

Daidai turned back to the small rectangular plaque that covered the screen door midway up. "I'm looking for Sister Mary Agnes," she said, undeterred, but received no response to indicate whether she'd even been heard.

Using the counter ledge to hoist herself up, the nun dominated the room with impressive height, yet her brittle movements and the lines around her mouth defined her as elderly.

"Would you happen to know where I might find Sister Mary Agnes?" Daidai spoke slowly and clearly. Having dealt with older patrons at the museum, she recognized the problems generated by faulty hearing, and guessed it was to blame for the missed communication.

"We're closed to the public during the lunch hour," the woman repeated, her expression softening into a smile.

"I see," Daidai said, lowering her voice. "May I wait?"

"Visitors are not permitted inside the grounds during the lunch hour. The shop reopens at one o'clock."

Daidai wondered whether the nun's seeming inscrutability could be attributed to her own lack of experience with nuns or clerics of any kind. Turning to leave, she doubted it would do any good for her to return after the lunch hour.

"I only came to bring in the trays, but I can sell you a loaf since you're here."

Daidai turned back around, confused. "I'm afraid I don't know what you're talking about."

"Ahn-bread. Isn't that what you came for?" The nun leaned her elbows on the counter, seeming to find Daidai as strange as Daidai found the nun.

A smile that felt mildly insincere curved Daidai's lips. "How much is the ahn-bread?"

"One loaf?"

"Yes. How much?"

"Ten dollars."

Daidai opened her wallet and slid a twenty across the counter. "Don't worry about making change, you can just give me two." She had no idea what had been handed her in the dark, but collected whatever it was she'd paid for and thanked the nun before turning to leave.

"God bless you," the proprietress called behind her.

Once in the sunlight Daidai was pleased to see the shiny brown tops of two perfectly shaped loaves of bread. She'd planned to pick up something for Danji in J-Town before returning to the Valley, but having the bread meant one less stop. She could give a loaf to Gizo to bring to his father and take the other home to Hiroshi.

Driving the back way out of the hills to avoid freeway traffic, through side streets of Hollywood she'd never even set foot on, she thought how strange it was to have grown up in a city large enough to hold so many secrets. There were the familiar spots, the ones she'd been traveling to or away from all her life, and Hollywood was not among them. She was glad to arrive in J-Town. As if in recognition that she belonged there, a car pulled out in front of Akai Electric just as she approached, and before she'd even shut off the engine, Gizo appeared. Standing on the curb, he grasped Daidai's shoulder from behind, pulling her into a side hug. "What's up, Daidai?"

Daidai smiled, wondering if every female Gizo knew got exactly the same greeting.

Bending to open the passenger door, she leaned back into the car and pulled out a loaf of ahn-bread. "I brought this for your father," she said, presenting it to him ceremoniously, with both hands. "Louise said he's had some health problems. I was sorry to hear that."

"How nice of you." He seemed genuinely touched. "Come in for a minute, fill me in on the latest."

Inside, the shop didn't look like she remembered it. Nothing she could put a finger on, but brighter somehow, the aisles slightly reconfigured. "Nice," she said, though she wasn't yet sure if she liked how it had changed.

"You like it?"

"Yup," she decided at that moment. "I do. I like it."

"It needed fresh paint for years, but that's not so easy with all the stuff in here."

Seeing the shelves, full of items put in place by Danji's hands, Daidai recalled the tremendous amount of sorting that needed to be done after her father's death. One day soon Danji would be dead, and Gizo would have to do what she'd done. Only Gizo's task would be far more complicated. Danji was an iconic figure who'd tended his shop on East First Street for as long as she could remember—longer than she'd been alive. Behind the counter, on a high shelf, someone had left a piece of *omanju* as an offering in front of the lacquered prayer shrine. That and the contents of the shop, displayed in neat rows, created a sense of reverence about the place somehow lacking in other venues.

"How's your dad doing?" Daidai asked, catching a whiff of paint fumes.

"Dad's okay," Gizo said. Picking the bread up from the glass counter, he held the plastic wrap under his nose and inhaled deeply. "How'd you guess his favorite?" He smiled. "I didn't know they made *ahn-pan* in a big loaf. Where'd you get it, here at Mikawaya?"

"Nope." Not having seen the bread as Japanese, Daidai laughed to see that the delight Hiroshi took in Japanese confections was shared by Gizo. "It was made in Hollywood, by a group of nuns."

"No kidding. Holy bread?"

She could accept the bread as Japanese, but not that it was holy, and suddenly she regretted having told Gizo where the bread had come from. It seemed wrong to let him think she'd gone out of her way to get the bread for Danji when the choice of a gift had come about merely by chance. "I'm not religious," she said, shrugging and hoping to recalibrate the conversation. "Are you?"

"I gotta believe there's something out there bigger than I am," Gizo said. He puffed out his chest playfully, but at the same time his mood had turned serious.

"Same," she said, realizing she'd not expected his response. Shifting her gaze from the contents of Danji's store to the expanse of Gizo's chest, she considered how he'd matured through the years and was struck by a wave of fondness for him. Growing up together had resulted in a feeling shared between them, a belief that maybe they were made of the same thing, or connected in ways she couldn't have anticipated. "I rather like the idea of holy bread," she declared, deciding that a wish for Gizo's father's good health had been the hidden purpose for her visit to the monastery.

Gizo looked around the store for customers in need of something. With no one but them in the shop, now it was his turn to make a concession. "I thought about you after I ran into you last summer on the street," he said, facing Daidai with an earnestness she found unnerving. "I always looked up to Hiroshi. He got his education, his good job and pretty wife. Now you're thinking about starting a family. That's great."

Daidai hoped that Gizo was right. Flattered that he'd thought about her at all, she made her own concession. "Growing up, I always wanted to be part of your family," she said.

"Really?" he said.

"My dad died two years ago," she added, not remembering if Gizo had ever met her father. He'd worked long hours when she was growing up, which she supposed made him the Irish version of Danji: a hardworking, tough family man.

"I'm sorry about your father," Gizo said. The sentimentality between them having become uncomfortable, Gizo eyed the bread, reminding Daidai of the child he'd been. "Do you mind if I try some of this?"

"Of course not!" she said, relieved. "I've got another loaf in the car. I'll go get it."

She was about to swing around when he grabbed her wrist. "Save the other loaf for Hiroshi. Dad's not supposed to have too much of the sweet stuff, but a little's okay. If I bring it to him like this he'll eat the whole thing."

Untwisting the wire from the plastic wrap that held the bread, Gizo reached inside and tore off a chunk for himself and another for Daidai. She could still feel the heat of his fingers on her wrist. The warmth of the expert hands that had repaired the rice sack caused her to imagine that time had looped back, or maybe it had never moved. The bread had a sticky sweet smell, its taste reminding Daidai how hungry she'd been.

7

Pulling away from Akai Electric that afternoon, Daidai had the sad feeling that part of her life had just ended. She doubted she'd see Gizo again any time soon; he wasn't part of her daily life, and she dreaded returning to her husband. The wintry low that started the day had left behind a layer of clouds that hung over downtown Los Angeles, and the chill that rose up from her core vibrated in her teeth as she wrapped her fingers around the cold steering wheel. Checking the clock on the dash, she calculated that Hiroshi would still be on campus, which meant she'd have time for a nap before dinner. She needed a chance to let her feelings settle. But sleep was not to come that afternoon. She realized that as soon as her key turned in the lock and the door to the apartment swung open.

"Okaeri ni!" Satsuki poked her head up over the back of the couch, startling her.

Though she visited nearly every day, seeing her there, alone in the apartment, caused the blood to drain from Daidai's face. "Is Hiroshi here?" she asked, worried over what could have brought Hiroshi home in the middle of the afternoon on the first day of classes.

"Isn't he teaching today?" Satsuki asked, her response somehow not reassuring. "I was waiting for you on the doorstep, but I got cold. I hope you don't mind that I let myself in."

On the tabletop lay the spare key that Hiroshi and she kept in the planter outside the front door. Daidai had used it recently. She'd been with Satsuki when she'd locked herself out, but why would Satsuki let herself in? Was this something Hiroshi and she had discussed? A sense of decorum prevented Daidai from asking, and Satsuki seemed to understand this. Smiling over the back of the couch, she let Daidai's favorite throw fall from around her shoulders. "I see you're more prepared than I was for winter in sunny Southern California."

Daidai was still puzzled, but seeing Satsuki's bare arms, she decided to let it go. The unusual thing, after all, was not that Satsuki had shown up, but that on this particular afternoon Daidai had not been home. "I pulled my sweaters out from under the bed this morning. I can lend you something warm to wear," she said, heading off to the bedroom, needing a moment on her own to think.

"So where have you been?" Satsuki called after her.

First she'd let herself in; now she demanded to know where Daidai had been. Daidai hadn't planned to mention her visit the monastery, and now she resented Satsuki's questioning her about her day. "I'm exhausted," she said, without saying where she'd gone. "I was hoping to lie down for a nap."

"Poor Daidai." Satsuki rose from the couch and rushed to where Daidai stood in the entryway. "I understand. Do you want me to go?"

She appeared ready to leave, but instead began circling Daidai, the way she usually did upon entering the apartment. "What are you doing?" Daidai demanded. "Stop that!"

Leaning over to sniff at the bread she'd carried in, Satsuki seemed not to hear her. "Let's start over." She spoke sweetly, showing her irresistible smile. "Will you do me a favor?"

"What?"

"Go out and come in again."

"Why?"

"Because I think it will put you in a better mood. Really. I wouldn't ask you if I didn't think it would work. Please try?"

"Are you joking?" Daidai said, getting irritated again.

"No way."

After gently turning her around by the shoulders, Satsuki gave Daidai a little shove, key in hand, and shut the door behind her.

"Can you hear me?" she asked, and Daidai imagined her forehead pressed to the other side of the door. "This time, when you come in, say, '*Tadaima!*'"

But when Daidai opened the door the room was quiet, no Satsuki popping her head up from the couch to greet her. Could the woman have managed an escape while she stood waiting outside? In her fatigued state, anything seemed possible. She regretted having been so unwelcoming until she remembered her line. "*Tadaima!*" she called out.

"*Okaeri ni.*" Satsuki appeared from behind the door to the bedroom wearing Daidai's favorite white cardigan, tying the sash around her waist. "That's much better!" she praised Daidai, taking the ahn-bread from her arms. "Now sit down. I'll make us tea."

"That would be nice," Daidai said, acknowledging that the possibility of a nap was over. "Let's have the black stuff."

"Not today," Satsuki said sweetly. "This afternoon I'll make *genmai*. Brown rice tea goes best with this bread."

"What do you know about this bread?" Daidai asked, shocked.

"It's a big *ahn-pan*, isn't it?" Satsuki called over her shoulder, having moved into the kitchen to get the tea started.

"How do you know about ahn-bread?" Daidai asked again.

"*Ahn-pan* is my favorite," Satsuki said.

Daidai recalled the events that led up to the brief transaction she'd had with the tall, old nun. When Hiroshi arrived home she served up what was left of the ahn-bread for dinner. Evidently he knew about the stuff, too, going so far as to claim it was the best *ahn-pan* he'd ever tasted and getting Daidai to promise she'd buy more.

"So you went downtown today?" he asked, assuming that she'd brought the ahn-bread back from J-Town.

"Mm-hmm." Daidai nodded, watching Satsuki's attention shift from her to Hiroshi, as if needing to gauge his response.

"See anyone?" he asked.

"I took some bread to Gizo to give to Danji. He's been sick."

Hiroshi stared at her from across the table, clearly waiting for something more. "If you were in J-Town, why didn't you bring the bread to Louise to give to her father? The public defender's office is right there on Temple, isn't it?"

"I figured she'd be busy," Daidai lied, stumped by her inability to explain her actions, even to herself. "And it was easier to find parking along East First."

She felt relieved when Hiroshi shrugged. What harm could there be in a simple substitution? So what if she'd bought the bread from Holy Heart Monastery, not J-Town, and what did it matter whether Louise or Gizo delivered some to Danji? It was more important that Satsuki and Hiroshi liked the ahn-bread, because her curiosity about Ritsuko Suzuki had been piqued and she needed an excuse to return to the monastery. She'd ask the nun about Ritsuko and bring back more ahn-bread. But two events kept Daidai from returning to Holy Heart Monastery in the month of January: first she found out she was pregnant, and then, a week later, she miscarried.

8

Daidai's mother was elated to hear the news of her pregnancy. "I knew it!" she said. "I've had a good feeling about this month." Even over the phone Daidai could see the spritely woman dancing around her kitchen, planning in her head for the birth of her first grandchild. A week later when Daidai drove over to tell her she'd miscarried, Mako sat down and wept.

Taken aback by the dramatic display of grief, Daidai tried to comfort her. "I've been to the doctor—twice now. The first time for tests, all of which came back negative."

But Mako refused to accept assurances, wiping at her eyes even though she wasn't the one to have experienced the loss. "Are you sure there's not something wrong with you?"

Daidai shook her head. Feeling her heart rate quicken, she drew in a deep breath and counted down from ten as she let it out.

"There's nothing wrong, then?"

"Look," Daidai said, waiting till she'd gotten down to zero. "If I hadn't been monitoring my cycle so closely I might not even have known about the pregnancy. I'm told a quarter of all pregnancies abort spontaneously in the first weeks."

"I don't think so."

"It's a fact." She shrugged, hating to argue. "The miscarriage proves I'm able to get pregnant."

"Maybe you just don't want to have a baby." Having stated the underlying reason for her upset, Mako sat perfectly poised and erect, still dabbing at her eyes, letting Daidai ponder her assertion. Did she not want to have a baby?

"You'll get your grandbaby," Daidai said, unwilling to entertain her mother's doubt.

"You don't have to have a baby to be happy," Mako said, refusing to let up.

As far as Daidai knew, babies were, to her mother, synonymous with happiness. So why say the opposite of what she meant? "I don't think you mean that," Daidai said, careful not to let on to what she was really thinking. The way Daidai saw it, her filial debt to her mother increased every year in proportion to her age, so that by thirty she owed her mother a baby—at least one. That was just the way things were between women of Mako's mind-set and their daughters. Even though she'd lived on the West Coast from the time she was a teenager, her upbringing in Tokyo had prevailed. Her traditional Japanese father had picked her husband, then a line worker at the car plant he ran. Peter Flynn certainly wasn't Japanese, but he was loyal and hardworking.

Daidai could imagine her parents young from pictures she'd seen, but she doubted they'd ever been in love. As far as she knew, love was an acquired skill, brought on by familiarity and common goals. Or maybe it was instinct, tempered by effort.

"Don't talk to me that way," Mako snapped.

"What way?" Daidai tried softening her tone.

"*Baka!*" Mako bared her teeth and threw her arms up. "You never listen to me!"

"I always listen to you," Daidai said softly, befuddled. Did Mako actually believe that a miscarriage and not wanting to have a baby were one and the same thing? "Hiroshi and I have gone through a lot of trouble to have a baby," she said, unable to stop herself now, pacing the room, stepping out of the way of the towering black unit that spanned the length of the wall. Bolted to a stabilizing beam after it had toppled in the last big earthquake, the console housed a flat-screen television beside a set of model Toyotas (the first Toyopet Crown and Land Cruiser alongside a Corona and Corolla), photos of a young Daidai in various stages of development, and wooden plaques that charted Peter Flynn's rise up the ranks at Toyota. He'd been Production Manager of the Year in 2008, the year before he died.

Next to the Buddhist altar her grandfather had brought with him from Japan, the martyred Jesus caught Daidai's eye, placed there by a woman whose judgment she now called into question. It occurred to her then that her desire to curate arose not from the peculiarity of her origins, but from her inability to situate herself in the images she'd been given. Turning from the artifacts of her childhood back to her mother whose defiance had collapsed into sadness, she could see her contribution to the confrontation she'd sought to avoid. "I can hear what you say as well as what you mean," she said.

"I don't know what you're talking about!" Mako said. "Why don't *you* say what you mean?"

"I think you wanted me to have this baby, maybe even more than I wanted it, and you're disappointed that I miscarried."

"Of course I'm disappointed!" Mako said, no longer able to contain her anxiety.

Daidai bit her lip and turned away. "Have you heard how Mr. Hashimoto is doing?" she asked, suddenly remembering the question she'd meant to ask earlier.

"Maybe not so good." Mako shook her head. "I heard he was mugged. Hurt pretty bad."

"Mugged?" Daidai echoed, struggling to make the transition in her thoughts. "Inside his shop?"

"No, it happened in the middle of the night."

"Was his house burglarized?" Daidai asked, doubtful that Danji would be anything but asleep in the middle of the night.

"I know, that's what I thought, too." Mako nodded deeply, seeming satisfied that they'd found a point of agreement. "But that's not what happened. Evidently Danji was out on the street. He'd get out of bed, dress himself in the middle of the night like he was going to work, and leave the house. Who knows how many times he did that. The police got in touch with Gizo, and now they're saying Danji has dementia. He got mugged when he was walking, and they left him there on the street.

"Louise didn't tell you?" she added.

"No." Daidai shuddered, thinking it time for a visit with Louise.

Mako shrugged. "Gizo handled it. Probably just some drug addict looking for money to get a fix. Picked the wrong guy to mug. Dead now."

Mako's stories could be so confusing. She tended to jump from point to point without transitions. It was the listener's job to make them. Maybe because she thought in Japanese the problem lay in translation, but to some extent she was also just someone who expected a listener to make leaps of thought. She had an agile mind, so everyone else should, too. "Are you saying Gizo went after the person who mugged his father?" Daidai asked.

"I don't think anyone would have hurt Danji if they knew who he was."

"Do you mean no one would hurt Danji because he was such a nice man, or because they were afraid of Gizo?"

"Wouldn't you be afraid of Gizo?"

She could be so infuriating! "Why would I be afraid of Gizo?"

"Honestly, Daidai, I thought this time off might be good for you," Mako said, disgruntled by her daughter's inability to follow her logic. "You've spent so much time looking at *things*, but what has that done for you if you can't even recognize what's happening with the people right under your nose? Reminds me of how your father would come home from work talking about how that bumper looked wrong on that car or complaining about the shape of a taillight. He knew how cars were supposed to look and he could see them just fine, but the rest was up to me—I'd have to point out the people around him making friends, remind him that those were the ones who moved up in the company. It's a good thing that my father wasn't fooled. He noticed Daddy and made him manager. You're just like him. You see the thing just fine, just not the hand that made it.

"What?" she demanded when Daidai said nothing.

"I'm listening to you," Daidai said. "I just don't know what to say."

"Gizo, he's so charming, right?" Mako started in again.

"I guess," she said, not wanting to anger her mother further in case she wasn't supposed to agree.

"See?"

"No, I don't."

"Gizo's charming, but you don't think: people are charming for a reason. Well, Gizo has his own business."

"You mean the security company he runs? I've seen his office behind the store."

"You saw what he showed you, but how about what he didn't show you? Did you notice all the money he makes? Lets him be good to his father—a good son."

So Gizo ran some kind of racket. So what? What was she supposed to notice? Mako wasn't making sense, but Daidai knew better than to say so.

After her visit with her mother, Daidai headed for home along the 405 Freeway. She stared up at the clouds hanging still and low, unusual for Los Angeles even in winter. In the grayness of the afternoon, it was as if the old sights were asking her to look at them anew. The hillside cemetery maxed out on room for gravesites, the buildings that made up Westwood clinging tightly to their quadrant, the tram that snaked its way up to the Getty Museum—it all amounted to what Daidai perceived as loneliness. Her father, who'd expressed his fondness in overt gestures and impeccably timed appearances every evening, was gone. Her marriage to Hiroshi had come with the assurance that she would never be alone. But she'd been on her own since she'd gone on leave, and with the loss of the baby they'd worked so hard to conceive she felt bereft.

She had the company of her mother, however erratic Mako's behavior. But even that relationship had begun to feel shaky. Perhaps rather than separate her from herself, the miscarriage had dislodged her from her mother. Was that why she'd been inconsolable? Then there was Hiroshi, who'd barely looked up from his work, choosing to emphasize the same facts she'd spun for her mother's benefit: that rather than loss, the ordeal she'd been through had foreshadowed her luck by proving that she could get pregnant. But what was the point of generating the same information they'd paid the doctor to render? The pregnancy, rather than affirm a potential life, had been a prelude to death.

9

Daidai no longer had grand expectations of what she might uncover at Holy Heart, but on the first Tuesday in February, an entire month gone by since her first visit, she retraced her route, this time arriving well before the lunch hour. She'd missed a lot the first time. Peering in through the screen, she wondered whether she'd even wound up at the same location. Near the entrance, a circular stand held postcards and other religious artifacts, and a row of carved wooden crucifixes lined the wall, apparently for sale. Under white fluorescent lighting, everything practically glowed.

When the screen door clacked shut, indicating the presence of a customer, the sister behind the counter turned to face Daidai with a broad grin. "I hope you're not here for bread!" she called out, her dark eyes wrinkling into peach pits. Like the nun running the shop the first time Daidai had visited, this sister was old, though not nearly as tall, and she appeared to suffer from poor eyesight.

"Good morning, sister." Daidai smiled, approaching the counter ready for conversation. "I was here last month looking for Sister Mary Agnes. Is she in today?"

"May I help you?" The habited sister's voice was loud, shrill, and impervious. Had she not heard Daidai's question, or was she merely ignoring her?

Daidai braced herself for the exchanges that might have to take place before she could broach the business at hand. "I'm here to see Sister Mary Agnes," she said, still trying to smile.

"I'm Sister Elspeth," the nun said, hands clasped on the countertop.

In contrast to her unyielding stance, Sister Elspeth's eyes were a pleasing and uncomplicated shade of brown. "Nice to meet you, sister," Daidai greeted her once more before taking up with small talk. "My husband really liked the bread I brought home the last time I was here."

"It's good stuff, isn't it?" Sister Elspeth's features softened into a grin.

"It's sweet and very unusual," Daidai said, pleased by the sister's response to flattery. "How long does it keep?"

"It only stays fresh for a couple days—three at the most. You can freeze it, and we sell it that way, too, but we don't have any right now."

"You've sold out?"

"We do sell out sometimes, yes, that's happened. But we haven't been able to make any this week. You're not the first person I've had to disappoint this morning. The bread has been the main source of income for this monastery for many years now."

"Then why would you stop making it?" Daidai asked, struggling to keep up her end of the conversation.

"The prioress has hurt her back, and the rest of us don't have the constitution to haul the baking flour and cook the beans."

The nun looked defeated as Daidai thought alongside her. If the person who usually did the work was laid up, the ingredients could be divided into manageable units. Perhaps all they needed was a way to divvy up the workload.

"The bread is filled with adzuki beans, which must be boiled on the stovetop and stirred for several hours," the sister explained, as if Daidai had asked how the confection was made. "But I've never done the baking or the boiling. I just work mornings in the shop."

"I see." The woman looked ancient, Daidai thought, as she readied herself to speak the reason for her visit. "Did you know Ritsuko Suzuki?"

Sister Elspeth squinted into the light. "I haven't heard the name Ritsuko in a long time. If you're talking about Sister Bernadette, the ahn-bread was her recipe. Bless her soul. She did all the heavy lifting and took charge of the beans."

"What happened to Sister Bernadette?" Daidai asked, using the name Sister Elspeth had given.

"Heart attack."

The vaulted door at the back of the shop opened and a rush of light reflected onto the walls from an elaborately carved metal crucifix that hung over the counter. Sister Elspeth regarded the newcomer with a deferential nod. "Sister Mary Agnes is our Mother Superior," she said, introducing the taller woman, whose title suited her perfectly.

Daidai had been about to point out to Sister Elspeth what she knew from the death record, that Ritsuko Suzuki had been shot by a handgun, but turned instead to the shelf of curios while Sister Mary Agnes engaged Sister Elspeth with whatever matter she'd come to discuss. She'd made an error in asking if the sister knew what had happened to Ritsuko. Now she'd be forced to wonder whether the sister knew why she'd come, and why she thought Ritsuko, whom she called Bernadette, had died of a heart attack.

"How many nuns live here at the monastery?" she asked once the Mother Superior had left the store.

"There are just eight of us—three, including the Mother Superior and myself, to take care of the five who can't get around much. We don't mind the work, but without the proceeds from the ahn-bread sales, I expect that there'll be no reason to keep us here. What's the point of keeping things as they are just for a bunch of old nuns? We've been told this property is worth quite a lot of money."

Daidai didn't know what to do with the information Sister Elspeth had offered. A picture of the elderly nuns, Ritsuko among them, had emerged as the sister spoke. What would cause women to sequester themselves in such a mundane and rote existence? They were old now, so the simplicity of life at the monastery probably suited them. But they hadn't always been old. And how was it that Ritsuko had become part of their group?

"I'm late in attending to morning prayer. God bless you," Sister Elspeth said, rising to leave when the Mother Superior reappeared with a stack of receipts.

"Sister Elspeth was telling me about Sister Bernadette," Daidai continued on with Sister Mary Agnes in as pleasant a tone as she could muster, given her mounting frustration.

"God bless her," the prioress said, framing herself with the sign of the cross before turning back to her work. "She recently passed."

"I was sorry to hear that," Daidai said to the woman's back. "How did a foreigner come to live in this monastery?"

"She got here the way the rest of us did: we were called here by God."

Daidai bit her tongue. *Let me get this straight,* she wanted to say. *The bunch of you really believe you were called here? To make ahn-bread and pray?* Having recently been confounded by the simple life, Daidai doubted anyone would want to confine herself behind a wall and do the same thing every day. And even if these women successfully combatted their boredom, why would they believe their lives to be an act of God? She'd have to think about it. Daidai moved to leave the store.

"During the nearly twenty-five years Sister Bernadette lived at Holy Heart she followed the same rules as the rest of us."

Sister Mary Agnes's voice called Daidai back. She hadn't asked whether Ritsuko had followed the house rules or inferred that she hadn't, so what was the prioress trying to say?

"All the sisters were very fond of Bernadette, right up until the very end," Sister Mary Agnes continued, with a finality that indicated she was done speaking.

Her words echoed in Daidai's ears as she walked away.

10

Daidai sped down the hill that led away from the monastery with her gaze focused on the road in front of her. Why had Sister Elspeth said that Ritsuko (whom she had called Sister Bernadette) had died of a heart attack when according to the police report she'd been shot? And what had Sister Mary Agnes been trying to say? The nuns knew more than they were letting on; she felt certain of it, even without knowing precisely why. She wished she could mull things over with Hiroshi. They'd been the perfect team, feeding off each other's ideas about their work, and it upset her terribly to think of Hiroshi doing what he'd once done with her with Satsuki.

Waiting for her husband to arrive back at the apartment, she dozed off and fell into a strange dream. Walking along the sidewalk in a congested city, she was trying to get home. The right side of the block, lined with tall apartment buildings that housed shops on the ground level, was the side she had to walk on because the earth on the other side had been dug up. A plywood wall hid a construction site, ending where the two sides of the street merged, at the foundation of a building about to be erected. She tried to walk around it, but even on the periphery the dirt began to crumble beneath her. Excess water had collected, forming a ditch that had been horribly polluted by the construction. She carried a black briefcase, which she stuck down into the water like a cane, hoping to prop herself back up.

She knew she shouldn't use the briefcase because the water would seep inside and ruin the papers. The briefcase was all she had, but it wasn't enough. She started to sink and was waist deep in the muck when she felt Hiroshi standing over her desk.

"You fell asleep," he commented.

The color had all but drained out of the winter sky. "I don't have dinner made," she said, groggy and hungry.

"Don't worry about it," he said, and smiled. "I can fend for myself."

Daidai smiled back, pleased that at the end of the day Hiroshi had arrived home in a cooperative mood. After taking a minute to stretch, she walked over to the couch where he'd gone with an apple and propped her legs across his lap. "How was your day?"

"Fine. Yours?"

"Fine."

"What did you do?"

"The ahn-bread I brought you before," she began, easing herself into wakefulness, "I went to get some more of it, but they were out."

"Too bad." He looked perplexed.

"Sorry."

"See Gizo?"

Suddenly she felt confused again. What was he trying to say? "The ahn-bread is made by a bunch of nuns at the Holy Heart Monastery," she explained, startled by a thump.

"No kidding?" Hiroshi used the apple core as a pointer, directing Daidai's attention over her shoulder to where a misguided bird had flown into the sliding door. "That's the second one this week."

She would need to put up decals on the clear glass as a deterrent. "I went to the monastery for information about Satsuki's mother. Aren't you curious about why she'd turn up dead here in Los Angeles? It turns out she was living at the monastery. She'd become a nun."

"Her personal life is none of our business," Hiroshi scolded.

"Death belongs to the public sphere," Daidai countered. "Strange thing is, one nun thought Ritsuko, who went by the name Bernadette, died of a heart attack, even though the record shows she'd been shot; the other, the Mother Superior, seemed angry. But I couldn't tell if it was with her or maybe with me."

Hiroshi screwed up his eyebrows. "Why would she be angry with you?"

Daidai shrugged. "She didn't seem to like being questioned."

"Surely a nun would see the act of suicide as a sin against God."

Hiroshi's simple explanation for the head mistress's irritation seemed likely. "I'm curious about Satsuki's dad," Daidai said, expanding her picture of the family to include his role.

Taking hold of her foot, Hiroshi pulled each toe expertly, the way he always did, releasing the tension with a pop. "How so?"

"Because he lied to Satsuki. He claimed her mother was dead when in fact she was alive, which means he probably knew why his wife vanished. Do you think he had something to do with it?"

Hiroshi dropped her foot and sneered. Taking aim, he launched the apple core he'd been holding across the room into the waste bin before turning his attention back to his wife. "I'm sure Satsuki's father just wanted to protect her so she could move on. She was a young child at the time. The police have been in touch with her again. Did I mention that?"

He hadn't, of course; she would have remembered if he had. "I just saw Satsuki. She didn't mention anything to me."

Hiroshi shrugged. "She probably didn't want to burden you because she knew you were upset about the miscarriage."

Daidai gasped. "I didn't tell her about the miscarriage. That's personal, between you and me."

"She could see that you were distracted and upset. She asked me why."

"You shouldn't have told her." Daidai removed her legs from across his lap in rebuke. "I'm still upset."

"A detective called her after trying to get in touch with her father again," Hiroshi added, shifting the conversation back to Satsuki. "He's evidently away on an art-buying trip and Satsuki claimed he wasn't reachable by phone."

"Isn't everyone reachable by phone these days?" She smiled, and he smiled back in agreement

."The first time they'd talked to him at his home in Mito. But apparently they don't have his mobile number and Satsuki doesn't want to give it out. She came to me to ask if she could get in trouble for not giving the police what they asked for."

"For withholding information? Of course she can." Daidai was adamant, but Hiroshi waved her comment away.

"If it comes up later, she can just say that she hadn't understood. Use their assumptions about her foreignness back on them."

"Why are you telling me this?" she asked. It irked her that Hiroshi would use race as a bargaining chip where the police were involved.

"Because you asked."

He was right, she'd asked. But the information Hiroshi had given didn't help. What had begun as an attempt to engage Hiroshi in conversation over something that puzzled her had ended badly. Clearly, her husband's involvement with Satsuki extended beyond their academic life, and Daidai wasn't really part of either conversation. Feeling teased to be offered a glimpse of conversations she hadn't been part of, she was glad to have dinner to think about, a meal that needed to be prepared and eaten. Hiroshi set water to boil for pasta while she got to work on a salad. There was comfort to be had in the ability to prepare a straightforward dinner together. Working in tandem, without words between them, they could follow simple steps that would result in something satisfying to them both. He'd not been able to console her after the miscarriage, which had resulted in a loss of intimacy. Blame the obstetrician for instructing them to refrain from sex until her next cycle. But standing beside her husband, Daidai had an idea, which she waited until the food had been served up to announce. "Let's go away this weekend."

Hiroshi looked up blankly from his bowl of pasta. "Too busy."

"You don't have to do anything," she assured him. They'd been to an inn in Santa Barbara so close to the beach that the surf had been audible from bed. She could see about booking a reservation there. All they'd need to pack was a change of clothing.

"Let me check my calendar," he said, letting her know he'd dismissed the idea.

"Could be fun." Daidai leaned over the table, letting her breasts brush across his arm.

"Maybe."

She'd have to settle for this modicum of progress. They ate the rest of their meal in silence.

"I'll do the dishes," she said. Pushing back her chair, she stacked the dinner plates and carried them off to the kitchen, leaving Hiroshi behind to dispose of the leftovers.

She hadn't expected him to come up from behind while her hands were soapy with dishwater, a line of sweat beading her forehead from the steam rising off the dishes. "I do love you," he said, parting her hair so that he could kiss the back of her neck. It bothered her a little that she couldn't see him, that she had only his touch to gauge what he might be thinking. Shutting off the water, she leaned over the sink, trying to visualize his hands as he worked.

"We're supposed to wait a while longer," she said, unable to summon the proper feelings of arousal, reminding him that the OB said it'd take a month for her body to heal from the precautionary D&C she'd been given after the miscarriage.

"How much longer?" he asked, moving his hands to her nipples and finding them hard.

"I guess it doesn't matter." She focused on his hands, unable to explain to him or herself what difference a few days on either side of a month would make. She tried to feel something for him as he worked his way inside her, but felt only herself, the deep inside of her out of the habit of being touched. And because it would have been untenable at that moment to feel her loss, she wrestled not with what she wanted, but to understand what it was she seemed not to want. She'd wished to see her husband's face, to feel something of what he was experiencing, but she concluded that maybe it was better that he couldn't see hers.

She could feel his abdomen against the small of her back and buttocks as his hand traced past her stomach to her pubic hair. It was what she'd asked for. She'd wanted him, though, oddly, she'd stopped thinking of Hiroshi at all. With her mind traveling back over the events of the day, it was Sister Mary Agnes's voice she heard: *Sister Bernadette . . . followed the same rules as the rest of us. All the sisters were very fond of Bernadette, right until the very end.* So what had happened to change their fond feelings?

II

The next morning Satsuki arrived looking more cheerful than Daidai had seen her in a while. *"Ohayoo gozaimasu!"* she said in a singsong. She had with her the same Thermos she carried everywhere, along with a sachet of tea for Daidai. While they waited for the water to boil, Daidai mentioned her visit to the monastery. She'd told Hiroshi, which meant Satsuki would likely find out from him if not from her, and she hoped Satsuki would reveal the layer of information that seemed to be missing.

"The ahn-bread you sampled?" she began, going on to explain about the nuns at Holy Heart who sold it to keep the monastery afloat.

"You went to the monastery to buy bread?" Satsuki asked, her face blanched of color in the harsh sunlight.

"Not exactly." Daidai explained how this group of nuns who lived with her mother had been forced to stop making the bread. Now that Ritsuko, whom they called Bernadette, was no longer working with them, they couldn't handle the labor.

"You went to the monastery to find out about my mother and came back with ahn-bread." The statement sounded more like a question, though Satsuki's gestures betrayed no uncertainty. She poured water for Daidai's tea with a steady hand, her gaze fixed on Daidai with the intense concentration Daidai had come to count on from her. "You're interested in knowing how my mother lived," she said, sipping the tea she'd poured for herself. "You want to know what she was like when she was alive, and how the people around her responded to her. Does this curiosity come out of your interest in me?"

"Yes, of course." Daidai cast away the guilt she'd been feeling in an attempt to reassure her.

Satsuki nodded her approval. "I can see that you're very thorough in your approach."

"I can be, indeed." Daidai held Satsuki's gaze, deciding in the pause to have with Satsuki the conversation she'd intended to have with Hiroshi. "I don't understand why Sister Elspeth would say your mother died of a heart attack when the record indicates a gun shot. And if that's the case, why haven't the police ruled out murder? Where would your mother have gotten a gun?"

"It's puzzling, I agree."

"If this is none of my business, just tell me." Daidai focused on Satsuki's hesitation. "Or maybe there's something you don't want to tell me?"

"No!" Satsuki's eyes widened. "I want you to trust me. Your trust is important to me."

With her tea laid out and steeping, Daidai watched Satsuki. She admired the economy of the woman's gestures, but her natural elegance had been offset by a flaw, a slight tremor that rattled the saucer as she set her teacup down. Surely the news of her mother's death had taken its toll. Although she'd not said so, Daidai knew it had been a difficult time, and perhaps as a result an older, worn-down Satsuki had emerged.

"You might think this strange, but I've always imagined that people are born in invisible boxes," Satsuki said after a long silence.

Daidai nodded as strange images flitted through her head. A glass coffin, Sleeping Beauty style, followed by a freight box with a baby folded up inside.

"These boxes have nothing to do with a person's actual size," Satsuki continued, as if to point out where Daidai had gone wrong in her thinking. "A large person can be born in a small box, and a small person in a large box. The box determines how far a person can travel in life. If your box is very small, then chances are you're going to live your entire life in one place, like a canary in a cage. And if your box is big, who knows where you'll end up, but chances are it'll be somewhere different from where you started.

"Since the boxes are something anyone can see if they look hard enough, how life plays itself out in most instances is not a great surprise. People born in big boxes are the fortunate ones. They can go wherever they want. In extraordinary circumstances a person born into a small box will struggle and resist and perhaps eventually break free and live outside the box they were born in. In that case a person may go very far. But unfortunately, people who break free of their boxes are especially vulnerable, because the box—as well as holding people in—offers them protection.

"Do you understand?"

The associations that fed Daidai's thoughts as Satsuki talked satisfied her into believing that she'd known all along about the boxes Satsuki described. Perhaps it was a lecture she'd heard in Asian American Studies about the assimilation process, or maybe it was something more personal. "Tell me about you and me and Hiroshi. I think I need examples."

Satsuki nodded. "You're special. You're protected, so you can go anywhere. Hiroshi less so, but he's still somewhat free. As for me, if I could see my own box I'd tell you what it looked like, but I don't think people can ever really see their own boxes."

What Daidai saw was a mirror. She was being enticed by her own image, one she'd constructed, so that what Satsuki described made sense to her. She was Japanese, like Hiroshi and Satsuki, but her father was Irish. "Special" was therefore a euphemism for "excluded." The paradigm applied to Hiroshi and Satsuki, but not her. "What about your mother?" she asked, wanting to know how Satsuki saw herself through the lens of Ritsuko.

"I've thought about my mother many times over the years," she answered. "She was born into a small, cramped box. She managed to break free somehow, but she must have felt very lost in the world outside Mito. It's not surprising that she wound up at a monastery. She needed protection."

"I see." Daidai couldn't appreciate what Satsuki was revealing about herself, but recalling her conversations with the nuns, she felt sympathy for Satsuki's mother.

"You and I would not have been friends back then," Satsuki pronounced, emerging from her reverie. "I had no friends as a child. When I think back, I was probably a very peculiar little girl. But I believed my company to be absolutely indispensable to my mother's well-being and so I never left her side. I didn't spend time with my father at all, even after my mother disappeared. He was a stranger to me. He still is.

"Most four-year-olds probably love being around their fathers. I'm right about that in your case, aren't I, Daidai?"

"Yes," Daidai concurred, feeling herself implicated in Satsuki's story. Raising her teacup to her lips with an unsteady hand, she shifted her hips uncomfortably in her seat.

"The difference between us is that I have only one early memory of my father," Satsuki said. "It takes place in the darkened foyer of my father's home in Mito. I believe he is handing his suit jacket off to my mother, a scene I witnessed nightly from the doorway to my room. Because I was sent off to boarding school soon after my mother disappeared, I never really lived with my father. In fact, I've not spent even one entire day with him. But the time he and I have had together confirms that he is a fascinating man, and there are many others who have shared with me their high opinion of him. In fact, I think he's someone you'd like to meet. Would you like to meet my father, Daidai?"

"I'd love to, of course." Having come to feel that she owed Satsuki something, Daidai responded the way any caring friend would have.

"Then I'd like to invite you to come to Mito with me over spring break."

It was a generous gesture, and one that seemed to come out of nowhere. Had Satsuki considered what such a trip would entail? How impractical, let alone expensive, it would be? "Maybe your father will come visit you here."

"He'd never come to Los Angeles, unless some buying venture brought him here!" She laughed. "But seriously, would you like to come with me to Mito? I've told my father about you and Hiroshi, and how kind you've both been to me. You're welcome to travel as my guest, so there'd be no need to worry about booking a hotel."

"I'd like to go." While she'd hoped to visit Japan someday, Daidai hesitated, unsure about this arrangement. "Let me see what Hiroshi thinks."

"Good!" Satsuki winked and exposed the set of uneven teeth Daidai had come to love about her. "It's a plan then."

12

When Hiroshi arrived home after a seminar that evening, Daidai poured him a glass of the expensive wine she'd stored away for a special occasion, hoping to convince him that he should travel with Satsuki and her to Mito. From her spot on the couch she watched the stress of the day empty out of him as he tilted the glass to his lips, draining the luscious red liquid before setting the tumbler to rest on the high counter. After a leisurely stretch, he undid the top three buttons on his shirt and pulled it like a sweater over his head, exposing the lean cut of his frame. His erect nipples stood out almost black against his pale chest as he bent over his wife. Tucking his hand inside her shirt, he teased her breast with his warm fingers. When he dropped his pants in front of the picture window, she pulled the curtain closed behind him.

"Your students are probably still making their way home after seminar," she scolded, knowing all the while she'd relent. "What if one of them is out there?"

It was a good thing, wasn't it, that Hiroshi wanted sex again? He entered her forcefully, climaxing before she could find her rhythm or let him know in some way that she'd expected better from him, though she guessed she wouldn't have followed suit even if he'd kept going. That night having spun from the one before without interest on Daidai's part, she worried that the miscarriage had affected her in ways she couldn't account for. Or maybe she was just out of practice. When Hiroshi was done, Daidai mentioned how Satsuki had invited her to spend spring break at her father's home and asked whether he wanted to join them.

"Impossible" was all he'd say. He'd received a deadline from a journal that published his research and spring break was the time he'd set aside for revisions.

It was a good excuse, one that months before would have been inarguable. But how often did an opportunity like this come along? "You should go with us," she found herself pleading.

"You go."

"You go, too."

"No," he said. And she knew his answer was final.

"But I think you should go," he added. "It'll be a great opportunity to see Japan."

PART TWO

|

THE GRANDEUR OF
HIS LIFE IN MITO

13

Tokyo smelled of the sea. A briny dampness drenched the air and clung to the insides of the nostrils, and a single cloud hung over the skyline like a giant hat exposing beneath it a broad stripe of blue. The plane had left Los Angeles in the early morning. Arriving at Narita almost twelve hours later, it was still morning, though the time had moved ahead by an entire day and the temperature had dropped nearly twenty degrees. Where before Satsuki had complained about feeling out of her element during the last months she'd lived in the Valley, now it was Daidai's turn to feel displaced. Amid the expressionless throng, each individual seeming to avert his or her gaze just as she attempted eye contact, she was reminded of the stranger who'd approached her on the street in J-Town the summer before, offering assistance only to disappear before her eyes.

But this time there was no Gizo, no benevolence or familiarity in an airport that had been bleached of color, the bustle of travelers hushed, or perhaps her ears were still clogged by the change in air pressure, a congestive silence punctuated only by the sharpness of a saccharine-toned woman's voice broadcasting polite messages in Japanese. Next to Daidai, Satsuki had emerged from the hub with a close-lipped smile. Right at home in Tokyo, though cautious not to reveal too much enthusiasm if that was, indeed, what she was feeling, she navigated through the crowded airport like the denizen she was, taking the handle of Daidai's suitcase and dragging it behind her alongside her own after genuflecting appropriately when her roller bag scuffed the black polish off the shoe of an overdressed businessman.

Outside the terminal, Daidai joined the queue beside her traveling companion, feeling increasingly self-conscious as they moved toward a row of taxis. "How far is your father's house from the airport?" she asked, recalling, if she'd calculated the distance correctly, that Mito was a good two hours' drive.

Satsuki ignored Daidai's question. Reciting her father's address to a uniformed attendant, she slid into the metered cab beside Daidai. "We'll have plenty of time to take public transportation if that's what you wish," she said, and smiled, squeezing the back of her friend's hand for reassurance.

Having no idea where she was, Daidai said nothing more. It had seemed unwise not to take the public transportation that she knew to be available, but inside the car she felt warm and comfortable and safe in a way she hadn't when suffused in the airport crowd. Seated on a bench with a white brocaded backrest and pressed against the car window, she became the observer of her own experience, aware of Satsuki's presence, but not involved in it. The ride felt as if it had come straight out of a dream—new and colorful images colliding before her eyes suggesting all that she'd overlooked, that things were not as they'd seemed to her the day, or even hour, before. When the taxi pulled up at a wooden gate two hours later, it was as if no time at all had passed.

Satsuki handed the driver some yen notes, waving away Daidai's offer to split the fare. "You've taken care of me for half a year. Now it's my turn to play host. I don't know what type of hospitality my father will show you. He is not always predictable about sharing his money or his time. But whatever he offers there's no point in trying to deny him. Please just accept and let him treat you well."

The gate opened into a carefully groomed courtyard. Potted plants lined the cement walkway, which had been laid in a square around a tall and leafless tree that towered over the blue-tiled roof of the house. The house itself sprawled out from the main entrance located at its center. Through barren branches Daidai could see a row of low, square-paned windows framed in wood, which she stopped to admire. "That's my room," Satsuki said, and pointed off to the right. "The original house ended there. It was quite small in comparison to what it's become through the years. My father bought up the surrounding properties that became available as his prosperity increased. To tell you the truth, I never know quite what the house will look like when I return to visit it."

A woman who might have been the housekeeper met them at the entrance. She bowed graciously to Satsuki and the two exchanged words that Daidai couldn't understand.

"My father won't be home until late this evening," Satsuki explained once the woman, towing their luggage behind her, had disappeared at a jog in the hall. "This is a good thing. It will give you a chance to view the house without his presence, which might otherwise dominate your impression. My father, you'll see, is quite opinionated."

The first stop was a traditional sitting room where the only piece of furniture was a low table surrounded by floor cushions. On a burner in the middle of the *kotatsu* an iron pot was warming, from which Satsuki served tea. The sparsely decorated room gave off a tranquil mood. High windows let in the natural light and a series of woodblock prints in muted colors lined the walls. Daidai would have been happy to spend more time sitting at the low table drinking tea and examining them, but when the housekeeper came to replenish the hot water Satsuki sent her away. "Now, if you're ready, let's move on with your tour."

The intricate layout of the house had not been apparent from the outside. Each room led to another chamber, all adorned with traditional Japanese artwork, which filled the interior spaces in abundance. Some paintings were familiar to Satsuki; others she stopped to ponder, remarking on a detail or soliciting Daidai's opinion of what constituted her father's livelihood. "A few pieces, the ones he feels attached to, are permanent," she explained. "The rest rotate when he discovers a new artist or tires of an old one."

Though Satsuki seemed to expect a professional evaluation of the work, Daidai found herself hard-pressed to render an appraisal. Her eye simply wasn't drawn to any one painting or even the collection that had been amassed, which was in many ways hodgepodge and unremarkable. Instead, what seemed abundantly worthy of comment was the house itself. Neither lavish nor commodious, it bore none of the markings that anyone might have expected of a wealthy art dealer. But what was lacking in extravagance and excess somehow heightened the effect. Daidai wished she could call Hiroshi and narrate the rooms along with their contents, but she had no words to articulate to Satsuki what she felt.

After enough turns and stops to leave a viewer utterly disoriented, a long hall dead-ended into a square, windowless space as darkened and dank smelling as an unused closet. Satsuki turned a dial, causing light to spill boldly against the wall opposite the doorway, where a canvas hung from near the ceiling almost to the floor. Even with ample lighting the background was dark, accentuating the figure in the foreground, larger than life, which in its stillness and formal posture suggested a statue. Naked, and revealing a shadowed, downturned profile, the silhouetted woman turned over one hip in the direction of the viewer. Daidai recognized her at once as a prototypical broad-cheeked woman from the Heian era—her strong, high nose and fine, arched eyebrows, the curvature of her long, slender nape and delicate feet the hallmarks of Japanese beauty. But something outside the tradition she came from marked her. Hollow-cast eyes shone no light back in the direction of the viewer. Moving closer, Daidai saw that the irises had been faceted. Like the blind men made famous by Hokusai, so the woman appeared, yet her surroundings suggested sight in the direction of her gaze, angled back at the viewer, and in the foreground, a vanity mirror turned to reflect the soft angle of her hipbone.

"What's wrong?" Satsuki's voice called Daidai from contemplation, her brow furrowed in concern.

"Who is the artist?"

"Do you like it?"

"Of course. It's exquisite."

"I'm glad you think so." Satsuki brushed her cheek against Daidai's shoulder like a cat, and Daidai was glad not to have said what she was really thinking, that she found the image deeply disturbing.

"This is the only painting made by my mother that my father kept. He designed this room."

"Remarkable." A tremor raced up Daidai's spine, settling in her jaw.

"Perhaps it is his inner sanctum, I don't know. The room is strictly off-limits. You mustn't tell him you've seen it."

When Satsuki spoke again, it was to comment on the materials used in the construction of the unit that housed the painting. Daidai nodded politely, though she'd stopped listening. Not having found a work of art as deeply affecting as this in quite some time, she doubted anything she'd see in Japan would leave a stronger impression. The lead-up to its discovery had contributed to the experience. In hindsight, the other pieces had been merely ornamentation, fetes on the way to the main event. The care taken to construct the unit indicated that Satsuki's father valued the piece, yet why had he chosen to preserve this particular painting? If it was a tribute to his wife, why keep it in a dark and airless room? Did its placement mark her value in his life? The entire setup, along with the painting itself, seemed incriminating. Satsuki had shown it to her, but it was as if Satsuki hadn't *seen* the work, remarking on a Christmas tree where Daidai saw a golem.

"What would you like to do next?" Satsuki asked as she guided Daidai back down the meandering hall.

"I'm suddenly very tired," Daidai confessed, gazing out the row of high windows into the courtyard through which they'd entered.

"Of course. I forget how far we've traveled."

Daidai nodded, having not thought of the distance as contributing to her exhaustion.

"I'm afraid my father's house is a bit like a museum. Too much to take in all at once."

She'd not been so far off in her analogy, though Daidai had never experienced the kind of fatigue she felt then, her body shuddering as Satsuki led her past the main living area down yet another hall. The room she was shown was the area of six tatami mats with a single window that faced the adjacent property.

"My room is on the other side of the hall—that way." Satsuki pointed. "Once you've rested come get me and we can talk about how you'd like to spend the rest of the afternoon."

Daidai crawled into bed and shut her eyes. The next thing she knew Satsuki was tapping on the door. "Daidai," she whispered, "you must be thrown off by the time change, but if we don't go out now, you'll miss things that can only been seen at this hour."

Too tired to inquire what those things might be, Daidai lay speechless. Waiting for her head to clear she noted the Kabuki mask that hung on the wall across from where she slept, illuminated by the afternoon light.

"Maybe you're hungry?" Satsuki suggested when there was no response.

"Do we have to go out?" Daidai called through the wall, not yet ready to leave the house.

"We can stay in," Satsuki called back, sounding disappointed. "At least until you get your bearings."

Satsuki ordered in sushi, an assortment of raw fish glazed with a sheen that attested to its freshness, set atop a black lacquered platter. They were just about to wrap up the pieces they'd been too full to finish when Satsuki jumped up and scurried out of the room, leaving Daidai behind at the low table.

Greetings were exchanged in rapid-fire Japanese; the father's low murmurs sounded like bass notes against Satsuki's chirp, which was a full octave higher in Japanese than it was in English. It took several minutes for their footfalls to approach the room where Daidai sat waiting. She considered standing, which seemed like the right thing to do, but feeling improperly dressed without her shoes she stayed seated, opting to conceal her bare feet beneath the folds of the *kotatsu*.

Satsuki's father greeted Daidai with a warmth that eased her nervousness and brought on a new set of concerns. "So you're the museum curator Satsuki has talked about. What an honor to have you as our guest."

"I'm delighted to be here." Daidai smiled warmly, hoping to convey humility and, at the same time, to steer the conversation away from her profession in case he wanted to engage her about his collection. "Thank you for having me," she said. "Your home is extraordinary."

"So it's my home that catches your eye?" He nodded.

Surprised with his attention to nuance, Daidai concluded that the man's comprehension of English was better than she'd assumed it would be. "You have an impressive collection of art," she added, taking care not to mention the one work in particular that interested her. A stone in her throat, she felt it there, threatening to surface if she spoke. "Do you ever offer public viewings?" she asked, referencing the work on display.

"I'm not understanding," he said curtly, turning his attention to his daughter. It was hard for Daidai to believe, as she watched him with Satsuki, that this was the man Satsuki had brought her across the Pacific Ocean to meet. From what Satsuki had said about him, she'd conjured an elegant older man, someone impeccably dressed and self-assured. But she found him instead to be almost grotesquely ugly. He was tall, she'd gotten that right. But every other detail, including his protruding forehead, disheveled mass of hair, and rugged appearance, she'd imagined completely wrong.

When at last he turned back to face her, it was as if she'd just then entered the room. "I'm sorry not to have been able to meet your plane at the airport when you arrived this morning." He smiled kindly from across the table.

"It wasn't a problem," Daidai said, a soreness in her throat causing the words to stick there.

"I see you've had dinner." He glanced down at the *kosara*, lined with bits of rice soaked in *shoyu*, as he spoke, his tone implying that they should have waited to start dinner. "Are those leftovers for me?" he asked, pointing down at the colorful pieces of fish and vegetables that had gone uneaten.

Daidai looked up, ready to contend with his disapproval, but was relieved to see that he was smiling.

14

No sooner had he mentioned food than a second tray of sushi was brought in, this time by a woman Daidai hadn't yet seen. After transferring the leftovers onto the fresh tray and silently filling three ceramic cups from a decanter of sake, she turned to leave. Daidai would have to ask later how many women worked for Satsuki's father.

The sound of the sliding door clicking into place resonated through the quiet room. Turning her gaze from the patterned rice paper door to Satsuki, Daidai grasped Satsuki's wrist, caught off guard by a sudden jolt. Satsuki's smile put her fear in check. She brushed her fingertips lightly across the back of Daidai's hand, stroking it like she would a cat.

"In Japan, it's customary to call people by their last name, but since Satsuki has already told me that you go by Daidai, you should feel free to call me Ichiro. Your unusual nickname reminds me that I, too, was given a nickname as a child, Ichiban."

"Thank you." Unable to think of him as anything other than Satsuki's father, Daidai didn't bother mentioning that her name was one she'd thought up herself and that it had long ago ceased to be a nickname.

"Let's drink to your visit!" he exclaimed. After placing a small ceramic cup filled with sake in Satsuki's hand and another in Daidai's, he raised his own cup. *"Kanpai."*

Daidai wasn't in the habit of drinking alcohol. She hadn't drunk at all since she'd been trying to get pregnant, but when prompted she drained the liquid from her cup, pleased to feel the warmth ease the soreness in her throat as it spread down into her stomach. A second round was poured. From the corner of Daidai's eye she saw Satsuki looking at her, but as soon as her eye caught Satsuki's she turned away.

"The plane ride from Los Angeles is twelve hours, and I believe the one from Oslo is double that, from the opposite direction, isn't it?" Satsuki asked.

"Yes, because of the two inconvenient stops where passengers are forced to disembark. I slept most of way."

"You just arrived back from Norway?" Daidai asked, unable to hide her shock.

"My business was in Sweden, but the work I carried home with me comes from a location closer to Oslo than Stockholm. I landed in Japan hours ago." He laughed, checking the time on his expensive watch. "I even made a stop along the way."

"I'd like to see what you brought back," Daidai remarked, curious about his buying venture.

"I'm sorry? What would you like to see?"

"The artwork you purchased."

"*Mochiron*, of course." Satsuki addressed her father in Japanese and Daidai in English, apparently trying to cover for some blunder her friend had made. "You should show it to both of us."

"The Swedes are among my best clients." He seemed not to hear the request and changed the subject as he refilled the ceramic cups with sake. "But what do you think of Japan so far?"

"We came straight here from the airport." Satsuki spoke in Japanese, cutting Daidai off before she could respond.

"I'm fascinated by your home," Daidai said, finding that her thoughts had returned to the banished portrait, to the place Satsuki had warned her not to go. No longer in the mood to hear Ichiro pontificate, she'd grown weary of her spot at the sideline, and the alcohol had weakened her tolerance for small talk. "Please talk to me about your artwork."

Turning to his daughter to indicate that she should do the talking, Ichiro murmured something in Japanese.

"Hai." Satsuki responded in Japanese with a remark Daidai couldn't understand and proceeded to engage her father with a series of polite questions.

Their back-and-forth continued in a sonorous tone as he ate, she refilling his sake cup twice before the woman who had brought the tray of sushi appeared to replace the sake with beer. How had Ichiro summoned the servant? Everything about the night and their interactions was strange. Most of all, why would Satsuki invite her all the way to Japan, ostensibly to meet her father, just so that she could ignore her? But perhaps Daidai was being overly sensitive. After all, as far as she knew, Satsuki had not seen her father even once during the eight months she'd been living on the West Coast.

As Ichiro talked, the ugliness that had overwhelmed Daidai upon her initial observation of him abated and she found him to be quirky and unique looking as opposed to arrogant and grotesque. She watched his animated features shift as Satsuki responded to him and noted that in contrast to his effortless speaking style, her expression remained guarded and unnatural. Perhaps the customs were simply different between family members in Japan, but there seemed to be no genuine affection between father and daughter. Each was merely playing a part in keeping the conversation going until finally Ichiro rose and excused himself to bed.

Once the door slid shut behind him, Satsuki refocused her attention. "So what is your impression of my father?" she whispered.

"He was different from what I expected" was all Daidai could think to say.

"He used to be quite handsome," Satsuki said, seeming to read her friend's thoughts. "In my childhood there was a coldness about him that was stunning, really. I equated his stature with physical perfection. But his facial features have become exaggerated over time. Now, rather than handsome, he looks ravaged. Don't you agree?"

"Maybe your mother's disappearance has taken its toll on him," Daidai said, the striking image she'd viewed earlier in the day creeping back into her imagination. What had Ritsuko intended to signify with the pose?

"Quite the contrary," Satsuki said. "Once my mother was gone he never spoke of her. Everything of hers was removed from the house as if she had never existed."

"Except for the painting," Daidai said.

"Including the painting." Satsuki shook her head to indicate that this was something she'd thought about. "He considered that painting *his*. He'd *bought* it, so it was his to do with what he pleased. He had it specially hung in an airless space, where it would be confined to the darkness. You might find it perverse, but that's simply the way he is, a man devoid of sentimentality. I've often wondered if there is something missing in his character, and at times I've worried that I might turn out to be like him. He and I are the same in that way: something in each of us prevents us from feeling the pain of the other's losses. Were he to vanish, I wonder if I'd miss him. Were I to vanish, I doubt he'd miss me."

"How could you say that?" Daidai asked, though Satsuki appeared to have chosen her words carefully. The strangeness of Satsuki's observation made her regret having had the sake earlier on. She'd need to sort through the interaction she'd witnessed later to understand what Satsuki had been trying to tell her about her father. Outside, rain had begun to pelt the thin walls of the house, accompanied by sudden gusts of wind.

"My father has no deep affections. Or if he does, he reserves them for his art."

"I see." Daidai nodded, still struck by the level of formality between Satsuki and her father, a stilted quality that seemed to permeate the core of her interactions with him.

"Although his materialism is likely what drew me to graduate study."

"Hiroshi says you're a good scholar," Daidai said.

Satsuki smiled, pleased by the confidence her mentor had shown in her, and the conversation ended there. Claiming the sake had left her feeling ill, Satsuki retreated to her room after dropping Daidai at hers. Not yet ready for sleep, she found herself wishing she hadn't taken such a long nap earlier in the day. Parched from the alcohol and the *shoyu*, which contained too much salt, she ventured off in search of the kitchen to pour herself a glass of water and almost bumped head-on into a woman hurrying down the hall from the opposite direction. Dressed in a white robe tied at the waist with a bright red sash, she appeared to be the housekeeper who'd brought trays of food and drink into the sitting room earlier in the evening, though Daidai couldn't be sure whether it had been her or a different woman.

Back in the room where she was to sleep, Daidai wondered how many women like her were living in the house. She wanted to call Hiroshi to report on her first afternoon and evening in Mito, but the walls of the house seemed quite thin, and she worried that a conversation could easily be overheard. As it was, the wind showed no signs of easing up and rain continued to beat down on the roof and outer wall. Through the interior wall Daidai could hear the murmurings of a conversation. Lying in the dark, she swore she could even hear Satsuki breathing, which should not have been possible given that their rooms didn't share a wall. Closing her eyes, she tried to conjure images of familiar objects that might calm her before sleep, but the darkness beneath her eyelids seemed only to intensify the noises that entered the room from all directions.

With her eyes back open the Kabuki mask sent an orb of light into the room, its simple shape enough to transfigure the darkness into a drama. Perhaps, Daidai thought before she finally fell off to sleep, it had been a mistake to accept Satsuki's invitation.

15

Daidai awoke early the next day to find that the storm from the night before had blown through, leaving the air chilly but spectacularly clear and still. The fine weather seemed a negation of the night and day before, promising that everything might turn out just fine were she simply to accept the day in all its loveliness. Stretching from the futon where she'd slept, she reached a hand over the side of the bedding, brushing her fingers along the tight weave of the tatami mats. She'd lapsed into a daydream when she heard Satsuki's voice calling tentatively from the other side of the sliding door. "Daidai, if you're awake, may I come in?"

"Come in, of course," she said, wrapping the thick bedding around her shoulders.

After removing her house slippers, Satsuki scooted herself beside Daidai while Daidai worked her hair into a loose knot. The two lay side by side, Daidai beneath and Satsuki on top of the bedding. "Did you sleep well?" she asked sweetly.

"I did," Daidai told her, groggy but unable to remember the dreams from the night before that had disrupted her sleep. "You?"

"I woke before the sun was up thinking of all the places we need to go."

Daidai refused to give in to the queasy sensation she got when she woke too quickly, trying to convince herself that her suspicion that she might not be ready for whatever Japan had to offer was really just hunger.

Finding Daidai's hand, Satsuki brought it to her cheek, which felt unusually smooth and cold. "I'm very excited today!" she said, perched upright like a cat before she settled back down on the futon. "Do you know that you are the first friend ever to visit me here?"

"Really?" Daidai guessed she was exaggerating, or qualifying the visit to mean overnight guest, or perhaps she meant first visitor from abroad.

"Tell me what it was like for you growing up," she said, clasping Daidai's hand in her elegant fingers. "Did you have friends who stayed overnight at your home? I've heard that American girls 'do sleepovers.' I used to fantasize about what it would be like to have a best friend. I was very lonely."

As Satsuki talked, Daidai thought of Louise. They'd spent most weekends at each other's homes, a fact of her childhood she'd taken for granted. "Did you really never have a friend over?" Daidai asked, her thoughts wandering back to the painting Ichiro kept apart from the rest of the house.

"I'm not lying," she said.

In the stillness of the room, pinned beneath the covers, she could feel Satsuki's heart beat. She'd matched her breathing to Daidai's, and the scent of her freshly washed hair along with a bitter base note that was uniquely Satsuki swelled Daidai's senses. Her mention of loneliness brought to mind the strange sounds Daidai had heard the night before and her tour of the house Satsuki had grown up in, where she'd become privy to a part of her life she'd not shared with anyone.

Pulling herself up and sliding her feet back into her house slippers, Satsuki clasped her hands together with a child's glee. "*Saitoshi-ingu e ikimasu ka?*" she called. "I want to show you everything, and it's a perfect day for sightseeing."

That morning, as they filled their stomachs with a traditional Japanese breakfast of rice, steamed fish, and soup, accompanied, of course, by her signature tea, Satsuki outlined the travel plans. They'd start with Kairakuen, a park where she and her mother had once taken their daily walks.

The experience of the day before, of feeling herself to be such an oddity, had left Daidai less than excited about venturing into the outside world, but her hesitation dissipated as Satsuki and she traversed the nearly deserted path that led away from Ichiro's home. It was a beautiful morning, indeed, and unlike the airport crowd the day before, the locals didn't appear to notice her at all.

"The plum blossoms are reported to be in full bloom." Satsuki's pace quickened as they approached the entrance gate. "I haven't taken this path in twenty-six years, but I still think of Kairakuen as my home. It's the place my mind travels to when I long for something familiar. It might seem like a strange thing to say, but I don't really have a home. My father's home is more like a museum than a home, and my father more of a curator than a parent."

Reaching behind her, Satsuki took hold of Daidai's hand. This was the path she'd taken with her mother, she said as they walked along the interior wall, turning into a small child again as she matched her pace to Daidai's. Daidai felt as sorry for her as she did for Ritsuko, who according to her daughter had ventured out from the small box she'd been born into, and whose life had ended abruptly thousands of miles from where it began. Having slept in the house that Satsuki described as a museum, she felt the loneliness of Satsuki's childhood. Bit by bit, Satsuki's history had taken root in Daidai's consciousness, replacing her own past for one more compelling and refined and, most important, more knowable. "I think I can imagine what it was like for you growing up here," she said, aware that being in the park had kindled Satsuki's recollections of her early childhood.

"I was content to be with my mother," Satsuki said, seeming to have retreated further into memory. "I don't like to think of what life was like afterward, on my own."

"You said you grew up at a boarding school." Daidai recalled the night the police called to inform Satsuki that her mother had been found dead, how she'd pressed her for personal information, risking Hiroshi's disapproval. She hadn't known enough then to be able to imagine how Satsuki had lived, but Satsuki's childhood felt palpable here, in Mito. "Isn't it rare for children in Japan to live away from home?"

"I spent nine years at Shodai Gakuen. You're correct that children who attend boarding school in Japan are at once set apart from the rest. The vast majority of Japanese children are raised by their parents. But even at Shodai I was different. From the start I learned to evade personal questions to save myself from humiliation."

"It must have been hard to adjust."

"It was."

"But how about later? You're so beautiful. I'm sure you had boyfriends."

"I had only one. Unlike you. I'm sure you had many boyfriends before Hiroshi."

"Not really. I was always very focused on my studies."

"Clever Daidai." She smiled. "Bookworm Daidai. I wasn't like you. Not nearly so smart or well versed. When I think back, I've always been a person who required social contact, even though I held a part of myself back. I felt tremendous shame at being on my own at such an early age, but I managed to coast along, even amid such a socially charged atmosphere as Shodai. I think anyone there at the time would have said I was well liked. I was popular because I made sure that the facts of my past never came under scrutiny and therefore no one had reason to think ill of me.

"No one had the slightest clue what I was made of, but people liked me because I offered back a pleasing reflection of themselves. This wasn't a difficult thing to do. I've always believed there's something to like and admire in just about anyone, and it's far more pleasant to see and cultivate the good than to dwell on a person's fallibilities and personality tics that can't be changed. It's also human nature to avoid being ridiculed or shunned. I had seen classmates being made fun of for shortcomings that seemed far less grievous than mine. I learned from them what parts of myself not to reveal."

"You felt inadequate because you weren't with your mother?" Daidai asked, recalling the blind figure from the portrait.

"I believed there must be something wrong with me—for her to leave me," she said. Satsuki spoke of her sadness, yet her tone was even and devoid of emotion, the same quality she'd referenced when speaking about her father the night before.

"Do you find it strange that the figure in the portrait painted by your mother is blind?" Daidai said, wondering aloud.

"A painting is like a wish," she said. "A blind person represents a desire not to see."

Clearly, she'd thought this through. "But what would your mother not want to see?" Daidai asked.

"Perhaps you should tell me." Satsuki smiled, exposing the full set of her overlapping teeth. "You are the curator, the one who understands far better than I do about art."

Satsuki was flattering her. But why would she goad Daidai to speak something she most likely already knew? "When you were talking just now about how you offered your classmates back a pleasing reflection of themselves, I thought of the mirror your mother painted," Daidai mused, speaking candidly of the image that came to mind.

"A mirror can be deceptive," Satsuki remarked, indicating that Daidai had gotten close but not hit her mark. "A person can never really stow away the significant details of her life. Memory may become dislodged, but it doesn't vanish."

Was she talking about her mother? Herself? What connection was there between the mirror and memory? "I'm afraid I don't understand," Daidai said.

"A person's interior can grow stagnant, just like any room left for too long without air or sunlight. People need human interaction to verify the fact that they are alive. I learned that at Shodai. I was very lonely after my mother disappeared. I'd been alone in the world until I met you and Hiroshi. Before the two of you, I never had people I considered true friends."

The subject had shifted, or perhaps it had merely broadened to include Daidai. They had stopped walking, ensconced in a thick forest of plum trees. The graceful arches and darkened boughs contrasted sharply with the delicate blossoms of the plum trees, which highlighted Satsuki's fine bone structure. Under the clear blue sky a spray of petals fell to the ground, shaken loose by the storm the night before. "This day, and your company. I'm so happy,"

Daidai said, feeling the world open up and any space between them dissipate. "I don't think I'll ever forget this moment. Thank you for bringing me here."

"Japan is very beautiful," Satsuki concurred. "I doubt there is anything like this elsewhere in the world."

But just as she'd spoken, a gust of wind caused a flurry of pink petals to spin upward into the air, and a chill ran up Daidai's spine. Standing beneath the branches, looking up at the sky, she wondered if Satsuki had felt it, too. "Wasn't that strange?"

Satsuki smiled, then changed the subject as if prompted to do so by the shifting wind. "During my sophomore year, long after most girls had begun to date, I decided to let my guard down. With ten years at Shodai behind me, it was rare to encounter an unfamiliar face, but a new boy came in that year. He was one of a handful of students who entered Shodai as a high school student to increase his chances of getting into a good university. I met him in a history class that spring term and he seemed to have a kind heart. He'd wait for me outside the classroom door, walk me in, and take the seat next to me. He had gallant manners and a restrained and observant nature unusual in boys that age that allowed me to trust him more than the others."

"What was his name?" Daidai asked, struggling to keep track of what Satsuki was telling her. It didn't help that Satsuki was no longer addressing her directly, instead speaking off into the distance as she talked. But rather than take Daidai's interruption for what it was, a sign of her desire to be attentive, she twisted her lips and focused her glare in the distance.

"What does it matter? Is there any chance at all that you would have known him?"

"Of course not!" Upset that she'd given offense, Daidai stepped back and crouched against the slender trunk of a plum tree, hoping to give Satsuki the space she needed to continue.

Conscious of her breathing, Daidai waited, staring straight ahead until the flash of Satsuki's white teeth indicated that her breach of etiquette had been forgiven. "It turned out that his family owned a vacation home on the Izu Peninsula," she began, allowing Daidai to breathe comfortably once again. "When he asked if I'd like to spend a week of summer break with him in Atami, he was shocked to hear that I'd never been there. Up to that point, I had turned down offers to go to classmates' homes, figuring such visits would open me up to questions of a personal nature. Since my father often left Japan to go on buying trips during the rainy season in June, I simply remained on campus over the long summer break. I didn't mind it that way. With no home to return to, I learned to find pleasure in having the space ordinarily filled with others all to myself.

"But that year I had considered writing to my father to inquire about returning to Mito for the summer. I was old enough to stay in the house on my own. Yet at the same time I felt a strange aversion to being alone.

"For that reason it seemed fortuitous to be asked by Kenji to accompany him to Atami.

"That was his name, by the way—Kenji."

"I see." Straightening her spine, Daidai pushed off from the tree trunk, for after issuing a chiding, Satsuki had begun walking away.

"I agreed because the invitation meant I'd spend one less week on my own," she said, glancing over her shoulder to catch Daidai's response.

"You'd been lonely," Daidai said, indicating her attentiveness as unobtrusively as possible.

"Yes." Satsuki stopped abruptly and turned to face her. "It turned out that the home was quite large, a castle by city standards. I was given my own room, with a view lovelier than anything I could have imagined. A bay window to the east looked straight down over the shoreline, and beyond that the Pacific Ocean stretched out as far as the eye could see. His mother rose early to prepare breakfast, and after Kenji and I had eaten we'd venture out together on foot carrying a lunch box she'd packed for us. I can still remember the taste of those delightful treats inside that box, and the way the sunshine felt on my bare shoulders as I walked along the narrow road that wound down to the shore.

"Each morning of my visit I'd walk a circle around an ancient camphor tree that stood in our path on our way to the shore," she said, embedding the massive tree in Daidai's imagination, and alongside it Satsuki, circling Hiroshi and her apartment. "Then we'd stop at Kinomiya Shrine, where he'd light an incense stick and I'd say a prayer. But at the end of the week, he began asking the inevitable questions about my family.

"Deciding it best to be candid, I told him simply that I hadn't grown up with my mother. In response, he merely shrugged, but I can still feel the way his small gesture reverberated inside me. It felt like a wave, cresting then crashing to the ground beneath my feet. I'd erected a barrier so as not to have to feel so sharply the profound isolation that was part of my existence, but in his questioning of me he'd managed to cross over it."

Turning her gaze to the branches of a plum tree, Daidai watched its leaves flutter in the morning breeze. Satsuki seemed to be telling a story she'd heard before, though Daidai couldn't place where.

"In that moment I knew I'd made a mistake.

"'Maybe you're lucky,' he said, chuckling to himself. But his laughter did nothing to repair the fissure that had opened between us.

"'I believe I am lucky,' I told him. I am a proud person, and I tried not to take offense because I sensed that he genuinely liked me."

Pushing herself upright from the tree trunk she'd been leaning against, Daidai felt the ache in her jaw from clenching her teeth. Shivering in the cool morning, she moved out into the sunlight.

"Later that evening while he and I stood side by side eating our dinner at a noodle shop, he turned to me with a pitying look and said, 'I've often wished my mother didn't love me so much.' Kenji was such an immature person. I left Izu sensing that he knew nothing about heartbreak or loneliness, let alone love."

Satsuki walked on in silence, saddened and obviously troubled by an experience from her past. Daidai hadn't entirely understood the story itself, or Satsuki's need to tell it, but recalling the admonishment she'd received when she'd interrupted, she didn't dare ask questions.

A while later, as they neared the park's exit, Satsuki asked for a story from Daidai's childhood. By that time, her presence next to Daidai had begun to feel so familiar that Daidai believed they might have been friends all along. Had they really met only months before? Wanting to tell Satsuki something of her life, Daidai was disturbed to find she had nothing to say.

16

The plan was to return to Mito by late afternoon. Since they'd made the mistake of eating without Ichiro the night before, Daidai suggested they wait to have dinner, but this proved to be a bad idea. Ichiro arrived home having already eaten and, after stopping briefly to greet them, he went straight to bed. Satsuki seemed disappointed; Daidai certainly was. She was tired and irritable from hunger when Satsuki reminded her about her father being unpredictable.

Instead of ordering dinner in, they walked to the river and consoled themselves with sloppy, overstuffed burgers and cheese fries at MOS Burger, a Japanese version of In-N-Out. That night, Satsuki's intrepid spirit reemerged with an insistence that Ichiro not be apprised of future plans, which included a week of travel starting the next morning.

Liberated by a new sense of volition, Satsuki desired to move from place to place. But where a flurry of activity constituted her definition of a good time, constant motion caused details to blur together in ways that Daidai found dizzying and unsettling. Daidai preferred to take her time. Her position at the museum had involved staring at objects until they made sense to her, and her curatorial stance had emanated out of her approach to life in general; she liked observing more than participating. Robbed of the ability to observe during the day, Daidai couldn't be sure what she was feeling. Because of this, she lay awake each night pulling impressions from the day out for inspection, unable to sleep until she could make a deep connection between objects she'd seen during the day and thought. In this way, day and night became transposed in Japan, and exhausted from her thoughts late into the night before, she greeted each day with increasing hesitancy. Sidelong glances seemed to come from every direction, forcing her to contend with her awkwardness in public places. To add to her discomfort, her inability to adequately express herself in Japanese enforced her reliance on Satsuki. She, on the other hand, seemed to relish her role as tour guide, pushing Daidai out in front of her onto crowded trains, purchasing tickets and meals, and stating her wishes without Daidai speaking or expressing what might not have been her wishes at all.

Arriving at the Izu Peninsula, Daidai realized she'd entered the setting Satsuki had described. The tree Satsuki had circled with Kenji turned out to be the largest and perhaps also the oldest camphor tree in Japan. What Satsuki hadn't mentioned, according to information engraved on a site marker, was that circling it was said to bring good luck.

"What did you wish for back then?" Daidai asked. "Can you tell me? Did your wish come true?"

"My wish hasn't come true yet. So I can't say. But I can tell you that I've wished for it all these years without losing hope."

What Satsuki said made sense. In Kairakuen, Daidai had felt herself to be on the verge of recovering a memory, but perhaps what she'd felt instead was prescience. She'd intuited some aspect of the nature of her relationship with Satsuki just as earlier she'd perceived meaning in Satsuki's circling her apartment and even encircling her with whatever wish she'd hoped to make come true. Contemplating what had been confided to her, Daidai walked around the ancient tree wondering what there was to wish for. It was a beautiful spring day. Several days' travel had solidified her friendship with Satsuki, yet she remained completely oblivious of what was to come. A warning had been issued that day. Near the entrance to the shrine, a plaque commemorated the Great Kanto earthquake: ATAMI IS THE EPICENTER OF A MASSIVE EARTHQUAKE, WHICH PRODUCED THIRTY-

FIVE-FOOT WAVES THAT FLOODED THE TOWN AND DROWNED THREE HUNDRED PEOPLE. Later she would wonder: How had she failed to grasp the relevance of that sign as she stood facing the shrine and having encircled the tree without a wish?

Time had gone funny in Daidai's head, causing her to regret she had wished for nothing that afternoon when there was still everything to wish for. Rather than turn her eyes to the future when she had a chance to do so, she'd homed in on the past. Satsuki had been affected deeply by sadness, which might have had to do with Kenji, or perhaps the story she'd told about her interlude with him had merely been a marker of another sort of sadness caused by having been left alone at such a young age. She had shared something of her sadness with Daidai and in doing so had solidified their friendship. She was the one to suggest they take the photograph, which she forwarded along with others to Hiroshi for what she called "Hiroshi's virtual tour of Japan." Standing in front of the information marker, Satsuki and Daidai are nestled in each other's arms.

The day after Atami they rode the Tokaido Line train to Odawara Station to transfer to the Shinkansen to Kyoto. After spending the night there they rode an early-morning train to Hiroshima, where they spent the bulk of that day at Peace Memorial Park and the Peace Memorial Museum, Satsuki clutching Daidai's hand to keep them from being separated by the schoolchildren who traveled in droves. On a normal day at the museum, Daidai found groups of children unattended by parents to be troublesome, but Satsuki ferried her through the chaos with aplomb, affording protection from the closeness of other tourists and even from the horror of what they saw inside the museum. They spoke very little while viewing the exhibits, but Satsuki's fingers were locked threaded through hers, steadying and connecting them.

Each installation contained a common thread of consciousness, asking the viewer to acknowledge the potential for harm that existed in each individual. The acts of destruction resulting in so much death and suffering had been atrocious. But where Daidai viewed the exhibits from a curator's standpoint, Satsuki seemed to experience them personally, needing to take her time, then standing transfixed in the garden just outside the museum, at the larger-than-life mother and child statue.

For the first time since they'd begun their travels, Satsuki had been the one to linger, so that rather than reach Osaka by midafternoon, they boarded a packed train at the height of rush hour and were made anxious by delays.

The line for the overnight ferry to Kitakyushu wrapped around the terminal, the salt breeze that blew in off the sea at Osaka causing a shiver that left Satsuki's teeth chattering uncontrollably. Worried that her friend had caught a cold, Daidai huddled close to her for warmth.

"Thank you," Satsuki said when she'd stopped trembling, "I don't know why I got so cold."

"You need to eat more," Daidai said, noting Satsuki's thinness and wan complexion. "Maybe your resistance is down." In fact, while Satsuki had begun to look familiar, she looked that afternoon like a stranger. Seeming to sense Daidai's concern, she averted her gaze to the dock floor. Once they'd reached the ticketing window, however, her mood seemed to lighten. She purchased the tickets for the twelve-hour ferry ride and pushed Daidai out in front of her to navigate through the mass of bodies making their way down the walkway.

On the ramp that led into the ferry's middle deck, Daidai became aware of an unfamiliar sound of rapid breathing behind her and turned, surprised to find not Satsuki but a middle-aged, pasty-faced businessman. "Satsuki?" she called, stopping in her tracks, forcing the line of foot traffic to veer around her in both directions. Scanning the crowd as far back as she could see and not catching sight of Satsuki, she had no choice but to board alone.

Trying to contain her panic at being the only non-Japanese speaker on board, Daidai reached inside her shoulder bag for her cell phone only to find that the battery had gone dead. Recalling Satsuki's mention of taking dinner at the bar, Daidai set off to find it.

Approached along the way by a uniformed ticket-taker, she struggled to explain her situation: "My friend has it," she said, using the word *tomodachi*, then pantomiming about her friend wandering off. "I've become separated," she said, "lost."

He smiled, perhaps understanding, issuing Daidai a hand-printed receipt, which contained on the back a statement written in English: "If the coupons or reservation tickets other than the boat ticket of issue of our company remain as they are, please exchange for the boat ticket of issue of our company, after filling in the name on application form."

Information had always calmed her, but Daidai's anxiety mounted as she struggled to understand what these words meant. Without Satsuki, she had only her shoulder bag, which contained a dead cell phone and other useless sundry items. But rather than give in to panic, she reasoned that she'd either find Satsuki or eventually Satsuki would find her. A panel of mirrors reflected the room behind the bar where passengers gathered in clusters around bar tables, and in the distance the foot traffic passed from the sleeping quarters to the main hub, where groups that were mostly families lay on long rows of mats.

For the first time since she'd left L.A., Daidai thought of Hiroshi and the life she'd left behind. Sipping hot tea, she watched in the mirror as a mother ran a brush through her young daughter's hair in preparation for bed. It was with her gaze focused on the hairbrush that she glimpsed Satsuki, her eyes fixed on the same pair she'd been observing. But in the instant it took her to turn and look over her shoulder, Satsuki had vanished.

Once the ferry began moving, the chill from the ocean air increased dramatically, heightening Daidai's sense of urgency. Rising from her seat at the bar to search for a warmer spot, she caught a second glimpse of Satsuki; her uneven teeth gleaned in the mirrored bar lights before she turned away, the set of her shoulders and hips recognizable, even from behind. Finding a cramped spot deep within the ferry's hull in an attempt to avoid the draft, Daidai believed she might be hallucinating when a familiar voice broadcast her name over the ship's loudspeaker: "My Daidai friend, if you can hear this, please report to room 238."

As she hurried along the exterior corridor, the ferry glided south down the coast of Japan with only pinprick lights to mark the horizon, the darkened sky reaching down to touch the ocean, both having turned to black.

Satsuki offered no explanation as to where she'd gone. "I'm glad you found me" was what she said, smiling as she threw open the cabin door, as if she were the one who'd been lost.

"Where were *you*?" Daidai asked, irritated.

"I came straight here, to our room." She waved her arm to indicate their quarters, which consisted of two stacked beds with a small table pushed against the wall to hold the suitcase they shared. "Do you like it?"

"I couldn't care less about it," Daidai said, her anger shaking Satsuki momentarily from her demure posturing. She held Daidai's gaze, neither blinking, as Daidai attempted to edge her way beneath the woman's stoical appearances. "I saw you in the bar," she said, "and I think you saw me, too."

"I did go looking for you, of course," Satsuki confessed, running her tongue over the surface of her shiny teeth.

"Then why did you leave without me?"

"Why would I do that?" she replied, reminding Daidai of her conversation with the addled nun.

"Twice," Daidai said, increasingly agitated at having to recall the evening's events.

"I thought you'd find me," Satsuki said. Cowed by Daidai's displeasure, she climbed up to her bunk, apparently with nothing more to say, or not wanting to further the confrontation.

Daidai, unable to calm herself, listened to Satsuki, conscious of the moment her breathing lengthened into sleep. Had Satsuki ditched her and then watched from a distance in a game of cat and mouse? What reason could she have for doing that? Daidai's thoughts returned to the image of Satsuki in the mirror, watching as Daidai did the brush being pulled through the child's hair. Also, there had been the statue where earlier in the day Satsuki had stood transfixed. Had traveling to Japan brought back memories of her life with her mother? Perhaps the events of the day had been too much for her.

The rest of the journey passed in a blur with nothing to mark it except for a small gift Satsuki purchased for her the next morning when the ferry arrived in Kitakyushu. A ceramic bowl, rough hewn on the bottom, but polished around the edges into a vibrant, sea-toned blue, she'd insisted Daidai should have it, calling it a reminder of their time together.

17

At Daidai's urging, Satsuki had reserved two days in Mito without travel as recovery time before heading back to Los Angeles. It was late afternoon when they arrived back at Ichiro's home, but this time no one came to greet them at the door. Since Ichiro had not informed them of his whereabouts, they ate dinner without him. But once again he arrived home hungry, just as they'd finished eating. *"Tadaima!"* he called out from the entryway.

"Okaeri ni," they called back in unison.

Under his arm he carried a large black canvas bag. He seemed upbeat as he unzipped it. "It's a bird's-eye view of Mito," he explained, peeling up the cloth to reveal the newly framed perspective drawing he'd brought back from Oslo.

The geometrical markings depicted a city, with each structure rendered in a set of lines and shapes that spanned the broad parchment from a focal point just to one side. Though Daidai found it as underwhelming as the other pieces, it reminded her of the dream she'd had the afternoon she returned from her second visit to the monastery, the expanse of city street as she pressed forward to an unknown destination.

"Where will it hang?" she asked, unable to recall a wall space large enough to accommodate the drawing.

"Eventually it will hang in the gallery," he said, referencing a place Daidai hadn't seen. "But for now, I was hoping Satsuki would help me."

Daidai followed Satsuki down the long hall to her father's room. Expecting to see his most prized possessions, she discovered instead that his bedroom was practically empty—the most ordinary room in the house. The walls, painted ecru, had been left without embellishments, a traditional futon resting on a platform just inches off the ground taking up the middle of the room. Because the thin walls would not support the heavy frame, Ichiro climbed a stepladder to where a pulley had been attached to a weight-bearing rafter. He then stood back while Satsuki threaded a length of thick fishing line through the back of the frame. Daidai's job was to make sure the drawing hung at the optimal height for viewing.

That Ichiro should commandeer such a makeshift job seemed laughably out of character. Why not just wait for a professional framer to install the artwork in the studio? But he insisted that the drawing be hung and that his daughter and she should be the ones to do the job—his impetuousness a stark contrast to his demand for precision. Standing back to get a look at the work he'd been so anxious to display, Daidai could see marks left behind on the wall where other paintings had hung.

"Now we should celebrate," Ichiro said, clapping his hands together. "Your stay in Mito is coming to an end, is it not?"

"We leave in two days," Satsuki said, seeming perturbed.

Before ordering dinner for himself, Ichiro inquired whether food should be brought in for Satsuki and Daidai as well, but did not seem to care that they'd eaten. When his dinner arrived, Satsuki sat zazen beside him, just as she had the first night in Mito, listening to Ichiro talk about his most recent acquisitions. From what Daidai could make out, Ichiro had purchased work from three artists whose paintings were currently on display in Japan's national gallery. The work was to be part of an exchange between Sweden and Japan in a deal that would bring greater recognition and appreciation of the artists of each country to the other. "This is something that might be of interest to you," he said, drawing Daidai into the conversation for the first time that night.

But his overture had come too late. While Daidai remained polite, she could summon only a tepid response. "It sounds interesting. But this is an area I know nothing about."

"Yes, of course. Why would you?" He seemed pleased to let the subject drop, as if he'd gotten from Daidai exactly the response he'd wanted. Yet where Satsuki was concerned, he showed no sign of letting up his end of the conversation, enlivened perhaps by the knowledge that his daughter would be leaving Japan shortly to resume her studies abroad.

After sitting through the exchange silently for nearly an hour, Daidai excused herself to bed. Satsuki didn't need her help to keep Ichiro company, and Ichiro, having not looked her way again after his offhand comment, obviously didn't care whether she stayed around for his conversation with his daughter.

Having gotten halfway through the events of the day in her head, Daidai fell into a deep sleep but was roused by an argument. Believing she might even have heard Satsuki calling her name, she pulled a jacket on over her nightclothes and made her way down the hall, careful not to stumble in the dark, conscious that the voices had subsided, or perhaps she'd only dreamed them. Near the sitting room, a band of white light spilling into the hall called her attention to the space that she guessed from the paint fumes escaping through the crack to be Ichiro's studio. Sliding the door partially open to get a better look, she saw women working in silence, their backs to her. The scratching murmur of short-bristled brushes applying paint to large canvases—was that the sound she'd mistaken from her room for anger? The heavy smells of paint and brush cleaners made her light-headed until she saw what the five or six women were painting. On each canvas the image of a young Japanese girl of an indeterminate age, portrayed as a middle schooler, then in her late teens. In each instance she wore a schoolgirl uniform, which made her age hard to guess, but the recognition each time was in the eyes, which seemed to look outward from the canvas directly at the viewer, so innocent and seductive at the same time. The gaze as aloof as it was familiar invited Daidai into the room so that she could see the rest of the paintings over the shoulders of the painters.

On the nearest canvas, the girl in a dark blue school skirt slid back over bent knees, legs spread just enough to reveal white panties pulled to one side by her own hand. The artist had, with an eye for detail, painted a small amount of pubic hair. The girl's sailor-style top was white, the blue stripes around the neckline interrupted on her right shoulder by a man's hand with its fingertips disappearing under the uniform's neckline. In the background stood the figure of a middle-aged white man.

Farther into the room, the painters, each seated on a wooden stool at an identical easel, continued to work. If any of the artists looked up, they took no notice of Daidai; she might have been a ghost gliding behind the row of women. Though the setting of each painting was different, each featured the same Japanese schoolgirl. One scene with her uniform open, exposing a brown nipple on an otherwise flat chest and no pubic hair between her open legs. Another featuring an older Japanese man, but this time in the foreground with his lips pressed against the girl's knee, his suit jacket unbuttoned with one arm out of its dark blue sleeve, his hand grasping the girl's ankle. As if responding to her question of who these men were, Daidai noted photographs of different men tacked to the top of each easel. These men, all middle-aged or older, were the same as the men in the paintings, the depictions often of a good quality. The painters were obviously very good, rendering in their work something more lifelike than life. The colors deeper, the expressions accentuated by being intentionally frozen in time, not merely captured in transition the way a camera would have them. Daidai was invisible to the women, her presence unacknowledged for the second time that night, and her invisibility combined with the paint fumes left her feeling unsteady. Turning back to the doorway through which she'd entered Ichiro's studio, she'd gotten as far as the sliding door when Ichiro came lumbering from down the hall. Inhaling deeply, she readied herself for confrontation, but before she could do or say anything, Ichiro rushed past with his outstretched hand covering the side of his head closest to her. His bizarre behavior served as a frightening reminder that Satsuki might have been calling for help. Though she longed to reenter the studio for evidence of what she'd seen, Daidai proceeded on to the sitting room, where she found Satsuki still seated at the table, in the same position that she'd left her.

"Are you okay?" she asked, positioning herself across the table from Satsuki, unable to read her blank expression.

Looking up, Satsuki smiled vaguely in Daidai's direction. "Has the commotion gotten you out of bed?"

"Are you okay?" Daidai asked again, wishing to know what had upset her friend so that she could ask about what she'd just seen.

"I'm sorry to have woken you."

Satsuki's muted expression underscored Daidai's impression that something had gone terribly wrong. "What happened?"

"My father can be so aggravating."

"What has he done?"

"He's lied to me. He's been lying for a very long time. But there's nothing to worry about," she assured Daidai, choosing to keep on with her evasions.

"What did you argue about?"

"We weren't arguing." Her composure suddenly restored, she looked up placidly, as if to say that the matter had been resolved. "After our conversation, I think we understand each other quite well."

"Understand what?"

"It wouldn't benefit either of us for me to tell you, Daidai. I'm sorry to have woken you."

"I wish you'd stop apologizing!" Daidai said, exasperated. "Can't you trust me?"

"I do trust you. And I'm very tired. If you'd like, we can talk about this in the morning, but for now I need to sleep.

"Don't be angry with me," she continued, and rose from the table and came around to offer Daidai a side hug. "Tomorrow will be our last full day together. After that, Japan will be only a memory, so we may as well prepare ourselves to make the most of our last day in Mito."

Daidai walked with Satsuki back down the hall to her room, noting that the white light that had shone into the hallway was gone. Through the sliding door, she could hear the same angry voice that had woken her, a voice she now recognized as Ichiro's. "What's going on in there?" she asked, pausing outside the door.

"That's my father's office," Satsuki whispered, holding a finger to her lips to silence Daidai from further questioning and leading her on by the arm. "He's gone back to work."

Ashamed to have stumbled on something not intended for her eyes, still Daidai regretted not telling Satsuki what she'd seen. She'd made a decision to think it over before asking Satsuki about the women and their paintings. But it was a mistake to wait, an error that would seal off an opportunity that wouldn't come again until it was too late.

18

The next day, Friday, March 11, began with rain.

Even though the entire week before had been practically cloudless, Satsuki said the dampness was typical of springtime weather along the coast. Having laundered and packed up a week's worth of clothes, she and Daidai donned their rain gear and left the house. Daidai reminded Satsuki of her promise to tell her what she and her father had argued about, but once again Satsuki evaded her questioning. They ate in silence at a ramen stand, then walked along the Sakura River, each woman sealed from the other in her own private thoughts. Looking up, Daidai was startled to note that a section of clouds directly overhead had dispersed to create a small blue heart. It appeared perfectly formed, wonderfully symmetrical, and so highly unusual that as proof of what she was seeing Daidai pointed her phone camera upward and captured a photo, which she forwarded to Hiroshi with the subject line "Blue Heart in Mito" to be included in his virtual tour of Japan.

Most likely her husband had yet to receive the image when the rumbling began as a queer sound, which then clogged her ears with a fearsome roar. Having grown up in Los Angeles and lived through the Northridge quake in 1994, Daidai might have associated the familiar sensation with the past had the shaking not then increased to an urgent and unprecedented pitch. As she and Satsuki struggled to keep their bálance, the nearby houses shifted on their foundations, emitting terrible groans, and bits of tile flew from rooftops like birds hurled briefly into the air before crashing to the pavement, where they shot off like fireworks. Windows popped out of their frames, spraying the ground with shattered glass. The earth itself seemed intent on sucking everything down in its fury, an interminable and insatiably greedy fit that seemed as if it might never stop. Satsuki dove and pulled Daidai down with her under a sturdy bench, where they lay with arms covering their heads. Once the violent shaking had subsided, sirens began sounding almost immediately. Satsuki explained that an alarm had been triggered by the threat of tsunami. Human noises replaced the rumbling as people fled their homes and office buildings for the street, as if the bad thing had already moved to the past.

Not until the shouts increased in timbre and lengthened into wailing accompanied by another set of sounds did Daidai hear the torrent of water rushing in from the distance. Where before she'd felt comforted by the presence of the river, within minutes it began to swell. Defying the laws of nature, the rippling brown spirals transformed into a fierce and swirling black as the current reversed its course, dumping in its frenzy sediment from the ocean bottom along with debris from the coastal cities it had already visited prior to Mito—a full nine miles from the coast.

As if in slow motion, the river overflowed its banks, lapping at the trunks of the fruit trees, which clung stoically to their blossoms. Like two children chased by the tide, Satsuki and Daidai, their fingers locked, began carving a path inland on foot, the salt spray of water licking at their heels as they ran. Who knows why the mind associates the familiar with safety, for without knowing what else to do they ran back to Ichiro's home.

Even though the water never achieved enough depth to sweep their feet out from under them, the ocean came up through the soles of their shoes. That afternoon, it staked its claim as it charged inland, collecting things that did not belong to it like a thief, carrying stolen items as it fled the scene of its terrible crime. Seaweed and garbage floated down the sidewalks along with signs that had been ripped from stores advertising lunch box specials and pictured sale items. One object became indistinguishable from the next as the churning black water turned muddy, the way in front of them smelling of brine and sewage and seeping into everything the water touched.

Disaster had struck on the day the blue heart lit the spring sky. Satsuki and Daidai could see the gate that marked the entrance to the house when the cell phone in Daidai's back pocket began chiming its familiar ringtone that could only mean Hiroshi calling her out of the void.

The connection was lost almost instantly, though she hoped the sound of her voice had been enough to assure him of her safety, for the line would be dead for many hours to come.

19

The heavy stone lantern top had lodged itself whole in front of the wooden gate. It would take two people to lift it. Daidai saw frustration in the set of Satsuki's mouth as she used what strength she had left, attempting unsuccessfully to restore it to the spot it had for so long occupied. Later, she'd tell Daidai the story her mother had told her, of how the stone lantern had been placed outside the gate to guard the property. Though they did not have the strength to return it to where it had sat, they did manage to move it the ten inches required to wedge their way inside the property.

In the foyer, water rose ankle-deep. Though earthquakes were a common occurrence throughout Honshu, nothing Ichiro could have done would have fortified the house against the damage wrought by this one followed so closely by the tsunami. Paintings strung on pulleys had obviously swayed during the quake like passengers on a ship, so beautifully made up and yet now looking quite absurd as they hung crooked and seemingly stunned on their moorings. Going from room to room to survey the damage, Daidai recalled the path she'd taken when Satsuki had led her through the house for the first time more than a week before, only now her tour guide was speechless. Blue tile and plaster had fallen through cracks in the ceiling, through which daylight could be seen. Daidai's anxiety increased as they made their way down the hall toward Ichiro's bedroom. Perhaps responding to her own trepidation, Satsuki stopped outside the room she'd called her father's inner sanctum where her mother's portrait had hung, and she and Daidai gazed through the almost complete darkness at the sinkhole into which the painting had fallen, along with an entire wall.

Electrical wires lay awash in viscid sludge heaved up from the sea, and Daidai clutched Satsuki's trembling body to her chest, struggling to keep her friend safe. "You can't go down there," she murmured into her hair. *It can't be saved; you must be safe.*

Any remaining strength drained away from Satsuki's body as Daidai held her, and she allowed herself to be led away. Stopping momentarily outside Ichiro's private study, Daidai peered into the studio she'd entered the night before, surprised to find no trace of the paintings she'd seen. The women, along with the canvases, were gone, the room completely emptied.

Not knowing where to go for safety, Daidai pulled the thick blanket off the futon where she'd slept, and she and Satsuki huddled together in the courtyard to wait for Ichiro. It would be too cold to camp outside overnight, yet staying inside was not an option since the constant aftershocks threatened to bring down the already damaged roof. Believing that Ichiro would need to have his daughter present when he showed up to find his home destroyed, Daidai thought they should stay put, guessing that the chances of finding a vacant hotel room would diminish as the evening progressed, but Satsuki wanted to leave without waiting for Ichiro, and in the end Daidai deferred to her friend's reasoning.

As a compromise, Satsuki wrote a note to say that they were okay and that they'd return in the morning. Looking around for a place to leave it and deciding on the tree that rose up from the middle of the courtyard, she tacked it to the trunk, a place where he'd be sure to see it, and they took the suitcases they'd packed earlier that day and walked off in search of accommodations.

Down the road, a shopkeeper sat on the street using a battery-powered radio to broadcast news. The nuclear plant in Fukushima had sustained severe damage, and service to the rail system had been suspended. The two were mentioned in the same sentence, one attenuating the other, because where a transportation stoppage seemed calamitous, a nuclear meltdown was simply inconceivable. Farther down the road, two elderly neighbors who sat wrapped in quilts on folding chairs in the street recognized Satsuki and wanted to know how Ichiro's property had fared.

The smaller inns in the area seemed in no better shape than Ichiro's home, with the staffers scrambling to meet the needs of their guests, all the while wary of structural damage evident upon inspection. After being turned away at several hotels, they felt lucky to be able to rent the last room available at a newer high-rise built to attract tourists near Lake Senba, which, though equipped with only partial electricity, seemed to have survived the quake intact. That evening, when Daidai's call to Hiroshi finally went through, she was surprised to find that news of the quake seemed to have reached Los Angeles faster than it was being reported from inside Japan. After expressing his relief that she and Satsuki were alive and well, he warned Daidai to get to the airport the next day to catch her flight home.

"There's going to be a rush to leave Japan," he predicted. "If you miss your flight you might be stuck there for days or even weeks."

"We need to go back to Satsuki's dad's house to try to find him first," Daidai argued. "If he's okay, we'll head directly from there to the airport."

"No." His voice bespoke a kind of urgency that demanded Daidai's attention. "Satsuki can stay in Japan if she needs to, but you need to be on that flight."

"Okay," she said, sensing how upset he was and trying to pacify him.

"Stay safe and come home," he said before the connection went dead.

Judging from her sullen expression afterward, Daidai guessed Satsuki had overheard Hiroshi's part in their phone conversation and she was sorry for her. She had Hiroshi to worry about her, but who was there to worry about Satsuki? Pulling her friend close as they peered out the third-floor window, she committed the darkened cityscape to memory. She couldn't make things better for Satsuki or rectify the horrors taking place all around them, but in that moment they were the same person, breathing air at the same rate, their heartbeats synchronized. The earthquake made it clear that their lives were intertwined. That night, events once separated by time clung together in the lights flickering in the descending darkness.

As a practice drill in case a strong aftershock necessitated they flee the hotel in the dark, Satsuki sent her down the hall to count the steps to the service stairs. Then, with an escape plan in place, she insisted that Daidai rest while she procured dinner. That night they filled their stomachs with packets of rice crackers supplied by the hotel and drank water Satsuki had poured from the bathroom tap into fluted wineglasses. Before going to bed, they zipped their suitcases, which they left standing by the door, and they slept fully dressed and with their shoes on.

Considering the scenarios they'd planned for and the tremors that pitched throughout the night like waves beneath a boat, Daidai awoke the next morning surprised to have slept through the night. She took her post back at the window, craning her neck from side to side to clear the ache that had settled in her head and surveying the cityscape while her eyes adjusted to the light.

20

Japan is a place of relative opulence, at least on the surface. But the morning after the quake the streets were alive with displaced people. Families and strangers huddled together around small fires burning out of hibachi stoves in the streets as Daidai and Satsuki walked back to Ichiro's towing their suitcases. An occasional cry was met by a placating hush, the reality leaving behind a powerful impression of fortitude in the face of adversity. Life for so many had been destroyed, but there were no complaints—at the moment there was nothing to be done. The ocean breeze that normally blew northwest, in from the Pacific, had switched course overnight, putting Mito in harm's way for the fallout from the nuclear reactor that had melted down the day before. They had no choice but to breathe in radiation, absorb into their pores and blood and bones a disaster that might plague generations to come. But the people living in the streets shared a conviction that was stronger than the reality they faced, that the powers that be would protect them, and they rallied one another with certitude that they would get through.

Daidai's thoughts turned to Ritsuko as she walked. Her beliefs had no doubt been challenged, the sanctity of both people and place. She wondered if Ichiro had ever been a caring husband, caught up as he seemed to be with his own preoccupations. He seemed not to have been a caring father. Satsuki had talked fondly about her life in Mito only in terms of how she'd lived with her mother during the early years of her childhood, beyond which Daidai understood nothing.

Power had not been restored to the house, so that they arrived to rooms lit only by traces of orange light as the sun began its ascent. The lantern top still partially blocked the entrance, prompting Daidai to summon an image of Gizo, wishing for the brute strength that neither she nor Satsuki possessed. They'd done well enough on their own, but neither could deny needing more muscle than they had. The note still pinned to the leafless tree made it unclear whether Ichiro had been home.

Water that had filled the entryway had receded overnight, leaving behind a thick layer of sludge. In it prints from shoes that were too large to be Satsuki's or Daidai's led off to the main room, providing a map of routes. There was no question that the prints belonged to Ichiro. Standing in the entryway, Daidai visualized his arrival home, stopping first in the main room, where he'd walked the periphery, inspecting the damage before moving on. Though the muddy prints lightened as he worked his way down the hall, it was clear that he'd stopped in each room before retreating to his chamber at the end of the long hallway. With no prints to indicate that he'd turned around to exit the house, he'd wound up in his bedroom. Perhaps he'd deemed the structure safe enough to spend the night, or he'd been too tired to look elsewhere for a place to sleep. But even as Daidai had these thoughts, something told her she was heading down the wrong track.

Next to her, Satsuki stood with her hand covering her mouth, using the smell and feel of her own skin for comfort, and perhaps trying to avoid being sick. "I think we should go in," she said, coming to the conclusion Daidai had already reached.

Daidai followed her friend down the hall, listening as the door slid along its casters, breathing in the warm, human scent of Satsuki's scalp amid the damp, putrefying odor of the house as she peered over her shoulder.

Ichiro might have been a sculpture, positioned atop his bed, the covers around him flattened, his arms folded across his chest.

"Is he asleep?" Daidai asked, not wanting to enter the room.

"Tondemonai!" Satsuki gasped. Reverting to Japanese to express her disbelief, she rushed into the room with Daidai in tow. Hovering over the bed, she shielded her eyes with her forearm.

It seemed shameful to stare at a body so defenseless against her gaze, but Daidai couldn't stop herself from looking. Even in the desperate act of suicide Ichiro had dressed in his own meticulous style, a well-tailored black sport coat covering an iris-tinted dress shirt, dress pants with a crease running down the leg pointing to a perfectly polished pair of black shoes. If it were merely death that he'd wanted, he could have gone to any number of places to die amid the wreckage in obscurity. But instead he'd retreated to his bedroom, where the first rays of morning light now illuminated the display.

Satsuki closed his lids with her fingertips while Daidai looked on incredulously, having to remind herself that what she was seeing was real. The earthquake, followed by the flood, and now this. It would all be over soon, but already she knew it was something she'd need to go over again and again, and her thoughts flashed to the mirror painted by Satsuki's mother, how it reflected light back to the viewer.

Feeling Satsuki trembling, Daidai turned to face her, and they stood with their foreheads pressed together, huddled for comfort, waiting out the trembling that refused to subside. Satsuki was the one to pull away. Sliding the door shut behind them, she led the way out the gate. The last thing Daidai saw before it closed was the suitcases propped against the entrance wall, a reminder of the promise she'd made Hiroshi to be on the flight home that would depart later that day.

The images she'd memorized stayed with her as she walked on in silence. Hiroshi wanted her home; Satsuki could stay. She didn't know nor did she ask where they were headed, and was mildly surprised that they arrived at the entrance to Kairakuen, where they entered a police annex Daidai hadn't noticed the week before.

Inside, they stood at the reception area, waiting while the personnel went about their duties, until a young woman noticed them over her shoulder. "How can we help you?" she asked. Her smile was friendly despite her shirt collar being displaced and the mascara smeared beneath her eyes.

Satsuki spoke up promptly. "I've come to report a suicide. My father. I found him in his bedroom."

"What a terrible thing for you." The female officer approached the desk. "Ordinarily, we would treat such a matter right away. But just now we have our hands quite full. If you could fill out this form and wait here"—she designated two chairs near the entrance—"I'll try to find someone to accompany you to your father's home."

"Thank you," Satsuki said politely.

"I wish I could help you," Daidai said, staring at the Japanese characters printed on the form, unable to read any of them. Satsuki looked up and, with a wan, exhausted smile, squeezed her hand.

After waiting so long to be noticed, it took less time than Daidai expected for a paramedic to approach. "Excuse me." A hand was extended, first to Satsuki, then to Daidai. "Officer Hirada has told me about your father."

He seemed like a compassionate person, but Satsuki avoided looking in his eyes, staring down at the ground in front of her as she and Daidai followed him to an unmarked white van that served as an ambulance. He opened the door to the passenger seat so that they could ride next to him even though the seat was barely big enough for one person. "Excuse me," he said again, wiping his forehead with the back of his hand. "There has been so much damage. My own apartment is in ruins and my parents are being housed at the senior center while they wait to see which relatives can take them in."

"What a pity," Satsuki said, perfectly composed.

"Sorry, yes," he said, quickly matching his disposition to hers.

The paramedic was stronger than he looked on first glance. Clasping the stone lantern top with both hands, he heaved it back where it belonged, rubbing his hands on his pant legs afterward to restore the circulation. "It's amazing that something so heavy could have been thrown to the ground."

Satsuki led the way to the back of the house, stopping outside the sliding door for the paramedic to enter. Shortly after he'd gone in, he came back out to retrieve his medic's kit from the ambulance. Then he disappeared again, sliding the door shut behind him, leaving them behind in the darkened hallway. Daidai was relieved that Satsuki hadn't felt the need to follow him inside the room.

The dinner of rice crackers rumbled in the pit of Daidai's stomach, but she felt thankful not to have eaten breakfast. The last time they saw Ichiro, he was wrapped in a black body bag to be transported to the morgue. "Would you like to see him before I take him?" the paramedic asked matter-of-factly.

"No." Satsuki shook her head. "That won't be necessary."

Next he turned to Daidai, thinking that perhaps she deserved the same question, but Satsuki shook her head before he could speak.

"Ah! I thought you might like to have this," the paramedic said, reaching into his pocket and dropping something into Satsuki's hand. "I found it in the breast pocket of your father's suit coat."

Satsuki opened her palm to reveal a dull brown stone the size of a marble. *"Taihen desu ne."* She frowned down at the stone, closing it into her fist before turning to look up at the paramedic.

"What is it?" Daidai asked, unable to contain her curiosity.

"If you wouldn't mind, please return it to where you found it." Satsuki held the stone cupped in one palm, the other beneath it as if to support its weight. "It couldn't have gotten there accidentally, so he must have wanted to have it with him."

"Ii desu." The paramedic bowed apologetically. *"Moushiwake arimasen deshita."*

"Ieie. Daijoubu desu."

Turning around, the paramedic unzipped the body bag and returned the stone to Ichiro's breast pocket while Satsuki watched from a few feet back. She remained watching as the cart carrying her father was rolled into the ambulance and the paramedic took his place in the driver's seat. Daidai stood with her in the hushed quiet of morning until the van had disappeared.

Finding her friend's lack of ostensible emotion at her father's passing unnerving, Daidai recalled what Satsuki had said a week earlier regarding her relationship with her father: she doubted she'd miss him were he to disappear. "When I spoke with Hiroshi last night, he was adamant that I catch my flight," she said, suddenly understanding Hiroshi's impulse that she should leave Japan as soon as possible.

"Yes." Satsuki's voice, so slight, might have been the breeze. "Hiroshi is right. You should leave."

"How about you?"

"There's still a week before classes resume. That should be enough to straighten things out here. If not, I'll ask for additional time."

"Of course. I'm sure you could get some extra time, given what's happened."

"Only if it's necessary."

Perhaps Satsuki was in shock. Likely they both were. Daidai wondered if there'd be a funeral and, if so, who would attend. As far as she knew, Satsuki had no family left in Japan. Daidai thought of her mother; Mako would be worried. "I can stay and help you," she offered feebly. "Who knows if the airlines are even flying planes in and out of Japan. The airports might be shut down."

"Let's get you to the airport," Satsuki said. "It's best that way. Even if your flight is delayed, it'll leave eventually, and you should be on it."

"Are you sure?" Daidai asked. But the wavering in her voice bespoke the speciousness of the offer. From across the Pacific Hiroshi was calling her home.

"My father's lawyer will know what to do. He'll get me in touch with the accountant."

Once it had been decided that she should leave Japan, the fear Daidai felt amplified every tremor to an almost unbearable pitch. The imminent danger, she told herself, did not involve her. But it was as if the earth's trembling had entered her body and it refused to leave.

Without electricity to keep the refrigerator working, the perishable food had spoiled, but Satsuki insisted they should eat before departing for the airport. She ladled leftover rice from a cooker on the countertop, which she carried into the courtyard with a plate of pickles and cool tea.

After lunch, Daidai followed Satsuki to her father's office, where she rummaged through the top drawer of Ichiro's desk. She seemed to know what she was looking for, working with the speed and know-how of someone who'd performed this task before. With her hair tucked behind her ears, she had the focus of a teenager rooting through her father's contraband. Watching over her shoulder, Daidai's eyes alit on a scrap of notepaper. "Look," she said, calling Satsuki's attention to the scrap. "Your father had the address to Hiroshi's and my apartment."

"I gave it to him when I asked to have the tea sent," Satsuki said, looking momentarily befuddled.

Daidai nodded and happily shifted her focus to the set of keys that lay next to the scrap of paper. That Ichiro had a car, parked in a garage down the block, meant she'd be leaving Japan after all.

The retaining wall of the parking structure where the car was kept had caved in, but the car itself had not been damaged. Despite roads blocked by debris, many makeshift detours, and traffic backed up for miles, Satsuki seemed determined to get her to the airport. Daidai kept her eyes fastened on the road, where destruction revealed itself on a monumental scale, yet it all seemed like nothing after what she'd already seen.

PART THREE

|

THE AFTERMATH

21

Flying twelve hours out of Narita felt like getting a redo. After calamity, followed by many anxious hours of waiting, time had not merely stood still; it had obliged Daidai by working in reverse so that she could start back at her arrival in Japan and make her way slowly through the eleven-day trip, pausing where she needed to, calibrating at her own pace. By the time she arrived in L.A., she felt quite lucky to have returned safely to Hiroshi. And it turned out that Hiroshi had similar feelings about being reunited with his wife. Having come to the airport to wait, he sobbed openly into her hair when he greeted her outside the baggage claim.

The air in Los Angeles was mild and fresh and filled with goodwill and forgiveness. Hiroshi had kept in touch with Mako, and when Daidai called from her cell phone on the way to the car she could hear the enormous relief in her mother's voice. Rather than bother about dinner, Hiroshi stopped for Chinese food at their favorite takeout, then drove home clutching her hand across the gearshift, humming and tapping out drum beats to Los Lobos while Daidai wondered if the exigencies of travel had cleansed her mind of thought, or if there really was nothing to say.

She appeared from the bathroom to find Hiroshi already seated at the table, hands clasped expectantly in front of him, the food distributed evenly on two plates. It might have been a picture of their early days together, when he'd telegraphed her needs and sought her pleasure in the little things he did. She could feel him watching her as she ate, and she appreciated the obvious care he took not to ask questions she couldn't easily answer.

Having not thought of sex in the twelve days she'd spent apart from him, she was surprised by the deep desire she felt building as she waited for him to finish eating, and the way he clung to her at the foot of the bed even before they'd undressed. Seeing him so vulnerable, she struggled to understand precisely what she felt in response. She fought the vague suspicion that she'd returned not to the person he'd become, but to someone he'd been, someone she'd all but forgotten, though she wondered if what she was feeling might just be tenderness.

"I missed you." She lay next to him diagonally across their bed and he reached again for her hand, a sweet gesture she remembered from their early days as a couple, when they'd been new and unknowable to each other, when the very sight of their skin pressed together—the dark hue of his skin lined up against the paleness of hers—had thrilled her. The stark ridges of his profile and musculature still excited her, along with his hair shining blue in the half-light. Rolling onto her side, she ran her fingers through its thickness, soothed by the musk of his scalp on her fingertips. She'd fallen in love with him not for the ways he was like her, but because he was not; he was the complement, not the double, and she wanted him back if he still wanted her.

Hiroshi had left the TV on, something he rarely did, so that instead of music, news played in a loop, tingeing the mood with bleakness. Cooling off in the dark, Daidai tried to steer her thoughts away from the doldrums to the life she'd come home hoping to resume. "I'm glad to be back," she whispered up to the ceiling.

"I kept watching the news and wishing you home."

"I'd have found my way back to you no matter what."

"I thought you'd forgotten how much you love me."

Daidai sat up, shaken from her romantic moment. "What are you talking about?"

"Well, calamities, like the one you've been through, can take their toll or bring fresh perspective. Did you miss me?"

She lay back down, thinking. Why had Hiroshi cast her feelings into doubt? She'd wanted him there so that she could better gauge her impression of Ichiro's house. But after realizing that a conversation between them could easily be overheard through the thin walls, she'd shut thoughts of him out, determined to focus on the experience at hand. Had she missed him? It was true that Satsuki, not she, had shot photos, sent electronically from each tourist site. She'd been immersed in another world, in a life that wasn't her own, one she'd observed and participated in until it had spit her back out again, whole, but not unaltered.

"Daidai, is something wrong?"

"I missed you, of course!" she said, made self-conscious by Hiroshi's gaze.

"I hope Satsuki's okay." Changing the subject, he rubbed his bristly leg hairs against her naked thigh. "Can you tell me now what happened?"

"I'll tell you if you answer a question first," she said, wishing he hadn't moved so quickly from missing her to wondering about Satsuki. Staring at Hiroshi's elegant profile, Daidai thought about the story Satsuki had told about her brief relationship with Kenji and how it had ended with his admission: *I've often wished my mother didn't love me so much.* Hiroshi had said something similar with regard to his mother: *It's not that she didn't love me. If anything she loved me too much.* She remembered the uneasy feeling of standing beneath the plum blossoms, surrounded by beauty, yet one step outside of understanding. Perhaps what Satsuki meant was that she'd found Kenji selfish. "Why do you want to know?"

Hiroshi stared back at her unflinchingly, as if the answer had been clear and evident in the question. "Why do I want to know about Japan?"

"Yes, why are you asking?"

Rather than answer, he appeared as flummoxed as she'd been when called upon to say that she'd missed him. She'd wanted nothing more than for him to proclaim his undying love of her, to say that he wanted to know what happened because the events were a part of her experience, because he couldn't get enough of her, but that didn't seem to be the case. Instead, he no longer seemed interested in her at all. "I'm worried about Satsuki," he said. "I want to know about any danger she might be in."

Feeling her body shudder, Daidai reached down and brought the covers up to her chin. "Why do all our conversations end up being about Satsuki?"

"They do?" He seemed genuinely puzzled. "I'm worried about her because of the state of emergency in Japan."

Daidai curled into a ball facing away from her husband. Hiroshi was right, of course; he was not being unreasonable in his concern. But the way he insinuated Satsuki into their personal life—while lying in bed, making her the subject of their intimate conversation together—wasn't there something strange about that? Or was it just that he was worried about Satsuki and she was not. "What's happened to Satsuki is terrible," Daidai capitulated, realizing Hiroshi's concern was easily justifiable.

"It's pretty strange that you're not more worried about her in light of all that's gone wrong," he responded. "Her father's dead, and it sounds like the home she grew up in was destroyed in the earthquake. Now there appears to be an all-out nuclear disaster unfolding less than a hundred miles from Mito. And months ago her mother was found shot to death."

"You're right," Daidai told him, recalling that she, too, had been worried about Satsuki prior to leaving Japan. Hiroshi had not been part of the equation then. It had been she and Satsuki, forced to rely upon each other. But Hiroshi's questions reminded her that her friendship with Satsuki had merely been an offshoot of Hiroshi's relationship with her, as his student. So why then had she gone off to Japan with her in the first place? And what reason did Satsuki have for inviting her?

Daidai suspected that it had something to do with vanity. She'd wanted to show off her father's collection, to impress someone who knew about art. Having spent years acquiring pieces from personal collections, Daidai understood what all patrons had in common. They'd tell you things or show you things so that you'd see them the way they did, or the way they wanted you to see them. But what had Satsuki wanted her to see? And then there was Ichiro. What about him? Had he wanted her to see something when he'd killed himself? Daidai needed Hiroshi to help her figure things out: "Satsuki invited me to go with her to Japan so that she could introduce me to her father, but I think there was some other reason. Something she wanted me to see. I thought the same thing when her father turned up dead. His death seemed staged, almost as if he wanted to be seen."

She waited for her husband to formulate his thoughts and was disappointed when Hiroshi refused to see her perspective as legitimate. "I think you've been traumatized and need to sleep," he said, dismissing her.

Daidai shook her head, realizing she'd have to rely on her own intuition. "Ichiro's suicide followed a set of calamitous events. The earthquake and tsunami created massive confusion, so the natural conclusion was that Ichiro killed himself because his home and livelihood had been destroyed. But what if the two events had nothing to do with each other?"

"So you think something other than his possessions being destroyed by the quake led to Ichiro's suicide?" Hiroshi was following her now, excellent listener that he could be.

"Maybe. The house could have been repaired, or he could have found another one. The artwork might not have been replaceable, but most of it had been spared. I think there was something else, some other reason he had for killing himself that just happened to fall in with the earthquake."

"And it has something to do with Satsuki," he said, skeptical.

"She was really angry with her father the night before he died. She wouldn't talk with me about it."

"People get mad at each other all the time." Hiroshi's audible frustration let Daidai know that he was more interested in protecting Satsuki than in what she said. Would he go so far as to repeat what she said to Satsuki?

"There was one other thing," she said, composing a mock confession in her head.

Hiroshi stifled a yawn, not taking the bait.

"Do you want me to tell you or not?"

"Go on."

"There were a half dozen women living in Ichiro's house. I'd seen a few of them when I arrived, women I assumed to be household servants. But the night before the earthquake, the door to Ichiro's art studio had been left open a crack, and when I passed by I saw a group of women seated in front of canvases painting."

"Huh, like a painting class?" he asked, scooting himself up in the bed.

"No, more like a factory. The subject of the paintings was a young girl in various stages of development. The same child depicted as a girl, a preteen, or a young adult—wearing a Japanese schoolgirl uniform in each scenario. But painted always in a lurid context. On one of the canvases her genitals were partially exposed, on others she was involved in a sex act or revealed in a suggestive pose. Each time the girl appeared with a different man, someone whose photo was taped up above the painter's canvas."

From his flat expression Hiroshi appeared to have stopped listening.

"Do you get what I'm saying?" she asked, needing a response from him. "Because here's the thing: when Satsuki and I walked through the studio after the earthquake, everything was gone. The women, the canvases—everything."

"That's not so strange, given the earthquake," he said, letting her know he needed something more.

"It's *very* strange," she insisted. "Don't you think I know strange when I see it?"

"Tell me again how you happened to wind up in the studio," he said, off on his own story line.

Hiroshi had already decided that the problem was not Ichiro's activities, but hers. Deadlocked, they lay together, bare-skinned; it seeming to Daidai as the sky darkened that the face she looked at so close up belonged to a stranger. The first time she'd seen Hiroshi, she'd marveled at the light in his eyes, beams along whose path she swore nothing could be lost. Now something about him was different. She couldn't say whether the change had happened to him or her, only that the terrain of the marriage had shifted while she was in Japan. The feeling was as palpable as it was confusing. And it came to her then that she wasn't going to figure anything out that night, jet-lagged and irrational as she'd begun to feel. Hiroshi was right. What she needed was sleep.

Fortunately, Hiroshi stayed beside her for a long while, keeping her warm with his body propped against hers, combing his fingers through her hair while he read. Even after he'd slipped away, Daidai could hear him on the other side of the wall, tapping away at the computer keyboard. The next thing she knew he was beside her again, and daylight had entered the room.

Daidai tried to appear grateful as she sipped the green tea he offered her. She didn't say what she was thinking, that she would have preferred Earl Grey or even rooibos, something fragrant that spoke of her life in Los Angeles, not Japan. From the living room, the television funneled news of the earthquake and tsunami into the bedroom. The death toll was large and rising, the damage dramatic and inconceivable. An explosion at the TEPCO power plant in Fukushima had sent radiation into the atmosphere, and in its aftermath the leakage of nuclear particles was nowhere near contained. Hard to believe that this was the scene she'd left behind.

22

"Any idea what you're making for brunch?" Hiroshi prompted Daidai to remember that she'd invited Louise over as a thank-you for her help with the fall reception, a date that had been scheduled and changed so many times that it had become disconnected from the event itself. She would have called to postpone yet again had Hiroshi not continued with news of his own. "I went ahead and invited Martin, my TA, and his friend Leonard, Satsuki's housemate."

Of course, once he'd said it she understood why the tea hadn't tasted right. Taking time to fix her hair and giving her teeth an extra good brushing before she made her way to the kitchen, Daidai wondered if there had ever been any pure gestures between her and Hiroshi. "Remind me about your two," she said, as she cut and seeded tomatoes for a salad. She knew Leonard as the boy who'd followed Satsuki into the kitchen, and Hiroshi spoke occasionally about Martin, his go-to TA, but she still didn't understand why he'd invited them to brunch.

"Martin's collecting data for my research this semester, and he's my grader," he said, as if that explained everything. "I don't know Leonard as well, but he hangs out with Martin, and graduate students seem to like to go places in pairs."

It turned out that Hiroshi was right. Martin and Leonard arrived together, each more awkward than the other, making it clear that both needed each other in ways she didn't understand; perhaps they felt dwarfed by Hiroshi's presence. To ease the tension Daidai produced a sack of oranges for them to juice while she finished setting out the food.

Louise showed up just after Hiroshi and his two guests had sat down. "Am I glad to see you!" she said when Daidai greeted her at the door, her words mirroring Daidai's thoughts exactly. Daidai inhaled deeply as they pressed cheeks, and she pulled away, happy to see Louise looking as perfect as ever. After handing Daidai a bowl of fruit salad, she followed behind her to the kitchen. "I was so worried about you," she said.

"I'm sorry, I should have called you," Daidai said, feeling remiss as she poured Louise some coffee.

"I could have called you, too," Louise said, letting her off the hook. "I thought to, but I figured you had your hands full. Besides, if anything had gone terribly wrong I figured I'd have known it somehow."

Daidai smiled, finding Louise's idea about the bond they shared part revelatory, part romantic, and wishing she could feel as certain as Louise did about her instincts. "Ready to eat?" she asked, picking up the bowl of sliced fruits to carry to the table on the other side of the wall.

"In a minute." Louise took the bowl from her and set it back on the counter. "Let's talk a bit first."

"What's up, Lou-Lou?" Daidai teased her with the name she'd called her best friend when the two were children.

"It can wait," Louise said, changing her mind and leading the way out of the kitchen.

"What?" Daidai called to her back, suddenly concerned. "Is it Gizo? How's your father? Tell me."

But Louise didn't turn back.

"Hey-hey." Leonard looked up, his sudden lack of formality surprising Daidai.

"Hey," Martin said, similarly casual.

"How do you all know each other?" Daidai asked.

"Friends of Gizo," Louise said.

"Daidai just arrived last night from Tokyo after visiting Satsuki in Mito," Hiroshi announced, mending a gap in the conversation.

"No kidding!" Leonard went on to explain how just that morning he'd waited in a long line at the pharmacy behind people who were trying to buy iodine tablets. Evidently, they'd wanted to counteract possible poisoning if radiation from the Fukushima plant spread across the Pacific. "The crisis is all the way in Japan, and they were worried about *themselves*," he added, seeming disgusted.

"Maybe they're right to worry," Louise interjected.

"Is it really that bad?" Martin asked, turning to Daidai.

"I'm glad to be home," Daidai replied with a shrug, but worried that Leonard would feel slighted, she addressed him directly. "How are *you* doing, Leonard? How's your first year at the university coming along?"

"Fine. Are people angry, or are they still in shock?" Ignoring her question about his life as a student, Leonard referenced the pop-ulation in Japan with his elbows on the table, leaning in to show his seriousness.

"I think they're in shock," Daidai said, realizing she could speak only from her own limited perspective.

"I can't keep my nose out of the news," Louise confessed.

Daidai hesitated before responding, worn out but curious to know how people were characterizing Japan's crisis in the States. "What are you hearing?"

Louise looked puzzled. "Do you want to know what the newscasters are saying? Or what I think?"

"Both." Daidai glanced from Louise to Hiroshi and his students before helping herself to some fruit.

"There's no comparison in terms of severity, but maybe this Tohoku quake is to Japan what the September eleventh attacks were to most Americans," Louise said. "The Japanese should see it as a wake-up call."

"I agree," Hiroshi chimed in, causing Daidai to wonder what the two were talking about. There were such obvious differences between a natural disaster versus people killed or injured by acts of terrorism, but perhaps they were right, that the important thing now was the aftermath.

After slicing a bagel down the middle, Daidai smeared a generous helping of cream cheese across both halves and bit down, guessing that the conversation might become long and involved. As it continued, Daidai's thoughts wandered back to Satsuki and how everything had changed.

"The aftermath," Louise clarified, seeming to realize she'd left the door open for misinterpretation. "Japan is a series of small islands. The main one, Honshu, sits on top of a major fault line, yet the Daiichi plant was constructed just meters away from the shore. The equipment was faulty and had been outdated for years. The power plant should have been shut down long before this massive quake, but the engineers and businessmen in charge of oversight were making huge profits and ignoring their responsibility. Now information is being withheld and what really happened will stay covered up for a long time."

"Exactly!"

Daidai nodded, continuing along her own trajectory, her thoughts settling on the aftermath. There hadn't been more than an hour or two of daylight left when she and Satsuki had gone off in search of shelter. Early the next morning, when they'd returned, the footprints had been the first things she'd noticed. They'd outlined Ichiro's steps through the house, leading to his bedroom. But had they been Ichiro's footprints? She supposed anyone could have made them.

"I'm sorry for all the innocent people living inside the danger zone," Louise said. "Because much of this was completely avoidable."

"I can't remember, do you have family there?" Hiroshi asked.

Louise barely glanced in Hiroshi's direction. "My family's all here on the West Coast."

"Japan has a choice," Hiroshi pontificated. "It needs to scale back on its use of nuclear power. It's a wake-up call to live differently. People's priorities have to shift, and we'll see if that happens. Why should they be spared what happened to Americans after September eleventh? Naïveté is no longer an option."

"Can a tragic event really change people in a positive way?" Louise sounded lawyerly, closed off to conversation. "I don't know. Who knows whether recovery will even be possible."

Daidai's thoughts had homed in on Ichiro. She'd seen his dead body only briefly, but her mind had fixed on his shoes. The morning light had illuminated their sheen, causing him to appear more like an installation than a suicide. If he'd killed himself in a fit of despair, why had he taken so much care to stage his death?

"By the way," Leonard said, "how's Satsuki?"

Daidai felt her face blanch at the mention of Satsuki, and Hiroshi's gaze shifted from Leonard to her. "Satsuki's still in Mito," he offered, covering for her when she didn't respond right away. "She'll be back next week after her father's funeral."

So he'd been in touch with Satsuki, then? "Have you heard from her?" Daidai addressed Hiroshi directly, trying to sound nonchalant.

"Just a brief e-mail," he said, equally blasé.

"What did she say?" Daidai gripped the sides of her chair, struggling to keep the panic she felt from showing in her voice.

"Just that." Hiroshi met her gaze from across the table in what appeared to be a challenge.

"Am I the only one with no clue about Satsuki?" Louise looked from Hiroshi to Leonard and Martin to Daidai.

"I guess so." Daidai laughed uncomfortably while Hiroshi piled the unused flatware onto his plate, indicating that he was done.

"What's her story, anyway?" Louise addressed her question to Daidai, but Hiroshi spoke up as if she'd asked him.

"She's a graduate student from Japan studying in my program. She was here at the beginning-of-the-year reception. Weren't you introduced?"

"We were." Louise smiled. "So how did a foreigner wind up in Asian American studies?"

She'd asked a good question, one Daidai hadn't adequately considered, but Hiroshi apparently had. "There's a growing interest in Japan in the lives of Japanese in America," he said, before turning back to Leonard and Martin. "She makes a fine contribution to the program, wouldn't you say?"

"She's brilliant," Leonard said.

"Her interest in material culture parallels mine," Martin added, further defending his classmate.

"I still think it's a weird choice of study for a foreign student," Louise volunteered, her gaze fixed on Hiroshi.

Daidai had an urge to reach across the table and hug Louise for her willingness to state the obvious. But Hiroshi dismissed Louise's remark, going on to cite other students in the program whose families had immigrated from the Philippines and Vietnam.

"I guess you liked her enough to go to Japan with her," Louise said, turning again to Daidai.

"She's had a tough couple of months," Hiroshi cut in, unwilling to be shut down by Louise. "Her mother was found dead at the end of last year, and most recently her father killed himself after the tsunami."

"Really?" Louise stared at Daidai wide-eyed, and satisfied to have gotten the upper hand, Hiroshi turned away and began a conversation with Martin.

Once the table had been cleared, the two women excused themselves to the kitchen. Louise picked the remaining tomato slices out of the salad bowl, keeping her voice low against the conversation playing out in the other room. "So is Satsuki your new best friend?"

"You're my best friend." Daidai smiled across the counter at Louise.

"And you're mine," Louise said. But there was something else she wanted to say, too. Daidai waited, remembering how Louise had tried to tell her something before they'd sat down to brunch. "I started seeing someone," she said, her tone so sheepish Daidai guessed she was referencing a therapist.

"A man?" she asked, deciding to err on the side of romance.

"Actually"—Louise paused and smiled—"a woman."

It took Daidai a minute to collect her emotions. One thing had happened when another seemed more likely. The possibility of Louise dating a woman had never occurred to her. "I'm so happy for you," she said, though happiness was not what she felt. Was it betrayal? She couldn't be sure. "Who? How long?"

"Not long," Louise said. "And I haven't mentioned her because I don't know how important she'll turn out to be yet. There were others before her," she added. "In case you were wondering."

Others? Louise's love interests had nothing to do with her, but she felt implicated by the revelation. How presumptuous she'd been to decide that Louise had no personal life, rather than that she'd kept her personal life hidden. What was friendship, if not a place where you could lay yourself open? But that hadn't happened since childhood. Her life had developed in one way and Louise's in another. They'd encouraged each other's career choices and triumphs, but their point of intersection had been in the past. They'd bonded around their mothers' friendship, affection they'd witnessed and internalized and cultivated as their own.

Feeling herself on the verge of despair, Daidai wondered if she'd been sidelined in all her most important relationships. Her on the outside appreciating her mother's fondness for Hiroshi, but not being enough for Mako. Or for Louise. And apparently she wasn't enough for her husband either.

"Don't look so glum!" Louise quipped, causing Daidai to break from her ruminations.

"I'm not glum," Daidai insisted. "I'm furious with you for not telling me and with myself for not knowing!" Reaching across what had felt like an unbridgeable distance, Daidai pulled Louise to her, breathing in the familiar scent of her hair. "Wait till I tell Hiroshi," she whispered. "He's been looking to add a new point to his paradigm."

"Right?" Louise said, pulling back. "And what would this point represent?"

"Successful. Female. Gay."

"Is that what I am?"

Daidai shrugged, shaken. Laughter erupting from the other room reminded her it was not just Louise she needed to think about. She'd need to contemplate the nature of her husband's relationship with his student and Satsuki's involvement in Ichiro's death, and suddenly the headache she'd been courting since before lunch overtook her.

Once the lunch guests had left, Daidai took a heavy dose of pain relievers. Hoping to nap, she instead slept straight through the night. The next morning the headache was gone, replaced with heaviness in her chest, chills, and a fever that persisted for the next three days.

23

The bug that kept Daidai in bed ended on a Thursday. That same morning a letter arrived. Despite all that had gone wrong in Japan, its postmark indicated that it had found its way to Southern California in under a week.

Inspecting the envelope carefully before opening it, Daidai believed at first that the note had come from Satsuki, though she couldn't understand why it had been sent the day before she'd left Mito. Shielding her eyes from the glare hitting the row of metal postboxes, she read the address line again to verify that the envelope had actually been addressed to her. Perhaps it had been delivered to the wrong mailbox. It was 70 degrees out that morning and perfectly sunny, but a shiver ran up her spine and her hands trembled, contributing a layer of unpleasantness all their own.

Daidai [she recognized her name, printed in kana]*:*

I welcomed you into my home when Satsuki invite you to return with her to Mito. I hope you enjoyed to visit Japan. Now I like to remind you how good reputation takes years to build. I cannot hope to control what you do. This decision must belong to yours, but I would ask you to consider that the truth might be different from what you think. Satsuki might have made mistake to discuss things that are none of her business. However, I still wish to protect my daughter and would ask you to think of her when I say that I believe it would be a mistake to go to police.

Sincerely,
Ichiro "Ichiban" Suzuki
H22.3.10

How unnerving to get mail from a dead man! It was as if Ichiro were reaching a hand up from the grave to pull her under with him, or hovering over a place in the world he couldn't or maybe just shouldn't be occupying. The letter was dated, indicating it had been written shortly before Ichiro's life had ended. She would need to show it to Satsuki when she returned, but the thought of Satsuki arriving back in the States within a matter of days made her shudder. Satsuki knew about whatever situation had caused Ichiro to send her a letter asking her not to involve the police. Most likely it had to do with the women she'd seen painting in Ichiro's art studio. Since Ichiro was dead, he posed no direct threat, but his art business had a shadow side of child pornography and maybe even indentured women artists about which he knew she'd become aware.

It wasn't hard to pull up information about his business on the Internet. Though the name Ichiro turned out to be as common as a John or Thomas in the States, "Ichiro Suzuki" coupled with "art dealer" narrowed the list of leads considerably. After she'd eliminated hits related to the professional baseball player, the Japanese terms *shunga* and *ukiyo-e* appeared beside the top listings, and it turned out that both shed light on Ichiro's art business.

The Japanese had a long history of depicting sexually explicit acts in their artwork, which could be viewed as either perverted or erotic. During the six-hundred-year Shogun period, when Japan had sealed itself off to Western influences, artists like Hokusai found ways to smuggle in images from the West, along with methods of shading and coloring, which allowed them to refine and mass-produce art. Instead of depicting timeworn country landscapes, *shunga* artists examined cosmopolitan settings and used ordinary city dwellers as their subject matter, teasing their patrons with erotic fetishes. Ichiro, entrepreneur that he turned out to be, had taken this tradition one step further by personalizing paintings to cater to his wealthy and sick-minded clientele.

Recalling what Satsuki had told her about her father's humble beginning as a framer, Daidai imagined his emergence in the art world. Did Satsuki know about her father's dealings? If so, had she brought Daidai to Japan hoping she'd investigate? Perhaps it was not by chance that his body appeared in the wreckage of the quake. Perhaps he'd intended his death to be connected to that event to draw attention away from his child pornography business.

Daidai felt certain that Ritsuko's death was also connected. But how? Though Ichiro hadn't mentioned his wife's death in the letter, Daidai had a hunch that by finding out what had happened to Ritsuko, she'd understand what had gone wrong for Ichiro as well.

24

Wanting to uncover whatever information she could before Satsuki returned, Daidai wasted no time in doing what needed to be done next: she showered, dressed, and was out the door by noon, timing her arrival at Holy Heart for just past the lunch hour.

As luck would have it, the entrance gate had been propped open with a large stone, the path to the monastery shop newly swept and hosed down, sending up a pungent musk. But even more fragrant than the earth's petrichor was the yeasty sweet smell inside the shop, where bread loaves in their uniform and pleasing shapes lined the tall pastry shelves and several customers stood in a queue to make their purchases.

Taking her place at the end of the line, Daidai was pleased to see that the nuns were back in business and that Sister Elspeth once again stood behind the counter. Though she'd been less lucid than Sister Mary Agnes, she'd also been the more forthcoming and chatty of the two, and Daidai considered herself fortunate that no one entered the shop behind her, leaving her and the sister alone when her turn came at the register.

"Good afternoon, Sister Elspeth," Daidai called across the counter in a cheerful voice, genuinely pleased to see the old woman again.

"Good afternoon!" Sister Elspeth called back, her jovial tone infectious.

"I'm glad to see you're back in the bread-making business."

"Back and better than ever."

"I take it you found someone to help with the lifting," Daidai said, curious to know what had changed.

"Even better than that." Sister Elspeth smiled, showing a row of yellow but perfectly even teeth that must have been dentures.

"A new nun?"

"A new oven, a professional stand mixer, and a hydraulic lift."

"Wow!" Finding the nun's habited form discordant with her enthusiastic talk of kitchen appliances, Daidai stifled her laughter. "That sounds expensive."

"Donated," she announced proudly, as if she'd somehow brokered the deal herself.

"You must have friends in high places," Daidai commented, unable to resist her own feeble attempt at humor.

Sister Elspeth smiled. "Our benefactor was a relative of the sister who recently passed."

"Satsuki?" Daidai asked, taken aback by the nun's revelation.

"I don't recall the name. Apparently the donor had heard of our dire situation and wanted to help."

As if on cue, Sister Mary Agnes entered from the door leading into the storeroom. "Sister Elspeth, you may go to afternoon prayer," she announced, aware that she'd interrupted their conversation.

Sister Elspeth, ever obedient, excused herself. "My goodness, I didn't even get your order! But Sister Mary Agnes can help you."

"Thank you," Daidai called as Sister Elspeth turned away, noting something different about Sister Mary Agnes's appearance. The first time, she'd reminded Daidai of a fragile bird; this time her curved spine made her look more like a seated cat. Waiting for Sister Mary Agnes to tie an apron around her habit, Daidai wondered to what she should attribute the sister's figurative transformation.

Sister Mary Agnes wasted no time assuming her position behind the counter. "How can I help you?"

"Two loaves should do it!" she said boisterously before modulating her tone, self-conscious in Sister Mary Agnes's presence. "Good afternoon, Mother Superior."

"I remember you!" the prioress said warmly. "I never forget a face. It's a gift I haven't made much use of through the years, but a gift all the same."

Did she remember then why Daidai had come the first time? Aware that the purpose of her visit had been to gather more information about Ritsuko, Daidai suddenly felt unworthy of the prioress's unassuming disposition.

"Is something troubling you?"

Surprised by the question, Daidai struggled to ease her way into conversation. Letting the warm, sweet-smelling air fill her lungs, she tried to imagine the prioress's life. What would it be like to live in such seclusion? "I'm fine, thank you," she said. "It's nice to see you."

Sister Mary Agnes smiled, indicating she'd hit the right note. "What can I do for you?"

"It's lovely here," Daidai said, eyeing her surroundings. "Have you lived here a long time?"

"I've lived at Holy Heart for sixty-one years," the Mother Superior said.

"That's a long time," Daidai said, deciding it might be more accurate to regard the prioress as a living relic than an ordinary person. Still, the old woman wouldn't be easily fooled. "You might remember that I'd come asking questions about Sister Bernadette," she said, thinking it best to be honest about wanting information since stalling would only make the woman suspicious.

"I do remember that, yes."

"This was before you'd received the donation of the new baking equipment."

"Yes, our good fortune has come about quite recently."

"May I ask about that, where the donation came from?"

"The donor wished to remain anonymous," the prioress said, her expression turning serious. "I'd be going against the terms of the bequest to reveal personal information. I overheard Sister Elspeth just now, and I apologize if she misled you. She's old like me and can sometimes get carried away with her enthusiasm. Of late, I haven't had much success in reasoning with her."

"I understand." Seeing the importance of remaining sympathetic, Daidai found herself struggling to understand on her own what the new information meant. Sister Elspeth's disclosure had provided the second surprise of the day, but given Sister Mary Agnes's rebuke of Sister Elspeth, she knew she wasn't going to get anywhere by bringing up Satsuki. "In that case I won't ask questions about the donation or the person who made it."

"Thank you," Sister Mary Agnes said graciously.

"To be honest, that wasn't the reason for my visit in the first place, though I'm glad that the donation has made your jobs easier. It would be a shame not to be able to make the ahn-bread since it's something you do so well and so many people enjoy it."

"Thank you," she said again.

"The first time I visited, it was because I'd heard about Sister Bernadette's passing. I knew that the police were investigating the cause of Sister Bernadette's death, and now I'm wondering if there have been any findings."

"You'd have to go to the police for that information. But I'm not one to hide from the truth. I can tell you that Sister Bernadette took her own life and that her suicide came as a great shock to all of us. May God forgive her."

"I see," Daidai said. "So she'd been troubled, then?"

"When she came to us—" The prioress's stern expression broke then to expose both tenderness and sorrow. "When she came to us she was troubled, indeed. But that was many years ago. She spent more than twenty-five years here at Holy Heart, and during that time the Lord transformed her life. She set an example for the others through her discipline and devotion. We were changed by her presence, and we are changed again by her passing."

"She must have been a powerful presence here for you to have held her in such high esteem."

"I don't think any of us thought of Sister Bernadette as powerful." Sister Mary Agnes chortled. "God is almighty. Jesus is almighty. Sister Bernadette lived her life as God's servant."

"Powerful" had not been the right word. Sister Mary Agnes's response showed sensitivity to language, which had perhaps come from reading the Bible for so many years. Irked about being corrected, Daidai understood nonetheless that there was something trustworthy about a person who said what she meant. "Was there anything in the end to indicate that Sister Bernadette had been contemplating suicide?"

"No. But we were quite surprised to find out recently that she had a daughter. The child must have been quite young when Bernadette came to us. Had we known, she would never have been granted a vocation."

So Sister Mary Agnes knew about Satsuki. "What was your impression of her daughter?" Daidai asked, barely able to contain her curiosity.

"She came here to the shop one day, much like you did—to buy ahn-bread. Sister Bernadette was the one to receive her. As far as I know, they met only on that one occasion."

"How did you find out that Sister Bernadette's daughter had come here? I mean, assuming Sister Bernadette was alone in the shop when the visit took place."

"Sister Bernadette came to me to confess." The prioress held her hands in fists on the countertop, calling attention to her prominent knuckles. "The sin of omission is a serious one. Sister Bernadette was troubled by it. In hindsight, I believe contrition weighed heavily on her for the twenty-five years she was with us."

"Were you upset about the daughter, too?" Daidai had no idea about the Church's protocols, but was curious as to whether the prioress's personal response conflicted with her role as head mistress.

"I advised her to consider leaving the monastery," she said, her tone devoid of emotion.

"Why?" Daidai asked, feeling a pang of sympathy for Ritsuko. What a shock it must have been for her, first to be confronted by her grown daughter, and then rebuffed by a woman she'd lived with for so many years and had approached for succor.

"A woman who comes to live at Holy Heart makes a vow not only to God, but to the community she agrees to take part in as well. Sister Bernadette violated our trust by withholding information. We accepted her based on false claims she'd made about her past."

Sister Mary Agnes had obviously felt betrayed by Ritsuko, but Daidai wondered what else lay behind the bitterness she'd expressed. "If Sister Bernadette were forced out of the monastery, where would she have had to go?"

"Back to her daughter," the prioress remarked. "Back to Japan."

"Really?" No mention had been made of Ritsuko wanting to live with her daughter. In the real world Sister Mary Agnes's bitterness amounted to a kind of racism that Daidai found abhorrent.

"I am the prioress. I do not confuse myself with God. I recommended to Sister Bernadette that she pray for God's forgiveness and ask God for direction."

"I see." Daidai hadn't confused Sister Mary Agnes with God, but she decided it best to heed her declaration as a warning. She'd need to pay homage to the Mother Superior's authority or risk being shut out. "And how did Sister Bernadette respond?"

"She wept. She begged my forgiveness. She claimed the daughter had already forgiven her and wanted no further contact."

Shouldn't Ritsuko have begged forgiveness from God, and not from Sister Mary Agnes? Noting Sister Mary Agnes's slip, Daidai considered what the prioress might be leaving out. Had something else happened for which Sister Mary Agnes felt she was personally owed an apology? The night Satsuki received the phone call from the police informing her that her mother had been found dead, why had she not revealed then that she'd visited her mother at the monastery? And how did Sister Mary Agnes know that Satsuki had forgiven her mother for abandoning her? "Are the police aware of what happened?" she asked, befuddled.

"Yes. I'm not telling you anything I haven't already told the police."

"I apologize if I sounded accusatory," Daidai recanted. "I really do appreciate your talking to me. May I ask just one more question?"

"Yes," Sister Mary Agnes said, her blue eyes penetrating in their sharpness.

"Where would Sister Bernadette have gotten the gun?"

"I don't know." Closing her eyes, the prioress clutched the metal cross that hung over her chest. "The police asked that same question. I have no idea where the gun came from."

Sister Mary Agnes had turned pale. It had been wrong to upset the old woman. Placing her palms on the countertop to steady herself, Daidai felt the ground sway beneath her as she struggled to recall what she'd been thinking, believing it had somehow been important.

"You're not well," the prioress commented.

"I'm fine." Clutching the rim of the countertop, Daidai realized she'd inadvertently contradicted the prioress. "I'm sorry," she said, not wanting to be perceived as combative.

"You'll be okay," the prioress said, placing fingertips on Daidai's wrist to feel for a pulse. "I think you're hungry."

"Yes," Daidai agreed. She'd meant to stop for lunch and had forgotten. "I'm sure that's it."

"You need to get your strength back," the Mother Superior said, coming around the counter. "You can rest in the back room. There's no need to leave if you're feeling unwell."

Where before Sister Mary Agnes's penetrating gaze had seemed cold, her eyes now shone with compassion, and Daidai felt humbled by the elderly woman's generosity. The back room, which had not been set up to accommodate guests, bespoke the nuns' ascetic lifestyle. Except for the fancy industrial oven installed against the wall and the professional stand mixer and hydraulic lift that occupied the middle of the floor—monstrosities, both of them—the room held only a wooden chair and cot, set up in the corner, perhaps to allow the older nuns to take a break from their work in the shop. From where Daidai sat, perched on the cot, she recognized the simplicity of Ritsuko's daily life at Holy Heart.

"Why don't you lie back and shut your eyes for a few minutes?" the prioress suggested. Having shaken out a brown woolen blanket, which had lain neatly over a chair, she draped it across Daidai's lap.

"Really, I'm just fine," Daidai insisted, not wanting to take advantage of the prioress's hospitality. But after disappearing back into the shop, Sister Mary Agnes returned with a glass of water and a slice of bread and took a seat beside the cot. It was such a nurturing gesture, to sit and watch over a stranger. Appreciating the head mistress's unequivocal kindness, Daidai wondered if gratitude was what kept Ritsuko at Holy Heart all those years. "So you've lived at the monastery for sixty-one years?" she asked, trying again to focus her attention.

"I arrived just after my twentieth birthday."

"That's a long time to have lived in one place. Are you originally from California?"

"I was born in Oklahoma, the part of the world that John Steinbeck has written about, and from the same era. My parents' lives were devastated by the Dust Bowl and Great Depression. I'm sure their economic situation contributed to my departure, but I had my calling much the same as any other sister, I would expect. Jesus spoke to me. He speaks to me still."

The mention of a calling had shocked Daidai, though she guessed it shouldn't have, given the circumstances. She tried to imagine what it would be like to be spoken to by Jesus, to be called to live with other women, to have your wardrobe consist of a plain, formless habit and your time structured to be the same each day in a life of devotion and prayer. Surely nuns had their own deep toils, but for a moment she envied the simplicity and singular focus of Sister Mary Agnes's days. "How did Sister Bernadette come to live at Holy Heart?" she asked, wondering if Ritsuko, too, believed in a calling.

"The diocese supports monasteries in many countries. Sister Bernadette served her postulancy in Tokyo and left Japan to come to Holy Heart. The charism at this monastery serves women and children. Sister Bernadette identified those areas as being her primary interest."

What a hypocrite Ritsuko had been, abandoning her child in order to pray for the well-being of children! "I'm an acquaintance of her daughter," Daidai blurted out, regretting after she'd spoken how wrong she'd been to omit what she knew, then to reveal personal information so abruptly.

"I see," the prioress said, seeming to take what Daidai had said in stride.

"I believe she suffered greatly from having to live without her mother," Daidai added.

"That should never have happened."

"Do you think Sister Bernadette was really a believer?"

"She lived here for over twenty-five years. I don't know how a person without faith could do that."

"No, neither do I," Daidai agreed, and deciding to let the subject of faith drop, she collected her things to go.

25

Heading north on the Hollywood Freeway, Daidai eyed the Santa Monica mountain range, noting the old HOLLYWOOD landmark sign and, closer, in the cluster of foothills, Louise's bungalow-style house where she was headed. The two had discovered the house together shortly after Louise landed her first job with L.A. County and Daidai started work at the museum. Pulling off at the Silver Lake exit, she assumed Louise would be at work, but it was nice to be traveling back to the locus of so many fond memories, and she liked the idea of leaving a loaf of bread, made by a bunch of nuns, on Louise's doorstep. Louise would be amused, and she hoped that the gesture of goodwill would bolster their waning friendship.

And as it turned out, Louise's car passed into the driveway just as Daidai was maneuvering into a curbside spot, Louise waving as if she'd been expecting her. Daidai waved back, smiling out her window, until the dejection in Louise's expression registered with her. What could Louise be so worried about?

Leaning in for a hug on the sidewalk, Daidai whispered in her friend's ear, "You look like someone who just got laid off," hoping Louise would find the self-deprecating reference to her own unemployed status funny.

"News travels fast," Louise said, pulling back to search for her keys.

Daidai had fallen in love with Louise's house for its thick walls, immaculately kept spaces, and creaky hardwood floors, but stepping into the foyer, she had the feeling that she'd wound up at the wrong address. A half dozen pairs of shoes lined the entryway, overturned where they'd been kicked off. Farther in, a collection of used mixing bowls lay abandoned on the sideboard along with the wilted tops of carrots. What had happened to disrupt Louise's orderly life?

"Did your mother tell you?" Louise asked, as if in response to Daidai's disbelief. "I can't believe he's gone."

"Your father?" Daidai said under her breath. Danji. Gone. How could it be? Too shocked to contemplate the possibility that Danji had died, she recalled the excuse Louise had given for not being in touch, that she'd have known if Daidai needed her from Japan. Why then hadn't *she* known?

The afternoon sunlight pouring in through the window had lengthened the room in shadows, turning everything a burnished orange. "They said he'd had a stroke. They wanted to keep him at the hospital overnight, but he just wanted to go home. Gizo had to carry him inside, he was so weak."

Still standing in the foyer, Daidai felt the blood drain out of her face. Gizo had carried Danji into Louise's house. When had this happened? Almost two years earlier she'd brought her own father home to die.

"I wish we could have done more for him. He died yesterday, just after dawn. I was lying on the couch with my eyes closed, not really asleep. Weekday mornings, a bus stops down the hill. You can hear the neighbors packing up their children for school, doors opening and shutting, the kids talking outside, laughing. He always said that was this house's best feature."

Daidai listened for the children, combing the space with her eyes for traces of Danji in the blankets pulled back from Louise's bed, the glass of water untouched on the nightstand.

"Gizo had gone outside for a cigarette. He'd left the door open, and I could smell the smoke coming in from outside. When I heard my name, I thought I was dreaming."

Unable to focus fully on what Louise was saying about Danji, she remembered her last night in Satsuki's father's home in Mito.

She'd fallen asleep after dinner and awoken to the sound of Satsuki calling her name.

"Gizo had his head sideways on my father's chest. I knew he'd passed. It had happened while Gizo was outside. But so recently that a tear that had collected in the corner of my father's eye ran down his cheek. Gizo saw it, too. 'That says it all,' he said.

"Dad had such a peaceful expression; his facial muscles relaxed as if he'd just decided to let it all go. All that restraint, everything he'd held inside, gone with him, and just that tear rolling down his cheek."

"Do you think he was sad to die?" They'd moved by then to the couch, where they sat shoulder to shoulder, Daidai holding Louise's hand as they stared into the bedroom as if it were a stage set.

"Gizo thought so. He took it pretty hard. Despite how tough he seems on the outside, he's still our father's only son, and the baby of the family. But I think he died satisfied by how beautiful life is. I think he'd always believed that, and in the final seconds of his life he felt it, and it mattered to him."

What mattered? Daidai wondered, thinking about her visit to the monastery. "What about you?"

"What about me?" Louise seemed not to understand the question.

"How are you?"

Louise looked down.

"You're probably still in shock," Daidai said.

Louise frowned. "It's as if I've gone somewhere outside of time."

Daidai nodded, feeling herself on the cusp of understanding something important.

"Do you remember when we were little? We wouldn't see each other for weeks at a time. Then my mother would announce we were having lunch with your mother, meaning I'd get to spend the afternoon with you at your house, or you'd come to mine, and we'd be back together as if no time at all had passed. In a way, everything in my life is organized around those feelings from early on, when everything revolved around what people meant to me. I think deep emotions exist outside of time."

Louise was right. There was daily life, lived according to routine and necessity, different from the space occupied by friendship, a privileged space she'd occupied first with her mother, then with Louise, and later Hiroshi. She no longer knew the details of Louise's daily life, just as Louise had lost track of hers. But sitting together on the couch, they still shared that space. Trying to imagine what the morning had been like for Louise, Daidai pulled up an image of Satsuki instead. She was glowering, and Daidai fought the urge to rise, to wash the mixing bowls and scrape the remains of carrots into the trash.

"I'm glad I could be here," she said in defiance of her thoughts of Satsuki, rubbing Louise's back in wide circles.

26

Daidai had been furious about her mother's unsympathetic response to her miscarriage, but as if to say that her anger had been misguided, Mako came to the door looking worn down and a little confused. "What are you doing here?" she asked. Her face showed signs of aging, the afternoon sunlight exposing a map of lines that ran across her forehead and around her mouth, projecting Daidai's future.

"I came from Louise's," Daidai said, worried about the impact of Danji's death on her mother, knowing she'd stayed away too long.

"So sad, neh. I tried calling you, but your phone just rang and rang."

Daidai smiled, assured by the feeling that the web of connectedness between her and her mother remained intact. Mako listened patiently as Daidai went through the details Louise had described leading up to her father's death, leaving nothing out. When there was no more to say, she arranged slices of ahn-bread on one of her mother's fancy Imari plates while Mako stood by examining the hand-printed ingredients label. "I've never seen anything like this," she said. "Where did nuns come up with the idea to make loaves of *ahn-pan?*"

"It's a long story," Daidai said, anxious to know whether the bread would meet with her mother's high standards.

Mako sniffed at it and eyed it suspiciously before popping a piece into her mouth. "This tastes pretty good," she said, chewing contemplatively.

Daidai laughed. She never knew what she'd get from Mako. Danji's death had upset her, but she'd been uplifted by the sight of the ahn-bread, and she didn't seem to need to move backward over what had gone wrong between them the last time. "I was so scared for you when I heard about the earthquake. Tell me about Japan," she said, hands clutched in her lap.

"There was a tsunami and the nuclear reactors in Fukushima are in meltdown."

Mako nodded. "Tell me about your friend, the one you went to visit."

Rather than be pleased by Mako's interest, Daidai still felt her mother's betrayal. "I didn't go to see Satsuki. I went *with* her," she said, offering a correction that shouldn't have mattered. But even angry, she wanted her mother's sympathy. "Her father has a house in Mito. Actually, her father is dead. Satsuki and I found him dead the day after the earthquake."

"Terrible." Mako thrummed her tongue against the roof of her mouth a few times, a quirk Daidai remembered from childhood. "How come you never told me about this Satsuki?"

Didn't she know that Daidai avoided talking about any subject that might lead to confrontation? With Mako there was no way to win. Mako tended to be traditional in her thinking about how women and men should interact, and Daidai could already see where the conversation would lead: she'd want to know why Satsuki had left Japan to study at the university, and, of course, she'd be suspicious about the way Satsuki behaved with Hiroshi, which would in the end point at her not being a good enough wife. Still, having just heard the news of Danji's death, Daidai felt vulnerable, and she needed Mako on her side. She took a deep breath before diving in, hoping for the best. "Satsuki studies with Hiroshi," she explained.

"I see."

"I didn't want to involve you."

"It's okay, Daidai."

"What's okay?"

Pushing back her chair, Mako walked around the table and pressed Daidai's cheeks between her palms. "Sometimes you don't want to, but you can always tell me things. Don't ever be afraid to tell me."

It had been a long time since she'd done that, held Daidai's face in her hands and looked her in the eye. Daidai felt the warmth of her mother's palms on her cheeks even after Mako had returned to her chair. "I'm sorry for not coming by sooner," she said, knowing she'd been wrong to stay away.

"I know how busy you are."

Daidai bit the inside of her lip. "I'm not too busy."

Mako reached across the table for another slice of ahn-bread. "So she's a student?" She looked like a regular little Buddha sitting across from Daidai, her head slightly inclined, her calm and pleasant disposition the only indicator that she was listening. "I was wondering where you'd met her."

"She got her undergraduate degree from Bunka Gakuen University in Shibuya. Before that, she attended an exclusive boarding school."

"Abroad?"

"A place called Shodai Gakuen, just outside of Tokyo."

"I've never heard of it." Mako's disapproval showed in her knitted brow. "What's her last name?"

"Suzuki. Maybe you two are related," Daidai joked, offering up a deflection, then wondering what concession between Mako and her father had resulted in her winding up with Mako's family name instead of Flynn.

"I've never heard of a young Japanese girl being sent to live at a boarding school."

"Satsuki's circumstances were unusual," Daidai said, becoming serious, relieved to be able to talk with her mother about Satsuki. "Her mother ran off when she was just four. Her paternal grandmother moved in after that, to help raise her, but then the grandfather became ill and the grandmother was summoned home. Satsuki's father was unable to care for her on his own, so he sent her away."

"I see." Mako took her time registering the information Daidai had given her. "So what was your business at the monastery?"

Daidai smiled at how quickly her mother's thoughts had circled back to her. "The monastery was where Satsuki's mother lived after she left Japan. Evidently, for the last twenty-five years."

"But not anymore?"

"She recently turned up dead."

"So both parents are dead?"

"Yes."

"And why did you say she came here?"

"I told you, she came to study in Hiroshi's program."

"But why does she need *your* help?"

"Because she's alone, because she and I have become friends," she said, realizing as she spoke how complicated her friendship with Satsuki had become.

"But why does she need you to help her? Doesn't she have family?"

"No." Daidai sighed, exasperated at having to repeat herself. "I just told you. Her parents are both dead."

Mako wasted no time in coming to a conclusion. "I don't think you should get involved with her problems," she said, staring unflinchingly across the table.

"Why would you say that?" Daidai asked, shocked that Mako's sentiments should echo Hiroshi's warning, and by her mother's lack of empathy.

"She's trouble. I can tell."

"How can you tell?" Daidai had hoped that Mako would clarify rather than add to her confusion. "I'm telling you about Satsuki because I don't understand her. I'm frustrated. But what you're saying is not helpful."

"I am being helpful if you'd just listen," Mako said defensively.

"I'm sorry," Daidai said. "I'm listening."

"You can't help being naive," Mako explained. "It's not your fault. I raised you to want to help people. It's my fault."

"Right," Daidai said, rolling her eyes at her mother's martyrdom. Mako didn't feel guilty. She felt entirely justified in her accusations, even if no one but her understood them. "Since when is trying to help people wrong?"

"Most Americans are like you. I'm not saying you shouldn't be generous and try to help someone when you can. It's human nature to do that. I'm just saying that you don't know what you're getting yourself into. Things might not be what you think."

Hiroshi had hinted at what Mako was now saying outright. Daidai assumed her husband had been led astray by his self-righteousness posturing, but there was something else about Satsuki she wasn't understanding. Did being Japanese enable Mako to see what Daidai was blind to? It was true that Mako and Satsuki had a similar upbringing. Even though Mako's father had moved his family from Ishikawa Prefecture to Torrance, California, when she was a teenager, she still considered herself Japanese, and each had been a social outcast because of her family's circumstances, Satsuki in Japan and Mako in the States. Mako would have remained with her mother in Japan had her businessman father, Satoru, not succumbed to travel fatigue. Fortunately, she'd mastered English quickly, but the irony was that she faced rejection by her American peers for clinging to Japanese traditions and by her Japanese peers for being too Westernized. In response to her complaint that she didn't fit in anywhere, Satoru introduced her to his favorite line worker, Peter Flynn, whom she'd married believing that if she could not fit in, at least her daughter would.

Of course, the ingredient she'd failed to consider was Daidai's will; her preference for Eastern over Western thinking, along with the facial features and body structure she'd never have. Still, the relationship she had with her daughter fortified them both. This had become especially true recently. After the death of her husband, Mako had staked her claim on Daidai's life.

"Will you please just tell me what you think I might be getting myself into so that I can decide for myself whether to move forward?" Daidai demanded.

"You don't understand," Mako said with a touch of pity. "You were not there when Japan was trying to rebuild after the war, so you couldn't see all that had been destroyed. For decades people became obsessed with modernizing, and that meant acquiring wealth. A country that had been shut off to outside influence wanted to join in and show the world its high status, even with objects that weren't meaningful."

Daidai recalled the historic sites she'd visited, tucked alongside the trappings of city life. "It was strange seeing the old and new so close together."

"Since the earthquake, I've been thinking back to my childhood. I was raised to believe that life gets its meaning from traditions passed from one generation to the next. But the world has changed since then. Maybe it's outgrown my way of thinking. Now radiation has poisoned the land and seeped into the ocean. The toxic effects will be around for many generations beyond our lifetime."

Mako's reflections on Japan's nuclear disaster sounded like Louise's. "It's all horrible," Daidai agreed.

"Maybe it makes you think twice about bringing new life into the world."

Daidai had wondered how long it would take Mako to trace her way back to the disappointment she clearly still carried with her. "I see," she said, struggling not to let their conversation degenerate into another argument.

"But it's possible that people will return to a more sensible way of life. Maybe rediscover more traditional values, which might mean something good comes out of this terrible mess."

"So you think I shouldn't have a baby?" she asked, trying to get at what her mother was really saying.

"I could understand if you didn't want to."

Daidai reached across the table and gave her mother's hand a squeeze. Did all the doubts she'd expressed about Satsuki really boil down to her worry about not getting her grandbaby? She guessed that the softening of Mako's approach had less to do with the multiple disasters in Japan than it did with a need to keep her daughter close.

Pushing her chair back from the table, Daidai stood, prepared to leave.

"Can you give me a ride to the memorial?" Mako asked, ready with one more detail that needed figuring out.

"Of course!" Daidai said, having planned to do that without being asked.

But before she could leave, Mako insisted that her daughter follow her outside so that Daidai could admire her vegetable garden.

Stooping over a vine of Japanese eggplants, she talked about the natural repellent she'd concocted to keep away a species of beetle she'd never seen before and, knowing Daidai's fondness for eggplant, snipped a half dozen of the purple *nasubi* from their stems, catching them in the expanse of her shirt, telling Daidai how she should cook them at home.

Back inside, she took her time with the eggplants, shining each one with a drying cloth before transferring them into a shopping bag. "I don't think the tear Danji shed was about life being beautiful," she said, not looking up from her work.

"What, then?" Daidai asked, curious as to what her mother knew, or thought she knew.

"I just don't think Louise was right about that. That's all," she said. "Danji Hashimoto had a complicated life. Anyone who's lived to our age has had experiences that people your age just haven't had yet."

"Like what?" Daidai said, prodding Mako to say outright what she meant.

But Mako would say no more, not that afternoon, and Daidai guessed maybe ever. Having made her observation, she practically pushed Daidai out the door, sending her daughter away to ponder the news of Danji's death on her own.

PART FOUR

|

INSTALLATIONS

27

At the end of a long afternoon, Daidai arrived home at her favorite moment of the day. The moon sat atop the eastern horizon, turning the sky a dusky blue with the trees and buildings receding in blackened outlines. Hiroshi's car was parked in his spot, which likely meant he'd walked to campus. He'd said nothing that morning about dinner plans, but glancing up the three floors to their apartment, Daidai saw that it was dark. She didn't expect to find Hiroshi home, nor could she have anticipated what she'd find when her key turned in the door: the table set much like it had been the night Hiroshi, Satsuki, and she had prepared their celebratory feast to mark the end of Satsuki's first semester on campus, only this time candles she didn't recognize lit either end of the table. The aroma of a Japanese meal filled the air, and out from the kitchen with a white apron tied around her waist walked Satsuki. She threw her hands up, tossing Daidai's wooden salad bowl into the air.

"*Bikkuri shimasu!* You startled me!"

Daidai's hands reflexively found their way to her hips. "I could say the same."

Placing the salad bowl on the table, Satsuki rushed across the length of the room. Her body trembled and her heart beat against Daidai's as she pinned her in an embrace. The sharp bones in her arms reminded Daidai of the trauma they'd experienced in Japan. Reaching a hand up to her back, Daidai ran her fingers slowly up and down her rib cage. "Are you okay?" she said, feeling how thin she'd gotten.

"I'm fine." Satsuki pulled back, showing Daidai her uneven teeth. "I'm happy to see you."

"I'm happy to see you, too!" Daidai smiled, still wondering about Hiroshi.

"I made dinner," Satsuki said, taking her hand to lead her back to the kitchen. "Aren't you hungry?"

It was shocking to see the pots lined across the stovetop, their lids emitting a spray of steam indicating that Satsuki had been inside her apartment cooking for some time.

"When did you get back?" Daidai asked.

"I'm all thrown off. What time is it now?"

"Late."

"Yes." Satsuki squinted out the window, the good cheer she'd expressed moments earlier seeming to dissipate into the darkness.

"Where's Hiroshi?"

"He's taking a nap."

"A nap?" Daidai's heart skipped a beat as she turned toward the bedroom.

"I'm afraid he's already eaten," Satsuki called out.

Daidai nearly bumped into Hiroshi on his way out of their bedroom. "What's going on?" she demanded.

"I thought I heard you come in." Scratching his scalp, Hiroshi blinked into the semidarkness.

"Are you okay?"

"I had a headache. Where were you, anyway?"

"Me?"

She knew full well where she'd been. What she needed to know was what had been going on in the apartment while she was away. But rather than Hiroshi, Satsuki was the one who spoke. "Hiroshi tried to call you on your cell phone but we found it ringing in the kitchen. You must have left it there on your way out. We'd planned to wait for you. Let me get you something to eat."

"I'm not hungry," Daidai told her.

Hiroshi slid a hand under his wife's elbow and ushered her to the couch. "What's wrong, Daidai? Why are you so upset?"

"I'm not upset!" she said, aware of the agitation in her voice.

"Satsuki," Hiroshi said, "would you mind leaving Daidai and me to talk?"

"I was just doing the dishes." Holding up the same salad bowl she'd had in her hands when Daidai walked in, she returned to the kitchen, sullen.

"Dishes? Really?"

"It's just for a week," he said, "a month at the most."

"What?" Daidai's voice rang above the sound of water running into the kitchen sink.

"She can't afford her room right now," Hiroshi said. "The money she has is tied up until the lawyers can sort through her father's finances."

"No." Daidai clutched Hiroshi's arm, fearing what was coming next. "There's no space here."

"She can sleep in my office. She says she'll cook and clean in exchange for rent."

"No." Daidai's mind raced ahead. Could he really not see what was happening? What would Louise say? Daidai saw her best friend, the public defender, pleading her case. "You didn't even ask me, Hiroshi, before agreeing to share our apartment?"

"She's in a pinch. She's your friend. I assumed you wouldn't mind."

Still thinking of Louise, she asked, "You did this because she's my friend?"

Hiroshi merely shrugged.

"Hiroshi," Daidai whispered to him, her tone pleading, "you have no idea what's going on."

"What?" he whispered back. "I don't know what you're talking about."

"Exactly." Daidai glared at him, penetrating the darkness with her gaze. "Neither do I. But until I do, I'd prefer she not live with us."

Hiroshi shot back instantly. "Given the circumstances, don't we owe her a little kindness? Didn't you just spend more than ten days with her in Japan?"

"I owe her nothing," Daidai spat in a whisper, "and neither do you."

Flinging her back against the couch, Daidai imagined herself in the taxi with the white cloth hung over its seat coverings, on the way to Satsuki's father's home in Mito. *My father can be rapacious.* Wasn't "rapacious" the word she'd used? "Satsuki told me that the trip to Japan was payback for the hospitality we'd already shown her," she explained to Hiroshi straight from memory, "before I went with her to Japan, before her father's death and this whole mess we now find ourselves in."

"What are you talking about?"

It was evident from his tone that he wasn't following her logic. Sometime during the day, while she was at the monastery or visiting with Louise or her mother, he'd departed to some other reality and she'd returned home to some simulacrum of her life. As if to illustrate that this was indeed true, Satsuki entered the room for a second time, the white apron still tied around her waist. "I'm done with the dishes," she said, smiling, her teeth gleaming in the darkness. "Are you sure I can't get you some dinner?"

28

How had Satsuki wound up in the apartment? Had she surprised Hiroshi by greeting him when he got home? Or had the two of them planned it out in advance of her arrival, so that he'd been at the airport waiting for her plane? Daidai fell asleep mulling over what might have happened. She felt terribly betrayed by Hiroshi, but sometime during the night he'd returned to their bed and curled himself around her, and in her sleep she'd accepted his gesture of affection. The next morning, when she awoke with his arm around her waist, she slid out of bed and substituted a pillow for him to hold so he wouldn't wake up. Needing to confront Satsuki, she made her way to the kitchen where, true to her word, breakfast had already been served up.

"Good morning, Daidai," she said warmly. "Did you sleep well?"

In fact, she had slept well. Far better than she imagined she could have, given the circumstances. But she was still angry with Hiroshi, and it couldn't have been hard for Satsuki to see that Daidai's resentment bled over to her.

"I hope you don't mind leftovers from last night's dinner," she said, a hint of contrition in her voice. "I tried to make it up nice for you. Hopefully you'll think it tastes okay?"

Though Daidai hated to admit it, everything tasted delicious. She really had been very hungry, and eating went a long way toward quelling her anger. "When did you get in?" she asked, attempting to restart the conversation she'd wanted to have the night before with more equanimity.

"I've been in Los Angeles less than twenty-four hours." Satsuki glanced at the hands of the clock on the kitchen counter. "I don't think I've ever felt as relieved to be anywhere."

"Been tough, has it?"

"You were smart to get out when you did."

"It was Hiroshi's idea, to leave when I did."

"Yes, I remember." Satsuki eyed her thoughtfully from across the table. "If you don't mind my asking, have you gotten pregnant? You don't look the same to me. Your complexion is rosier and your cheeks are a bit fuller. And of course last night I couldn't help but notice that you acted irrationally when you came home."

"I don't know what you're talking about!" Daidai was indignant, but at the same time a part of her had to admit it was possible.

Satsuki shrugged. "Of course, I hope you and Hiroshi will both get the baby you deserve."

Daidai's impulse was to rush back into the bedroom, if only to get away from her, but then she remembered that Hiroshi was still in there. It was seven in the morning, and the situation at the breakfast table felt too complicated to think through. She wished someone other than Satsuki could have raised the possibility that she might be pregnant. "I doubt I'm pregnant. And besides, I don't know how you could think that's an appropriate question to ask someone."

"I'm sorry." Satsuki averted her gaze. "It's just that you seemed so different to me last night. I was worried about you, but when I came to that conclusion I felt better. I hope there's not something to be worried about. Is there?" Satsuki smiled attentively, her hands folded on the tabletop, waiting for Daidai to respond.

"I got a letter from your father." Daidai maintained eye contact to gauge Satsuki's response, just long enough to note that her expression gave away nothing. "It arrived yesterday."

"How puzzling." Biting at her lower lip, Satsuki furrowed her brow. "Are you wanting to tell me what it said?"

"Basically, he asked me not to turn him in to the police."

"A little late for that now, isn't it?"

Had Daidai not been so startled by Satsuki's comment, she'd have acknowledged that Satsuki was one step ahead in her thinking. Instead, she probed for what she already knew. "Can you tell me what he was referring to? I mean, he seemed to think I knew something about his personal or professional life that might cause me to report him to the police."

Daidai felt her presence ceasing to matter. Satsuki fixed her gaze on a point behind Daidai's head, looking like a suspect giving a police statement. "My father was involved in a number of unethical business dealings. If you're wondering whether I threatened to expose him, then yes, I did. He believed he was above the law. He used his power over me the same way he used it over my mother and other women."

"What are you talking about?" Daidai demanded, taking Satsuki's response to mean that she'd likely known about the paintings all along.

Satsuki raised a hand to her forehead to wipe away a strand of hair that had fallen into her eyes, her pinkie trembling slightly. "I'm not surprised to hear of his attempt to bring you to his side. That's the way he was, always working to have people on his side. But he's dead now. He left it to me to tie up the loose ends of his business dealings. Having done that I'd prefer not to have to think of him."

The irony of Daidai's rebuking her for asking whether she was pregnant, then proceeding to solicit information of an equally personal nature, had not been lost on Satsuki. "I'm sorry," Daidai said. "Of course."

Reaching across the table, Satsuki grasped Daidai's hand and squeezed it. "Is that what upset you, the letter?"

"In part." Daidai pulled her hand away, startled by how cold Satsuki's fingertips felt to the touch.

"Okay, my Daidai friend," she said with a sigh. "What's the rest of it? I can't stand the thought of living with someone who's troubled because of me!"

After a slow start, the tea and breakfast finally signaled to Daidai's brain that it should resume functioning, but was it wrong to tell someone who considered her a friend that she wasn't welcome?

She had no need for a roommate, and Satsuki hadn't asked her before moving in.

"Is something going on between you and Hiroshi?" Daidai whispered across the table.

"Is that what you're worried about? I see."

"What do you see? What's going on?"

"Nothing's going on, Daidai." Satsuki's eyes met hers across the table. "Nothing at all. I think my father's letter led you to do some research on him. That's what's troubling you, isn't it? What you found out?" Perhaps sensing she was losing her audience, Satsuki cast her gaze downward. "What you probably don't yet know is the level of ability of the painters who worked for my father. He'd seek out the most talented young women in Japan, and the most destitute. He knew the type that would be willing to paint what he requested for a small commission.

"Did you also find out what a huge market there is among businessmen for schoolgirls painted so explicitly? So big that it caused my father to expand his enterprise to include foreign markets. The most lucrative was Sweden. For a fee, a buyer could take home a personalized memento brokered by my father. Sickening, isn't it?"

"How long have you known this?" Daidai asked, wanting her to continue.

Satsuki smiled, her gaze shifting upward to meet Daidai's once again. "I might not have found out had you not decided to go with me to Mito. There were so many things I never would have dared to ask him. But your questions made me see the gaps in what I knew about him, and about myself. I went through his business ledger when we were there.

"He'd made no attempt to hide things; he'd grown sloppy. The connections were not difficult to make. He'd barely taken the trouble to hide the canvases that had been commissioned most recently.

"He was very angry when I confronted him," she continued, reminding Daidai of the night they'd returned to Mito from sightseeing and she'd awakened, somehow believing Satsuki needed her. "He said I had no business going through his things. He accused me of being like my mother. It was the first time he'd mentioned her name in twenty-five years. I wanted to understand what he was saying. But he perceived my questioning him as insolence. He called me a stupid, ungrateful child and threatened to cut me off financially."

"I see." Was Satsuki innocent, then? A child stumbling upon her parent's secrets? Daidai dropped her shoulders in an attempt to disperse the tension that had been building in her head and neck. "I'm sorry for what you've had to go through."

"I understand." Satsuki politely accepted her apology. "As I mentioned, my father and I were not close, but even so we were not estranged. I have a hard time explaining my relationship with him—even to myself. My feelings are still very complicated. Is that what it was like for you with your father?"

The events of the previous day had left Daidai feeling overwhelmed: the news of Danji's death, followed by the visit to her mother. Now she was being asked to think about her father. "Our relationship was fairly straightforward. He wasn't a complicated man, I don't think. He worked hard."

"Yes. That makes sense."

"Makes sense, how?" Daidai asked. But she was no longer really thinking about Satsuki. "He loved cars. I can't remember a day that he went off to work without a smile on his face. I remember him coming home after he'd won the Production Manager of the Year award. This was after my mother's father had died, so my father no longer had to live in my grandfather's shadow. He brought the plaque home and my mother cleared a place for it on the wall.

"That night I went out with my parents to celebrate at my father's favorite restaurant. The waitress must have noticed his good mood because when she came by our table with his mug of beer, she asked if it was his birthday. He laughed and put his arm on my mother's shoulder. 'I'm just happy to be out with my beautiful wife and daughter,' he said. He didn't tell the waitress he'd just received the plant's highest honor."

"I don't remember ever going out to celebrate with my father," Satsuki said, the tone of her voice slightly bitter. "There were always women, my mother followed by many others, to wait on him. Going out is what he did for his business. For him, staying home was for pleasure."

Daidai nodded, still not understanding entirely what Satsuki was trying to tell her.

"I think my father's problem was that he was spoiled. His mother waited on him without complaint, so he expected that all women should do the same. At the end of my grandmother's life he fulfilled his obligation to her by sending money to take care of her and my grandfather. He was a filial son. They were very proud of him. But he cared only about himself. I don't think it ever occurred to him to consider how the women in his life suffered because of him."

A different, more vulnerable Satsuki had emerged as she spoke. She hadn't lived with her father for most of her childhood years, yet even after she'd discovered how unscrupulous he'd been, even as a dead man, he held her under his sway. Ichiro sounded like the opposite of Daidai's father. Satsuki's ambivalence had been apparent in her narrative; yet along with contempt, she seemed to regard Ichiro with a type of awe.

"My father knew that you had worked as a curator. I told him you planned to use your influence in the art world to destroy him," she added. "Either that or you'd go to the police. I threatened him by saying that his reputation would be ruined. But the fact was that I'd lied. I'd never have told you anything about his business. The next day, I was still trying to clear my head when the earthquake struck.

"I couldn't help but think that fate had intervened. My father held himself in too much esteem to have done himself harm. But even more than the artwork he commissioned or the pieces in his private collection, he loved being the one in charge. He controlled his clients' fantasies along with the women who worked for him. My father enjoyed playing the role of proprietor."

Satsuki had offered a chilling depiction of her father. Yet it made sense somehow and freed Daidai to ask a more pressing question: "You say that your father held himself in too much esteem to have done himself harm—"

"That was before the earthquake," Satsuki interrupted, before Daidai could phrase her question. "I take responsibility for the heartache I caused when I confronted him with the truth, but the earthquake and tsunami led to a cataclysmic reversal of his fortune."

"I see," Daidai said, even though she felt that Satsuki was hiding something from her. "I'm sorry, Satsuki."

"Don't be," she replied, her tone turning harsh. "Japanese have a saying about attacking a wild dog only after it's fallen into the river. My father was the dog who, as a result of the earthquake, fell headfirst into the river."

"Still, it's surprising, isn't it, how things turn out." Daidai no longer knew what else to do but agree.

"I'm guessing my father thought of me before his death," Satsuki surmised. "And now it's only natural that he should be the focus of my thoughts. Had you and I left Japan a day earlier, I might never have confronted my father. Perhaps then he'd still be alive."

29

Satsuki acknowledged her role in the events leading up to her father's death in a conversation that had been only partially satisfying, and Daidai would certainly have followed up with her questions had Hiroshi not appeared in the kitchen just then. "What're you two arguing about?" he asked, rubbing his eyes.

Satsuki's attention refocused instantly on Hiroshi. "Ready for breakfast?" she asked, pushing back from her chair and proceeding to clear a spot for him at the table.

"We weren't arguing," Daidai said defensively, wondering what her husband had heard.

"Good."

Hiroshi stretched and yawned as Satsuki set down a newspaper and cup of coffee. Where Hiroshi was concerned, she seemed unable to control her impulse toward servitude. Perhaps, Daidai considered, what she'd perceived as a crush was attributable to a faulty interpretation caused by her cultural bias.

Spring had arrived. Hiroshi noted from the weather section in the morning paper that the afternoon temperature at the Santa Monica Pier was forecasted to be in the low 70s. With his work out of the way and no plans, he suggested a drive to the beach.

The three of them walking along the shore together? Was he joking? But knowing Hiroshi's preference for keeping things simple,

Daidai wondered if perhaps she'd been wrong about the nature of his affection for Satsuki.

Hiroshi parked at the pier, where Satsuki bought them giant pretzels. Contrasting so sharply with the delicacy of food items in Japan, their size must have seemed irresistible. But finding their bland taste unappealing, Satsuki fed bits to the seagulls. Daidai wondered what the gulls made of their configuration, she in the middle with Hiroshi on one side holding her hand and steering the threesome inland from the tide, and Satsuki on the other side preferring the dry sand. Following the coastline as it curved south, their hearing congested by the sound of the surf and salt breeze, Daidai felt like a live conduit for whatever chemistry lay between Hiroshi and Satsuki. Unable to know for sure what they had going on, she sensed only that whatever there was between them, she was deeply implicated, a predicament she didn't know whether to find reassuring or perverse.

The beach should have been crowded, given the excellent weather. Looking west over the Pacific as they made their way back to the car, Satsuki was the one to remark on the three sets of footprints left behind in the sand when they'd walked in the opposite direction. Except for the antic skittering of seagulls and mounds of seaweed brought in with the tide, the usual beachgoers had chosen inland spots that Friday afternoon. Perhaps they'd been scared off by fears of radiation leaking into the Pacific from the Fukushima Daiichi nuclear plant. It seemed almost inconceivable that the toxic nuclear particles could be making their way across such a vast expanse of ocean on that beautiful spring afternoon. Yet it was an undeniable fact: five thousand miles away, emergency workers had begun flushing the Daiichi nuclear reactors with seawater to prevent the meltdown that had already happened, the highly radioactive material spilling into the ocean just yards from the reactors and swirling through the currents that make up the Pacific.

30

Daidai blamed Satsuki for both the small and large things that went wrong that week. A feeling of claustrophobia inhibited every interaction in the tiny apartment and exaggerated her misgivings about Satsuki, along with her suspicions about her husband's relationship with his student. And though she knew Hiroshi liked to have advance notice about events he needed to attend, she couldn't understand his annoyance over being asked to attend the upcoming memorial.

"I don't think it will matter if I don't go," he said simply, when she reminded him that the service for Danji had been planned for the next afternoon. "It'll be a big crowd, every shop owner in J-Town and then some."

He offered up a second justification—"I'll go if you want me to, but I could use the time to prepare this week's lectures"—apparently forgetting that he'd spent the Friday before last at the beach to celebrate having nothing to do.

"Don't go if you don't want to go," Daidai told him. "You do what you want."

Of course, she meant just the opposite, but apparently he hadn't been listening. "You sure?" he called after she'd turned away.

Daidai nodded over her shoulder. "I'll ask Satsuki to go with me." It might have been crazy thinking, but she wasn't about to leave the two of them together in the apartment.

Hiroshi raised his eyebrows and shrugged, not seeming to care what it would look like for Daidai to attend the event without him.

Daidai worried that her mother would disapprove of Satsuki, but the two women appeared to get along fine. Mako turned her head over the passenger seat to make eye contact, and Satsuki poked up from the back, seeming to anticipate the funeral like a festive event. They conducted their conversation in nonstop Japanese, each sounding more high-spirited and polite than the other. Satsuki would never know the unkind words Mako had spoken about her, and no one looking in from the outside could have guessed that the two women were not intimately acquainted.

Driving inland on the Santa Monica Freeway, away from the beach, Daidai noted the familiar exits: La Brea, Fairfax, La Cienega. She'd gone with her mother to the farmers' market, Kobe Pharmacy, Paul's Kitchen, Tenri. Now Satsuki had taken her place, her economical gestures mirroring Mako's, her jet-black hair and fine features fitting just right next to Mako's fair complexion, sharp eyes, and enigmatic smile.

By the time the car pulled into the lot on East First and San Pedro, Daidai had observed her way into a state of dejection. But fortunately the afternoon had turned beautiful; though chilly along the streets of downtown with the buildings sending down shadows, the weather was warm enough to walk with only a light wrap. Flanked by Satsuki on one side and Daidai on the other, Mako took her time, pleased by the reception she received from local shopkeepers who rushed into the street from behind their shop counters to greet her. It had been that way with Gizo, except that Mako showed off for Satsuki's benefit.

"You're so popular," Satsuki flattered her. "Everyone is so happy to see you."

Mako waved away her remark. "Not really. This is nothing."

They nearly missed the turn off East First Street, down the narrow walkway barely visible from the street. It was always surprising to see the ornately decorated gold pillars and Japanese-style black-tiled roof, which came into view just as the sharp smell of incense wafted out onto the street. With most of the guests already seated inside the temple, Mako and Satsuki fell into the kind of model behavior they'd seemed incapable of during the car ride or on the walk.

Once the door at the rear had been shut, the only natural light came from a row of high windows. It was a formal affair, with men dressed in dark-colored suits and women in close-toed shoes, stockings, and long, stiff dresses; the darkly attired guests with their black hair sat in rows amid the temple's darkened interior. Satsuki had ducked behind Daidai as they were ushered to their seats near the back, so that Daidai sat wedged between her mother and friend. The reverend clanged a small cymbal to signal the beginning of the service, and the crowd fell into complete and overwhelming silence.

After, when the bodies rose in unison to allow the family to file out to the street, Daidai could hardly wait to be back in the open air. From her spot in line, she watched Louise at the front entrance, receiving condolences. She was as poised as always, but up close Daidai could see the black smudges under her eyes. "I'm so sorry," she whispered, leaning in to brush her cheek against Louise's, then blotting at the rims of her own eyes. Turning toward Gizo, she leaned in to him and suspected that the strength of his arms, briefly touching her waist as she bent to hug him, steadied her more than her presence did him.

"Hey, Daidai," he said solemnly, though in typical Gizo fashion. "Thanks for coming."

Mako passed through the line after Daidai, pausing longer than most of the others, encircled by Louise and Gizo, who nodded with downcast eyes as she spoke with them. When Satsuki reached the front of the line, Daidai looked back to note the exchange, observing the way she bowed deeply, in traditional ceremonial fashion, fingers pressed together, palms touching, hands lowered at her hips. Gizo barely acknowledged her, but Louise excused herself from the reception line, pulling Daidai behind her back through the rectory. "Did you think this was a party?" she demanded, her eyes beaming the sharpness that marked her as Louise.

"I don't understand," Daidai said, needing to apologize and not knowing for what.

"Isn't that your friend Satsuki?" she said, a drop of spittle flying from her lipstick-stained mouth, the warmth of her breath like heated metal.

Daidai braced herself, but rather than chastise her further, Louise began to cry. Tears ran down her face for the loss of her father and for the state that both her parents being dead had left her in: less protected, bereft. She needed more than Daidai had offered her. Louise had helped her through the death of her father, calling to check on her, taking her mother to lunch. The organ thrummed its low notes amid the murmurings of mourners outside the temple, amplifying the horrible confusion that had encircled Daidai in the last months and now threatened her friendship with Louise.

Daidai recognized her mother waiting with Satsuki in the street and was glad not to be asked where she'd gone off to, or why she'd returned with swollen eyelids. Mako would have sided with Louise in their exchange, and perhaps she understood something of the rift, claiming to be too tired to attend the banquet being catered just down the block. Held at the local restaurant that had once hosted most of the weddings of local Japanese, it was now serving food for the funerals of many of those who had once been guests.

31

Daidai noted the traffic piled up along the northbound 405 as they headed south to drop her mother off. There didn't seem to be an accident, just too many cars, but it meant she wouldn't arrive back in the Valley till after dark. Having given his study over, Hiroshi had moved his reading chair into their bedroom, where he cluttered up the floor space beside the bed with his books and papers. He barely glanced up when Daidai entered, but her level of distress must have signaled to him that something had gone wrong, because he appeared at the door to the walk-in closet they shared as Daidai removed her black shoes and stockings. Less than three months earlier, the morning of his first class of the new semester, she'd watched him undress for a shower hoping he'd come back to bed and seduce her; now he stood still and silent, watching her.

"What's up, Daidai?" He spoke in a gentle tone. "How was the service?"

Having not been able to stop weeping, she felt vulnerable and oddly uncomfortable standing exposed in her black underwear, which, on another occasion, he might have construed as a turn-on. "It was unbearably sad to see Louise," she said, then, in a lower tone, "Bringing Satsuki was a mistake. I regret it. And you should have been there."

Turning away from him, she cried some more as she unfastened the hook on her bra, proceeding with what she'd gone into the closet to do in the first place, and let Hiroshi sort out whether she was sad for Louise or angry with him. Searching through her nightclothes, she found the most comfortable item she owned, a gray cotton T-shirt with rips and stains that would have been noticeable in the light. Brushing past him, she went next to the bathroom, where she tied her hair back and rinsed her face with cool water.

Hiroshi kept his eyes fastened on her back, causing Daidai to wonder what he saw. Had she ceased to be attractive to him? Had he always, in the six years of their marriage, been so clueless?

"It was wrong of me not to go with you." He made this concession reluctantly, as he held up a towel for her to dry her face. "I'm sorry."

"You should be," she whispered, keeping her voice down so as not to be overheard by Satsuki on the other side of the wall, turning from him to hang the towel back on the rack.

"Maybe I needed this time alone to think. I've felt badly all afternoon."

"Good." Slightly relieved, Daidai perched herself on her side of the bed, allowing him to resume his post in his reading chair. "I'm glad you're upset."

"I don't think you understand," he said, startling her. "You're in this, too Why are you so worried about my relationship with Satsuki? She's my student, but you're my wife."

She drew in a deep breath before responding. "So why is your student living with us?"

She guessed it wasn't a good thing that he didn't jump to answer her. "Are you trying to manufacture something about Satsuki to keep your mind off Gizo?" he finally replied.

"Are you kidding?" she nearly shrieked.

Hiroshi shrugged. "It was the only thing I could come up with."

"No," she said. "No, no, no."

"Same."

Grabbing the book he reached to pick up, she tossed it aside. "Why would you think something's going on between Gizo and me?"

"Maybe for the same reason you think I'm having an affair with Satsuki."

Daidai looked at him incredulously. This was about their marriage. Why make Gizo into a sideshow? "Do you still love me, Hiroshi?" she asked point-blank.

"I could ask the same of you."

"You could, and if you did I'd tell you. I'm here sitting in this room because I love you. There's no other way to look at it. Everything I've done comes out of what we've built together. I'm trying to make you happy, to figure out what you need to be happy, and to give you what you need. Why can't you see that?"

"My turn?" He smiled as she bit the inside of her lip.

"Go."

Hiroshi shrugged. His face went still. She'd asked him if he loved her, and he hadn't responded. She had no idea what he was thinking, and they could go no further until she understood his feelings for her.

"I need you to tell me what's going on between you and Satsuki."

Hiroshi stared back at her blankly, his right eye spasming almost imperceptibly, his lips pursed as if he'd forbidden them to speak his thoughts.

"Let me put it another way," she said, speaking to his muteness. "I think there's more to Satsuki than we know."

"I told you that before," he reminded her, "when you were so determined to look into her background. Don't open yourself up to things you might not want to know."

"What are you talking about?" she demanded, no longer caring if Satsuki heard.

"You don't need to know everything," he whispered, as if showing her by example how to modulate her tone. "Trust me on that."

"I want to know what you know," she insisted, meaning that he should fill in the gaps.

Hiroshi only shrugged once more.

"I don't trust her." She took in a deep breath, willing her voice not to betray her. "I feel threatened by her. I don't want her living in this house."

"This is all just temporary."

In her confused state, she didn't know what temporary meant. There didn't seem to be anything more to say. Picking up the book she'd tossed aside, he resumed his reading and she sank down into the bed with her back turned to him, furious and more determined than ever to figure out what was really going on.

32

The next day Hiroshi and Satsuki both returned to their academic schedules. Having lain awake much of the night, irritated to hear rustlings on the other side of the wall and wondering why Satsuki wasn't asleep either, Daidai poured a second cup of tea and tried to remember why she'd thought leaving her job at the museum would be a good idea. Hiroshi and she had wanted a baby, but in the time she'd been off, had that changed? More to the point, if he understood what Satsuki being in the apartment did to her—to their marriage—wouldn't he have thrown her out himself? Thwarted by her inability to convince her husband that Satsuki needed to go, Daidai had come to believe Hiroshi merely needed proof, for her to assemble what she knew in a clear and compelling fashion. Such a task was doable because she was good at collecting and organizing data. And since she'd moved from questioning Satsuki's integrity to the even less tenable position of suspecting her husband of infidelity, she set her course on finding out the truth.

Not knowing where to turn for evidence, Daidai's thoughts wandered back over the last installation she'd curated. After being with the museum for nearly four years, a couple of big grants had given her the go-ahead for an internment exhibit she'd been waiting to host. Over the years, potential donors had contacted her with gifts that ranged from cash to personal keepsakes. It was the perfect opportunity to go back through the list. Her first thought had been the corsage pins made by internees at Tule Lake. Ever since she'd seen them, she'd been interested in them. Tule Lake was the internment camp where the alleged troublemakers were sent. She imagined them arriving in the desert by the busload, dejected and with nothing to do but stare at the dirt and patches of sagebrush. But there'd been a treasure trove of tiny shells in the sand, buried where the water had once been, available by the bucketful to be bleached or dyed and crafted into jewelry. Daidai saw ingenuity in those beautiful little corsage pins. And it seemed fortuitous that just as she'd started collecting them, the daughter of an issei woman got in touch to say that her mother, who'd lived in Arkansas since the war, was holding on to a large collection.

Of course, communicating with donors always took time, but this woman being a ninety-five-year-old with hearing loss complicated matters even further. At the daughter's suggestion, Daidai wrote a letter detailing the plans she had for the exhibit, which involved both a display at the entrance and a large sand tray in the children's wing where kids could dig for the shells and use them to create their own jewelry. Though the daughter said she'd read the letter to her mother, Daidai had nearly given up on hearing back when a month later the response she'd waited for finally arrived.

Overjoyed with the news that the old woman intended to lend out her pins, Daidai booked a flight, figuring it best to go herself to retrieve the collection as a show of appreciation.

She knew things were not going to go well when little Mrs. Hattie Fujioka stood blocking the doorframe, hesitant to let her inside. Dressed in a patterned gray polyester blouse, knit pants, and black nursing shoes, she came to the door seeming ready for action, with a firm set to her puckered mouth. She wasn't unfriendly, and Daidai didn't get the sense that she was crazy; she just seemed to want to take her time deciding about things. Having already introduced herself by name, Daidai added that she'd come from the museum, trying to remind the woman who she was in case the visit had slipped her mind.

"Yes, I know who you are," she said at last.

When she finally moved aside so that Daidai could enter her home, she led Daidai into the kitchen, where a plate of food that had probably taken all morning to prepare had been set out. She'd seen to every detail, including two perfectly arranged place settings atop a white tablecloth with hand-embroidered purple flowers. Daidai was touched by her obvious efforts, guessing by her surroundings that the woman operated on a tight budget.

But the meal proceeded without mention of the corsage pins. Daidai waited until they had finished eating and tea had been served to remind the old woman of the reason for her visit. "I'm looking forward to seeing the pins."

Mrs. Fujioka lifted an unsteady hand to wipe at the corner of her eye, causing Daidai to wonder whether sentimental attachment to the collection had given the woman second thoughts about lending it out. Then came the head shaking, gentle at first, becoming more violent as reality set in. "I'm afraid you can't have them."

"Why not?" Daidai tried to be gentle, guessing the brooches had been misplaced or, worse, stolen.

"Because I destroyed them." The woman's confession issued strong and clear. "This morning, before you came—crushed them under a hammer."

"Why?" Daidai's voice was barely audible. "They were so beautiful. Many people were looking forward to seeing them."

"I know."

Daidai gave Mrs. Fujioka a minute to compose herself, and to think things through: several hours till she needed to be back at the airport to board her return flight to L.A., nothing to pack up.

"I don't know what came over me," Mrs. Fujioka said after a while, apparently shocked by what she'd done. "In my entire life I've hardly swatted a fly, let alone smashed something with a hammer."

Perhaps she'd gone crazy after all. "I'm sorry. I'm afraid I still don't understand."

Mrs. Fujioka stared hard across the table through eyes that were half glazed with cataracts. "Maybe you have to be Japanese to understand."

"I *am* Japanese," Daidai explained, taken aback. "My mother immigrated to California from a suburb near Tokyo."

"You can't understand." Mrs. Fujioka shook her head, either not hearing or not caring what Daidai had said. "I'd kept the shells tucked away in a drawer. I never looked at them. For all those years, I never brought them out.

"We Japanese experienced such deprivation during the war years. It would be impossible for someone just seeing the pins to know what that was like back then."

"I understand," Daidai said, knowing even then that she understood something different.

Now, as Daidai replayed what Mrs. Fujioka had said, she saw the image of Ritsuko's painting. Maybe it was the figure's eyes, occluded by blindness, or the mirror, representing something the viewer could see that the subject could not. Or maybe it was the notion of keeping something of value hidden away: What would cause someone to do that?

Ritsuko's painting seemed to exist on the level of memory. By looking into the mirror the viewer saw not the subject, but his- or herself. And why had Ichiro kept this particular painting, yet sealed it off from the rest of his collection? Satsuki had identified the impulse as the need to control something, to *own* it. Was that what Mrs. Fujioka did by crushing the pins? Owning her experience?

"I'm sorry you had to come all this way," Mrs. Fujioka had apologized.

"May I see them?" Daidai needed to witness the wreckage as proof that the pins had really been ruined.

"Why look at something that's been destroyed?" Mrs. Fujioka asked, still full of her own incredulity.

"I mean this without any disrespect, but how am I otherwise to know that you're not lying to me?" Daidai said, provoking the woman with the conceit.

Mrs. Fujioka folded her arms across her middle. "Why would I lie to you?"

Daidai waved away her question. "I'm not sure it matters if you are."

Mrs. Fujioka rose from her seat at the table. With all the energy that had caused her to stand so stoically in the doorway gone from her stance, she led Daidai down a short hall to her bedroom, where a cardboard box lay open beside a small hammer on the hardwood floor. Inside the open box, bits of shell littered the cotton packing, much of it crushed into sand.

Daidai bent to touch a broken flower. Compelled by her unsatisfied desires, she couldn't say what caused her to mislead Mrs. Fujioka, or to need to see what the woman had done. The old woman's bedroom smelled like the musk her own parents' room had picked up since her father had become ill. Crouching to examine the ruined corsage pins one last time, Daidai picked up the hammer that lay beside the open box and slipped it into her handbag. Standing beside Mrs. Fujioka, she'd thought to express her regret, but she didn't want the old woman to feel worse than she already did. After holding Mrs. Fujioka's hand between her palms, she left in silence.

The word "deprivation" repeated in her head. Daidai drove away from Hattie Fujioka's clapboard house, past other houses scattered along the two-lane highway that appeared from the outside identical—most of them falling into decay—and past broken-down cars, beyond which children played amid the wild beauty of untended fields. She had no idea what had compelled Mrs. Fujioka to crush the artifacts from her past.

In light of the events of that day and her musings about Ritsuko's life, Daidai's own life didn't make sense to her. Her mother the child of a wealthy businessman, her father a hard worker who'd risen up the ranks in her grandfather's company, she had no ancestral connection to the internment, except through Hiroshi: her ancestry linked through his. The installation had stemmed from that feeling of being removed, of a vision compelled by distance. Instead of corsage pins, she'd showcased a collection of contemporary photographs of the internment camps taken by a Japanese American photographer. Simple, direct, their horizons maintained at midlevel throughout; the scenes juxtaposed camp ruins and found objects with the present-day landscape, allowing the viewer to interact with the sites as they were and as they'd become.

Mostly the reviews were negative, though one critic seemed to get it when he wrote of the curator's attempt to "substantiate that which might not otherwise be seen."

What hurt most was Hiroshi's comment: "They're just not ready." He'd sided with the public and its tepid response to the exhibit, implying that his wife was out of step with the community, that she didn't belong. The thing he knew and didn't say—the thing that Daidai knew—was that any child born between them would be more Japanese than its mother. His consolation lay in a paradox she found treacherous.

Still, her vision had been seeded that afternoon, in Hattie Fujioka's home. Another memory came to her then. Halfway to the airport she stopped at the edge of a grassy expanse and stood along the highway. Reaching into her handbag for the hammer, she hurled it into the sky, satisfied to see the grasses tremble where it landed. In the end, why did the logical mind always succumb to the yearnings of the heart? A part of Daidai still wanted to believe she was wrong about her husband and his involvement with Satsuki. Entering Hiroshi's office that morning with the purpose of searching through Satsuki's belongings, she felt like a criminal. Intent on finding some sort of proof to offer Hiroshi, and suspecting that she might turn out to be the dangerous one, she stood in the doorframe for a long time like a dog, sniffing the air, looking around for evidence in the absence of evidence.

It shocked her a little to find only a single black leather duffel spread open on the floor. A few items of clothing, toiletries, and a mirror were all Satsuki had brought with her. Thinking back to her interaction with Mrs. Fujioka, Daidai realized there was nothing she could do to make her husband see. A person who believes things are a certain way is not susceptible to proof. Still, Hiroshi would do well to remember what had drawn him to her; he needed to trust her instincts. What Daidai suspected was there was floating closer and closer to the surface—only a matter of time until it became visible.

33

Satsuki arrived back before Hiroshi that afternoon. *"Ohayoo goza-imasu!"* She entered using the standard greeting exchanged between coworkers at the beginning of a shift, meaning literally "good morning," and gave Daidai's shoulders a squeeze as she stood over the kitchen sink. "What've you been up to today, my Daidai friend?"

"You're home early," she remarked.

"Time to start cooking," Satsuki said, referencing the arrang-ement she'd made with Hiroshi, to exchange cooking and light housekeeping for a place to stay. She started unpacking a bag of groceries onto the counter. "By the way, I couldn't do any of this without your help."

"You worked it out with Hiroshi, not me," Daidai said, rebuffing her flattery.

Satsuki's averted her gaze, her expression full of misery. "Are you angry with me for imposing, Daidai?"

"You shouldn't have gone behind my back."

"I'm sorry. You're right. But I think it's more than that. Am I right?"

Was she giving Daidai an opportunity to call her out? "You're right."

"I think you don't trust me because you can't be certain what happened to my parents. It's natural to distrust a person without parents. I've found that over the years, so I am not surprised by your response to me."

"It's not the fact that your parents are dead that makes me distrust you," Daidai clarified, unwilling to abide any longer by oblique statements that turned the malefactor from Satsuki to herself. "It's that I don't understand why they're dead."

"And therefore you blame me?"

"How can I not wonder?"

"Who would you like to know then?" She sat and clasped her hands on the tabletop. "My father, my mother? What would you like to know?"

Daidai sat across from Satsuki and leaned back in her chair. "Tell me what you think I should know."

Satsuki mirrored her posture, though she looked awkward seated in repose. "Lately I've been thinking about my mother. Would you like to hear about her? She was an idealist. She wanted a better life than the one she had."

Daidai stopped her. "But how would you know?"

Satsuki's expression flattened, and she stared back in silence.

"If you're going to be forthright, so will I." Daidai held her hand up, palm out, to indicate her earnestness. "You should know that I went back to the monastery. The day you flew in from Mito, that's where I was. It's why I was so late getting home."

"Why would you do that?" Satsuki tilted her head to one side.

"Your father's letter made me curious to know more about your mother's death."

Satsuki's hand, visibly trembling, shot to her hairline. Daidai had her full attention.

"I did mistrust you," Daidai went on. "You're correct about that. I wondered what you hadn't told me, and since you weren't here for me to ask you, I wanted to see if the nuns could shed light on what happened to your mother."

Seeming satisfied with Daidai's response, Satsuki shrugged. "I supposed you would do that. It's something I admire about you, your thorough nature."

"Is that why you took me with you to Japan?" Daidai asked, suddenly understanding. "To keep me with you so that I wouldn't go off exploring on my own?"

Satsuki's expression turned sad again. "Maybe that was a small part of my reasoning."

"What was the other part?"

Satsuki smiled. "We were talking about your visit to the monastery, were we not?"

Accepting the bait, Daidai continued. "The sisters have a brand-new industrial oven, a professional stand mixer, and a hydraulic lift—all of it donated."

Satsuki's expression did not change, though her voice rose in pitch. "What? No kidding?"

"You didn't know about the new equipment?"

"How do you think I could have known?"

Daidai shrugged, frustrated by the failed rhetoric that had allowed her questions to slip away. "You'd been there, to Holy Heart."

Satsuki's fingers trembled as she reached a hand up to wipe the stray hairs from her forehead again. "Not since last fall."

So Daidai had been right. The night the call came from the detective saying that Satsuki's mother had been found dead, Satsuki had known her mother had been living at the monastery. "You knew she'd left Japan, that she'd been living here in Los Angeles."

"Of course." She knitted her brow again, nonplussed, as Daidai reconstructed the evening: the phone call that Satsuki had gone off on the terrace to take, the shock. "How could I forget such a life-changing event as that?"

"So why hadn't you told me that your mother was living at Holy Heart?"

Satsuki stared into her lap, perhaps considering how best to continue. "Actually, I wondered myself why. I don't know if you will find my explanation satisfying. I can only say that those first months here in Los Angeles were very confusing for me. I'm sorry to have made you upset with me."

"I'm not upset." Daidai took a deep breath, needing to get her bearings back. If Satsuki had been American-born, someone who'd grown up with familiar customs and values, Daidai would have pegged her at once for a fraud. But instead she regarded her as a foreigner, and at that a Japanese foreigner; she played Daidai back and forth against herself. What's more, she had the same knack as Daidai's mother did for avoiding questions she didn't like. "I just hadn't understood," Daidai said, hoping Satsuki would indulge her in a new line of questioning. "So you came to the West Coast to find your mother, is that right?"

"I came here to enter the graduate program at the university."

"Were you interested in Asian American Studies because of Hiroshi?" she asked, recalling Louise's suspicion about what had brought Satsuki to the West Coast.

"I attended a lecture Hiroshi gave at Bunka University last spring."

"I thought that might have been the case."

"Have you ever heard Hiroshi lecture?"

"Yes, many times."

"So you're aware of his colloquial style." Satsuki's eyes shifted to the ceiling, her thoughts seeming to trail off from the conversation. "But are you aware how your husband speaks of you, of your life together?"

"What are you talking about?" Daidai asked, stupefied.

"He has a way of incorporating his daily life into his lectures. I'd never encountered a style like his in my education in Japan. I was most intrigued."

Daidai was glad to hear her life with Hiroshi meant something to him, but that wasn't part of the discussion she was interested in having. "Can you tell me more about your mother? I was interested in what you were saying."

"Even though my father told me that my mother had died, I think I always knew she was alive. In the years after she disappeared, I came to believe she'd left me in search of a new life, but now I wonder if maybe she hadn't just given up on life and retreated into her imagination."

There she was again, the shadowy figure from the painting who'd been appearing in Daidai's thoughts since she'd toured Ichiro's installation. "Are you talking about how she wound up at the monastery?"

"I'm talking about her selfishness. She was essentially a selfish person."

"Didn't you just call her idealistic?" Daidai asked, recalling how Satsuki had described Kenji.

"Women are complex. They aren't like men. Women become resourceful in order to survive."

"So your mother was a survivor."

"She was certainly that," Satsuki mused. "But anyone who would abandon a young child—which is what my mother did—is selfish."

"I can imagine how betrayed you must have felt by her." Daidai hoped that Satsuki would offer insight into her relationship with her mother, but instead she changed the subject.

"The interesting part of her nature had to do with a human quality that allowed her to believe she could make things right for others through correct action."

"Are you referring to prayer?" Daidai asked, befuddled.

"This has nothing to do with religion," Satsuki said. "My mother was selfish."

Daidai was having a hard time keeping up. "Because she neglected her responsibilities?"

"Because of what she did to me I'm not sorry for what happened to her."

Daidai had been inclined to disbelieve everything Satsuki told her, but at that moment, as she waited for the deeper reality that lay hidden from view to be revealed, she read in Satsuki's expression the fragility and earnestness of a child, her eyes wide and full of credulity, and she felt her belief shifting.

"Wait," Daidai interrupted her, needing to confirm that she was on the right track. "When did you find out your mother was living at Holy Heart?"

Satsuki stared back blankly. "I'd visited her in the fall."

"Had you met the other nuns?"

"No. But my mother spoke of them."

"In what way?" Daidai asked, wanting to gauge Ritsuko's comments against what she'd seen. "What did she say?"

"My mother wasn't the type of person to speak badly about anyone. But I could tell from what she wouldn't say that the director of the monastery hadn't liked her. Maybe it was because my mother was foreign. Mary Agnes pitied her and gave her the jobs that no one else was smart or strong enough to handle."

"Like the baking."

"I'm sure all the sisters living at the monastery benefitted from the contributions my mother made. The ahn-bread was her idea, you know."

"Yes, the prioress acknowledged that."

"No," Satsuki corrected her. "The director would never have acknowledged my mother. You must be referring to Sister Elspeth."

Daidai had been mistaken. Satsuki seemed to know the sisters quite well. "That's right, Sister Elspeth."

"Elspeth and my mother were friends. I think that made the Mother Superior jealous. The old woman had probably wound up at the monastery and stayed there because of her need to be in control. It's such a cramped little world, who else but a control freak could have stood it? No contact with anyone from the outside and only eight women left to keep the place going. To a large degree the person who ran it had free rein. But I'm thinking that when my mother confessed she'd had a daughter it was too much for the Mother Superior. She felt personally violated."

Daidai didn't know enough to judge Ritsuko's relationship with Sister Elspeth, but what Satsuki said about Sister Mary Agnes being jealous seemed plausible. "So the prioress took her revenge on your mother?"

"Possibly."

"Where did the gun come from?"

"Did you ask Sister Mary Agnes that question?"

"I did."

"What was her response?"

"She said she didn't know."

Satsuki nodded.

"How did she wind up with the kitchen equipment?" Daidai asked, her mind wandering back to the image of the monstrous appliances that occupied much of the back room, so out of place there.

"I sent it."

"How did you do that?"

She shrugged. "I used my father's money."

"But why?"

"To show the Mother Superior who was really in control."

"You mean, make her feel guilty?"

"People like Sister Mary Agnes are able to justify their actions no matter what. She isn't capable of feeling guilt."

Satsuki could have been Hattie Fujioka, referencing the dark impulses that had led her to smash the shell corsages. But the image of industrial-sized kitchen equipment was less mutable than corsage pins. "What do you mean?" Daidai asked, trying to follow her.

"She regarded my mother as deficient, but my mother was the one who did everything. She's the one who came up with the ahn-bread recipe and the one who took care of the older sisters. She worked harder than the others, and she got less credit. That was the shame."

"So you sent the kitchen equipment?" Daidai asked, still trying to get the facts straight.

"I wanted the Mother Superior to have to see the industrial-sized appliances every day, to remind her of my mother every time she touched them."

Buoyed by Satsuki's counterintuitive thinking, Daidai felt her shoulders drop, and the air eased back into her lungs. "But how did you afford all that?"

"It wasn't my money," Satsuki said, as if that explained things.

"Even though you didn't have enough to pay rent at Leonard's?"

"Ah." She smiled. "That is a different matter."

"Personal?" Daidai asked, evoking her husband's thinking about boundaries.

"Not in the least," Satsuki replied. "Have I mentioned how much I appreciate your curiosity about me? Please don't worry, my Daidai friend," she added. "Things have a way of working themselves out in the end."

There seemed no point in speculating further about the nature of her friend's complicated finances. Instead, Daidai felt the irony of her assurances, since as far as she could tell not much had worked out in Satsuki's favor.

34

Each morning that first week, Satsuki had left the apartment with Hiroshi, claiming she needed to use the library to catch up on late work as Daidai's unease mounted. While she suspected that there was more to Satsuki's life than long hours spent at the library, oddly she missed their contact and felt pleased each afternoon to fall back into a routine, joining Satsuki in the kitchen while she made preparations for dinner, accepting her role as sous-chef by peeling and chopping the vegetables that Satsuki cooked.

Satsuki was invariably at her best in the cramped space of the kitchen, moving seamlessly from sink to stovetop. "I've been wondering, my Daidai friend," she said, as she prepared dressing for a batch of cucumbers Daidai had been chopping, "do you believe in coincidence?"

Daidai scraped a pile of waxy green shavings from the cutting board into the garbage. Having had some time lately to think about her life with Hiroshi, she'd come to the conclusion that she held no special place for him. He'd met her quite by chance, just after the death of his parents when he'd been on his own for the first time, floundering. Had she not taken an active interest in him, she felt certain he would have wound up with someone else. "Things unfold pretty randomly if you ask me," she said, acknowledging a truth that only weeks ago had pained her.

"My meeting Hiroshi was not by coincidence," Satsuki said, wrinkling her nose as she twisted the top off a bottle of rice vinegar, releasing an acrid smell into the room.

Daidai liked Satsuki. It wasn't hard to see why Hiroshi would be attracted to her, but sometimes jealousy threatened to overtake her. "What are you getting at?" she asked, irked all over again by their unusual living arrangement.

"The lecture Hiroshi gave at Bunka is linked in my mind to an image. As you know, in Tokyo there is little room for greenery, but Bunka is known for its full garden, rendered in miniature, with trees pruned just so to simulate the natural world. As I was leaving Hiroshi's lecture, I stopped to admire the flowering plum trees that lead away from the lecture hall. I noticed a groundskeeper sweeping dead blossoms from the breezeway, so I complimented him on how well the garden is maintained. 'I learned how to take care of plants when I tended the trees in Kairakuen,' he said.

"'Are you the daughter of Ritsuko Suzuki?' he asked.

"At first I thought I had misunderstood. This man who was merely a groundskeeper—how would he know my mother?"

Recalling the plum trees blossoming in the garden at Kairakuen, Daidai's thoughts raced ahead as she attempted to recall what Satsuki had said about her mother's disappearance.

"'A long time ago, I was your neighbor,' he said, 'although of course you wouldn't remember me.'

"He was right, I didn't remember him. But his face recalled another image, a pile of decaying plum blossoms.

"I'd always believed my mother had been taken from me. It had never occurred to me that her disappearance had been staged, that my father had orchestrated the events of that morning. Apparently, Ichinose, whose wife had died a year earlier, had racked up debt from gambling. My father paid Ichinose an ample sum for his house, enabling him to move in with his son and his family, and in return, Ichinose agreed to bring me to the police station.

"My father never had any interest in raising me," she added. "His keeping me was just a way to hurt my mother. Still, I clung to the story he told me, that my mother had been found dead shortly

208

after she disappeared. I'd probably still believe it had I not run into Ichinose. It happened that same afternoon I met Hiroshi."

"How did you find out your mother was living in Southern California?" Daidai asked,

saddened to imagine the dealings that had led to her mother's disappearance when Satsuki was just a child.

"A living person is not that difficult to find," she said, holding out the serving bowl filled with *sunomono* for Daidai to sample before bringing it to the table for dinner. Her simple gesture ensured that Daidai would associate the taste of sweetened vinegar with misgivings about Satsuki's role in her marriage.

That night as Hiroshi ate, he jokingly referred to Satsuki as their factotum, citing her uncanny way of knowing when something was needed and producing it, especially, Daidai thought, when it was something desired by Hiroshi. It was Satsuki, not his wife, who made sure the couple never ran out of the foods they liked to eat, and it was her presence in their home that guaranteed they would never eat a meal that wasn't superbly and thoughtfully arranged. "We're lucky to have you here," he declared, raising his glass in a toast to their houseguest.

Raising her water glass, Daidai noted how entitlement had replaced the smugness in Hiroshi's gaze, and she counted a month forward to the end of the spring semester. If Satsuki hadn't moved out by then, she'd leave. Satisfied with her decision, which was motivated by self-preservation, still she'd timed it with respect to Hiroshi's profession.

Revisions of the essay Hiroshi had drafted during spring break had been finalized, and the piece was scheduled for fall publication. It was a quick turnaround for an academic press, which showed the editor's obvious enthusiasm about his writing. "Material Culture among Japanese Nationals: The Legacy of an Authentic Existence" was already making a stir. In it, Hiroshi made the timely argument that Japan must return to its traditional values to regain its credibility in the world marketplace. Of course, the devastation by nuclear fallout of whole swaths of land used for agriculture further reduced the prospects for such a shift happening any time soon, but no one was talking about that. What counted instead was his impeccable timing, with Hiroshi situating the crisis around theoretical paradigms ranging from material culture to post-consumerism.

Meanwhile, Satsuki detailed her plans to orchestrate relief efforts on the West Coast for victims of the Tohoku earthquake and nuclear disaster at Fukushima. Edified by Hiroshi's tutelage and grateful to Daidai for her hospitality, Satsuki praised them as the only two people she could trust.

The grandstanding was hard to take. Reminded of an online posting for a sabbatical year one-bedroom she'd seen advertised on the department listserv, Daidai rushed off to her computer. Returning to the table with the listing in hand, she described how perfect it would be. With an end-of-the-spring-term start date, Satsuki would be done with classes and have a month to prepare. "The estate is bound to be settled by then, don't you think?" Daidai added.

Hiroshi fell silent and Satsuki's face blanched as Daidai handed the printout to their wayward houseguest.

"I'd need a car," Satsuki said, after scanning the ad.

"A bicycle might work," Daidai said, volunteering to lend Satsuki hers.

"I never learned to ride a bike."

"Anyone can learn to ride a bike."

"Maybe." Satsuki shifted her gaze to Hiroshi, who didn't endorse his wife's plan but seemed to know better than to collude against her.

Looking dejected, Satsuki excused herself from the table. "Would you mind doing the dishes tonight?" she asked, the falsely sweet tone gone from her voice. "I'm not feeling well. I think I need to lie down."

"Of course," Hiroshi spoke up, for once taking the initiative.

Satsuki didn't come out of Hiroshi's office that evening, nor did she appear for breakfast the next morning. When the following afternoon passed without her, Hiroshi left the apartment in search of dinner and returned with burgers in take-out bags from In-N-Out—which Satsuki refused, claiming to have caught a summer cold.

A couple days later, when she finally emerged, she seemed to have forgiven Daidai for her transgression. During her period of seclusion she'd transformed Hiroshi's office into a workstation where vibrantly colored strips of cloth painted with flowers now hung, each with the words "Save Japan" printed in black Sharpie, strung together in a massive collage like Tibetan prayer flags. The plan was to give them away in exchange for donations. People could hang them in their homes as a reminder, and she'd send the donations she collected to Japan as her contribution to the relief efforts.

"What do you think?" she asked, her question rhetorical, the effect of them overwhelming. Patting the chair for Daidai to sit, she pointed at the computer display. "You need to hear this. In Fukushima a man sorting through rubble found two hundred sixty thousand yen. He approached all his neighbors with the money, but when no one claimed it, he turned it in to the police station.

"'Lowering our moral standards would be too terrible,' this man writes. 'We survivors are left to consider what makes us who we are, and what needs to be protected at all costs.'"

Days after the quake, a couple in Tokyo returned to the restaurant they'd fled to pay their bill; women with young children in their arms waited in long lines in the stinging cold to buy provisions; neighbors shared water and food and donated their blankets to the elderly.

The stories Satsuki needed to tell alerted Daidai to her friend's deteriorating mental state. Satsuki hadn't showered, which left the room smelling bad. Nor did she appear to have slept or eaten. Her hair hung down limply, her complexion shone waxy and gaunt, and her shirt sagged from her diminished frame so that Hiroshi's small office space, littered with the evidence of her project, seemed to swallow her up.

"Why don't you let me help you clean up?" Daidai suggested. "I think you've been working too hard. You need to take a break."

"Nonsense!" Unwilling to stop, Satsuki spoke with reverence about acts of kindness and the perseverance shown by those who had lost family members in the quake or tsunami. "Don't they look good?" She pointed at the flowers she'd painted, strung up and cluttering the walls.

At the end of the evening, after having spent much of the afternoon involved with the Save Japan project, Daidai shut the door behind her feeling pleasantly exhausted and relieved that her company seemed to have bolstered Satsuki's spirits. Before bed, Satsuki appeared back in the kitchen carrying a portion of her special tea leaves. She sprinkled them into the infusion pot she carried with her, filling the air with the bitter smell Daidai had come to associate with her. "I hope you're not angry with me," she said.

"Why would I be?" Daidai asked, still hopeful that Satsuki's spirit had been restored.

"It's not easy to have a third person around all the time," Satsuki acknowledged, keeping her gaze downcast, her hands trembling as she poured her tea.

"I'm sure you're doing your best to settle your father's estate."

"You know how much it means to me to be able to stay here with you."

"I know," Daidai said.

"You are always asking me questions," Satsuki observed, glancing over her shoulder. "Can I ask you one?"

"Sure." Daidai shrugged, ready to hear her out.

"Do you consider me a friend?"

"That's a strange question," Daidai said, but it occurred to her then that the obvious answer was yes. She didn't know if she trusted her, and she was not the friend that Daidai would have chosen; still, they shared a palpable connection. "Yes, I suppose I do." She smiled, having arrived at the correct answer.

Satsuki reached across the table to clasp Daidai's hand. Then, apparently deciding against the bedtime tea, she poured the water down the drain and dumped the steamed leaves into the sink, gathering up her belongings before disappearing back into Hiroshi's office.

35

After a solid week of wrestling with what Satsuki had said about Sister Mary Agnes being jealous of her mother, together with her not seeming to know where the gun that killed her mother had come from, Daidai turned to Louise. Surely a lawyer working out of the public defender's office would know what to do.

It was a rainy morning, typical early April weather, the decision not yet made about when spring should give in to summer. Louise picked up on the first ring, her chipper tone letting Daidai know she was in her full-on work mode. "I was just thinking of you," she said. "How've you been, Daidai?"

"I'm fine," Daidai said. "How are you?"

"I'm doing well, actually. I knew it'd take a while to get back on my feet, but it's been a relief not to have to worry."

Daidai's voice caught in her throat as she struggled with the real reason for her call.

"So what's up?" Louise asked after a pause.

She regretted not being a better friend and considered lying, or hanging up. But instead she decided it best to get to the point: "I haven't called you because things have been crazy. Hiroshi invited Satsuki to live here, with us."

A long silence followed while she waited for Louise to process the information she'd been given. "Are you there?" she asked, wondering if someone had approached Louise's desk while they talked.

"I'm here," Louise said. "I'm worried about you."

PART FIVE

|

HARD EVIDENCE

36

On a Tuesday, the last week in April, Daidai unwrapped the boxed pregnancy test having already guessed that she was pregnant; she'd just needed to wait to be alone to get the confirmation. Something felt different, not just the fullness in her breasts and a heightened sense of taste and sensitivity to smells, but a kind of levity, as if the ground rose a bit each time she set down her slow-moving feet. After waiting so long, then wondering whether she really wanted a baby, she didn't know how she felt about the news, only sensed keenly that the timing could not have been worse with Satsuki in the house and Hiroshi unavailable to her.

Hiroshi seemed more surprised than she when she told him that night, perhaps noting the irony of the copious sex acts they'd been asked by the fertility specialist to perform—which included many months of lunchtime conjugal visits—that had amounted to nothing, followed by a forgotten romp that had resulted in the pregnancy. "Looked at another way," he said when she noted how bad the timing was, "maybe you just needed someone around to take care of you."

"Are you kidding?" Daidai understood how easy his life had become with his wife at home and his grad student around to cajole him and cook his meals, but she'd never needed anyone to do her cooking for her and, until recently, had never relied on anyone but him for company. Looked at another way, wasn't caring for her, at least in part, supposed to be his job?

"I was making a joke," he said.

"Don't you want this baby?" she asked, truly needing to know. "Because if the timing isn't good for you, or if it's not the right decision anymore, it's not too late to back out."

"It's exactly what I want." He turned to face her, no trace of doubt in his steadfast gaze. "I can't wait till this semester is over and I'm done with teaching. Then I'll be able to focus on you."

"So what about our living situation?" Daidai kept her voice low in case Satsuki was listening from the other side of the wall, knowing that irrespective of his response it was going to be a tough few weeks.

"Do you mean Satsuki? I imagine she's just waiting till classes end to begin looking for another apartment. She hasn't said anything, so I don't know what her plans are for the summer."

Daidai just shrugged. Realizing she no longer had any idea about the truth, she stayed up later than she should have that night to ponder what it might mean that she was finally pregnant. Unlike the last time, when she'd miscarried so early on, she had a sense that this baby would be with her to term. She didn't know whether she was carrying a boy or girl, or what her life with Hiroshi would look like in seven and a half months, but she lay awake with a strange calmness and a feeling of inevitability that she mistook for resolve.

The next morning she awoke to the clatter of starlings in the tree outside her window and the smell of a salt breeze that made the ocean seem closer than it really was. For a minute she felt disoriented, recalling the first weeks after her return from Japan when she dreamed almost nightly of Ichiro's house and awakened believing she was still in Mito. But Japan had faded into the background, an event from the past, and in the hours since she'd found out she was pregnant, the familiar world—the one she could navigate with her senses—had come sharply to the forefront. Beneath the birdcalls, she realized that what she was really straining to hear was Satsuki, the rhythm of her morning activities sometimes audible from the other side of the wall, or perhaps Daidai even had the intuition that Satsuki was listening for her. It couldn't have been a coincidence that they tended to appear in the kitchen each morning within moments of each other.

Daidai hadn't planned to say anything until the pregnancy moved further along. But then, irritated as she was by the sight of Satsuki's smiling face and feeling the need to hasten her departure, she wound up telling Satsuki in a moment of weakness.

"This is wonderful news!" Satsuki, rushing around the breakfast table, leaned her head against Daidai's chest and squeezed her shoulders. "This is exactly what you hoped would happen, isn't it?"

"I guess so, yes." Taken aback, Daidai wondered if perhaps she'd underestimated Satsuki's fondness for her.

"I know how much you wanted this baby. Have you told Hiroshi?"

"Last night," Daidai said, her smile wavering. Did Satsuki really think she'd tell her before she told Hiroshi? "I guess we'll need to start thinking about converting Hiroshi's study into a nursery," she said, hinting at the news that would come next.

Satsuki's broad grin gave away nothing. "You need a house with a yard."

Satsuki was right, but first things first. The next person she needed to tell was her mother. But Mako called before she had a chance to, surprising Daidai with an announcement that she'd received a letter from Japan. It was waiting for her on the kitchen counter.

Daidai's first thought was of Satsuki's father. Could Ichiro have found a new way to contact her, this time through her mother? But that was far-fetched even in her imagination, since by that time Ichiro had been dead for over a month. "What are you talking about?" she demanded.

"You'll see when you read it," Mako said, cryptic as ever.

"I was going to call you to tell you I'm pregnant," Daidai blurted out, not wanting to dwell on her mother's obstructionist language.

"*Omedetoo!* I'm happy for you." Mako beamed her congratulations through the receiver, shifting her allegiance seamlessly back to Daidai.

37

Mako stuffed the letter into Daidai's hand like a wad of cash as soon as she arrived. Daidai had intended to read it right away, but with the excitement about her pregnancy building all the way over, she'd slid it into her back pocket and forgotten about it until she excused herself to go to the bathroom and it had fallen to floor. Picking it up, she examined the envelope, noting that the return address bore the imprint of Shodai Gakuen and that the letter, written by hand in neat, vertical rows of Japanese characters, was addressed to her father. Daidai would need her mother to translate. After returning to her chair at the kitchen table, she sat with her head propped in her hands while her mother read:

Dear Mr. Flynn:

I'm sorry it has taken a while to respond to your reference request. I appreciate the sympathies expressed in your letter. Japan faces hardships as difficult as those experienced at the end of the war. Even here at Shodai, where students are isolated from many issues facing the larger society, a month after the manifold disasters everything is far from in order.

Regarding Satsuki Suzuki, I have been asked to respond to your letter because I have been at Shodai longer than most other administrators and teachers. In fact, I was here to greet Satsuki when she arrived as a six-year-old child. Satsuki attended Shodai from her first year of primary school until her graduation from high school. A few children come to board without ever having attended a prefectural school, but this was not the case with Satsuki. If I recall, her paternal grandmother had supervised her education in Mito, until a death in the family caused the old woman to return to northern Japan. Immediately thereafter, the father petitioned Shodai administrators to have Satsuki admitted midsemester.

Many students arrive at Shodai from unusual circumstances. Fathers who are diplomats or businessmen whose occupations take them away from Japan. Or mothers who work away from the home so they cannot adequately care for their children. Many parents of Shodai students believe their home life would detract from a child's education. Teachers at Shodai work hard to instill children with traditional Japanese values and morals that will enable them to succeed throughout life. For parents who want their children to receive a traditional Japanese education in Japan, Shodai provides an excellent learning alternative to prefectural schools or boarding schools abroad, and many children, such as Satsuki, thrive in the school's setting. Satsuki placed into the top level in reading and mathematics from her first year. As a child, she had an introverted nature. However, her excellent grades reflect her spirit of hard work.

Shodai teachers described Satsuki as exceedingly clever and imaginative.

She took advantage of many of Shodai's excellent resources. She participated each year in the maintenance of the school garden and she was eager to learn the traditional Japanese arts. I believe she studied ikebana and chanoyu, as well as samisen, and she even performed in the school's sho-gekijo. *She loved literature. As a high school student she studied classics by Mishima, Kawabata, and Tanizaki. But she was particularly drawn to women authors such as Ariyoshi Sawako. I remember because when I lectured on Ariyoshi's novels Satsuki stayed after class and asked questions, which I found to be quite provocative. In particular she was fascinated by* The River Ki. *If I remember correctly, Satsuki was interested in attention paid to the changing role of women in postwar Japan.*

When young children arrive at Shodai, it is not unusual for them to experience a period of transition. Often children withdraw at first. Satsuki seemed to prefer seclusion through much of her primary education. Though she engaged fully in academics, she socialized less than other children and kept mostly to herself. For that reason, I'm happy to hear of the life she has made for herself in California. Maybe she needed to leave Japan to truly begin her journey with others.

I must before ending mention one incident that still disturbs me. Mostly, of course, because when one is in a leadership position and something goes wrong, it is natural to blame oneself and wonder what one could have done to prevent such an unfortunate outcome. In Satsuki's sophomore year of high school, she developed a close friendship with a student who had entered Shodai as a high school student. This is sometimes the case for children at the middle or high school level when parents wish for them to receive a more rigorous education than the one available to them at their local school, without distractions that can sometimes occur during the teen years. The boy entered in Satsuki's grade and was quite shy, like Satsuki, so I wasn't surprised that the two would find each other and develop a friendship.

Unlike most Shodai students, Satsuki remained on campus during breaks. This was the time that I got to know her, when the other children returned home and the campus was mostly deserted, and for myself there were no administrative responsibilities or class papers to grade. But during the summer break, Satsuki was invited to accompany this child to his parents' vacation home. The faculty was pleased to hear that Satsuki had agreed to go.

Of course I was anxious to hear from Satsuki about the vacation when she returned to campus. She was always polite in responding to my questions, and I recall that she told me her stay had been "pleasant." But in the weeks that followed Satsuki seemed more withdrawn than usual. She stopped spending time with the boy. Then, shortly before the end of that term, the boy's body washed up on the shore of a nearby lake. Naturally, everyone at Shodai was quite upset. An investigation was carried out for the sake of the parents, and counselors were brought in to talk with students who suffered the loss of their classmate and friend.

I don't believe Satsuki took advantage of counseling services, but I'm certain the tragic incident must have affected her. It is something I recall with deep sadness even so many years later, perhaps out of regret for whatever circumstances contributed to this boy's life coming to an end so prematurely.

I believe Satsuki will succeed at whatever she sets her mind to doing. Of all the students I have had the opportunity to work with in nearly thirty years at Shodai, I consider Satsuki to have been in the top tier. Her natural cleverness and ability to sustain hard work would make her an excellent employee. She is a capable young woman. She is also naturally a good observer and someone who can implement her observations into her work with good result.

I hope you find these thoughts helpful.

Sincerely,
Matsumoto Shuji
Assistant to Headmaster

"Why on earth would the assistant headmaster of Shodai write to Dad?" Daidai asked, dumbstruck, unable to concentrate on the letter's contents until she could first understand the context.

"I thought about what you said about Satsuki and realized that the administrators at the school Satsuki attended would probably know her better than anyone else. Isn't this helpful?"

"What are you talking about?" Daidai asked, still not understanding.

"I used some of your dad's stationery. I knew the letter would get here because his nice assistant still stops by once in a while to bring me his mail."

"Donna?" Daidai asked in disbelief.

"I'm glad you remember her. She is such a nice young woman! She worked for him for nearly twenty years, so I guess she's not that young anymore. What did you think of the letter?"

Having stopped listening, Daidai was trying instead to remember what Satsuki had told her about the friend she'd called Kenji. "I don't know if the translation was completely accurate. What did you say to get this Matsumoto-assistant-headmaster-person to write back?"

"I told him Satsuki had applied for a job at Toyota. I figured it couldn't hurt. I thought you wanted to know more about her."

"What you did is illegal!" Daidai said, worried already about how Hiroshi would react.

"Is it?" Mako shrugged. "I didn't know."

"You must have known!" Daidai said, assuming Hiroshi's tone with her mother.

"What did you think of the letter? After so many years not using Japanese, mine is no good anymore."

"Obviously, for him to have responded in such elaborate detail, your Japanese is just fine." Daidai lowered her voice, deciding to let the issue of the legality of Mako's actions drop in favor of what her mother had discovered. "What did *you* think of the letter, of what Assistant to the Headmaster Matsumoto had to say?"

"He found her clever." Mako's observation surprised Daidai. "He said that twice."

"He did?" She realized she'd need to review the letter on her own. "Can you translate the letter for me in writing?"

"Of course." Mako scanned the thin sheets to find the two spots where Matsumoto had referred to Satsuki as "clever." "Japanese, more than Americans, I guess, sometimes have an oblique way of expressing themselves when they find the subject matter difficult. This man chose his words thoughtfully, and there was something he was careful not to say. Would you agree?"

"Not necessarily," Daidai said. "Why would you think that?"

"A feeling I had, because the letter went on at length and the writer took care to describe the school and its educational philosophy. Why would he do that unless he was concerned about the school's reputation? He also found this student to be odd, for reasons he couldn't exactly point to or didn't want to say." Having picked out parts of the letter that Daidai hadn't really caught or understood, Mako surprised Daidai with her sagacity. "Why do you think he would have mentioned the drowned boy? Is that why you wanted me to check on Satsuki?"

Impressed yet again with her mother's ability to make connections, Daidai could tell that Mako was prompting her to share her concerns about Satsuki. Her inquiry had produced the letter; now it was Daidai's turn to reveal something. "That information came as a total shock to me," she admitted, hesitant to take the bait.

"I don't trust Satsuki," Mako declared. Putting the letter down, she withdrew her hands from the tabletop.

"You two seemed to get on well enough in the car," Daidai responded, recalling the nonstop talk that had pretty much excluded her the afternoon of Danji's memorial. "I thought you might want to replace me for her."

"Don't talk so silly. Of course I took an interest in her because she's your friend."

"Why do you not trust her?" Daidai didn't entirely believe her mother, but she wished to steer the conversation back to the headmaster's assistant's letter.

"I knew girls like her growing up, girls you wanted to be friends with but couldn't trust."

How much had Japan really changed from the time her mother had grown up there to the time Satsuki had attended school at Shodai? "Is that why you wrote, to check up on her?"

"I told you I was worried about you. Isn't it nice to see that your mother can still get things done?"

Daidai had never thought her mother the least bit incompetent. Just the opposite: she'd been shocked at how readily Mako had entered a territory she knew nothing about. Mako had spent her working years primarily as a secretary, but the method she'd used to collect data was not one learned from training, and it made Daidai anxious to get home to tell Hiroshi what she'd found out. News of the sudden and unexpected deaths of Ritsuko and Ichiro had not fazed him, but maybe Kenji's death would. Even given his unassuming disposition, he had to consider that now there were three deaths linked to their houseguest. Two might be considered a coincidence, but three?

As Daidai drove back to the Valley she tried to recall what Satsuki had said about Kenji the morning they'd walked together through Kairakuen. She could see the flowering plum trees, which served as a distraction, as if the blossoms had been laid over the memory she needed to access. Sometimes she hated how thoroughly memory resisted oversight. She knew there was no use working against her nature; she'd just have to wait for the moment to open itself up. But one thing was certain: Satsuki hadn't mentioned Kenji's death. She would have remembered that.

38

It was as she'd expected. Rather than appreciate the detective work Mako had shown herself capable of, Hiroshi was furious, insisting that Daidai, not her mother, had solicited the letter from Matsumoto.

"It's your choice whether to believe me," she said, knowing she had little chance of convincing him otherwise.

"I'm not saying I don't believe you, just that you shouldn't have involved your mother in our business. It's not even *your* business," he said, becoming moralistic.

"It's not my business that Satsuki is living here?" Daidai argued despite her promise to herself that she wouldn't. Why did Hiroshi have to be so patronizing? "I shouldn't care that she's sleeping on the other side of the wall and for all I know having an affair with my husband?"

"That's ridiculous. How come you're still going there?"

Seeing Hiroshi indignant did nothing to convince her of his innocence. "Your self-righteousness might mean more to me if you'd quit focusing on your own work long enough to think about me. You know, you could back me up."

He stared at her coolly. "We're allowed to have different viewpoints, aren't we?"

"If you don't back me up, we don't have a marriage. It doesn't matter whether you agree with me. I don't always agree with you, but I always back you up."

"I don't need you to back me up," he said after a long pause to consider what she was saying. "I need you to stand your own ground. Please don't feel like you have to back me up, okay? I'll back myself up."

Having made his point, Hiroshi laced up his running shoes and left, shutting the door loudly though not letting it slam behind him, and Daidai turned into the kitchen to make herself tea and replay for herself what he'd said. Might things have gone differently had she waited for her mother to translate the letter before approaching Hiroshi with what it said? Maybe he'd needed physical proof, because he'd dismissed her concerns, along with her mother's, for the wrong reasons, thus making sure that the letter did not get the attention it deserved. He'd gotten stuck on the fact that some administrator had been approached for information on Satsuki's background under false pretenses. He'd gone so far as to speculate that the university could hold him liable for Daidai's mother's actions. But rather than diminish Daidai's suspicions about Satsuki, his conjecture merely made Hiroshi seem unlikable.

Daidai was sitting at the kitchen table with her tepid tea when she heard the door reopen and saw Satsuki approach out of the near darkness. She visibly startled when she saw Daidai. "I didn't think you were home."

"Sorry."

"Are you unwell?"

"I'm fine."

Looking up at her in the dim evening light, Daidai thought to ask the same question. Satsuki looked terrible. Her hair seemed limp and thinning, like she could have used a thorough wash and blow dry, and her skin shone a pasty shade of gray. "You don't look fine," she said, worried.

Satsuki's lips closed around her gleaming white teeth. "Neither do you."

"Don't you and Hiroshi ever get tired of thinking so much?" Daidai asked.

"That's a very strange thing for you to ask," she said, staring quizzically at Daidai through the shadowy darkness. "I mean, is this a serious question?"

"I'm asking because I want to know," Daidai said, annoyed, though she didn't know over what. "What's it like to fill your head every day with abstract ideas?"

"I think ideas are all we have," Satsuki said. "Good ones, when implemented, are the only things that can elevate us as a species, and maybe save this world."

"Do you really think that?" Daidai asked, because she felt dejected. Having traveled from a place of confidence to despair, she no longer knew where she stood. "My turn to ask: Are you being serious?"

"Completely. Did you have a fight with Hiroshi?"

"How did you know?"

"I saw him going around the track when I was leaving campus. He was running like someone being chased, and here you are, sitting by yourself in the dark, all glum."

"You're very observant."

"Pregnancy is a hard time in a marriage."

"How would you know?"

"I read up on it. So I'd know what to expect."

"From me?"

"Who else?"

"What more did you find out?"

"Men frequently go through a period of regression in which they long for their youth, or they crave special attention from their pregnant wives."

"That doesn't sound like Hiroshi."

"Men are very childish."

"Not Hiroshi."

"In some cultures, women separate themselves from men during pregnancy."

"Why would they do that?"

"Because men are limited in their ability to understand women, and pregnancy should be a time when women feel liberated and embodied."

"Is this something you read?"

"It's something I know. Don't worry, my Daidai friend. I plan to take good care of you."

Daidai smiled, but at the same time a chill ran along the back of her neck, causing her to turn toward the window above the sink to look for where the draft was coming in.

39

Everything seemed to happen in slow motion in those next few weeks. Daidai called the fertility specialist (thrilled to hear of one more success for his record) to check whether he oversaw prenatal care and found that his fee ran way over what the insurance company allowed for her pregnancy. He gave her a referral, but that OB wasn't seeing new patients. Another with offices in West Los Angeles would have meant battling traffic, which was a stress she tried whenever possible to avoid.

After a week of thinking it might take the next seven months just to find the right doctor, Daidai remembered the name of the midwife a colleague had used. An MD oversaw her practice, shared with nurse practitioners. But more important, she had an opening on Monday of the following week and the office was less than ten minutes away. She hoped Hiroshi would accompany her to the first visit and was glad when he agreed. She was still angry with him, but they'd exchanged no further jabs and had refrained from communicating about Satsuki at all since their argument. She was still there in the apartment each morning and evening, with Daidai counting down the days to the end of the semester for a new phase to begin, or at least that's what she told herself.

The practice was more new age than she liked or could get used to, the low-lit green waiting room filled with pamphlets on naturopathics and various forms of massage and healing. The midwife, a thin, limber-boned woman in her fifties, struck a good impression. She seemed both knowledgeable and thorough during the initial checkup. But when she explained that each prenatal visit included a guided birth meditation, Daidai had to fight her impulse to get up and walk out.

"What have you got to lose?" the midwife asked, clapping her hands as if to break a spell. She must have seen the panic on Daidai's face. "Just think of it as ten minutes of free relaxation time that benefits both you and your baby."

Thinking instead about how many calls it had taken to get an appointment for prenatal care served to renew Daidai's patience.

When Hiroshi tried excusing himself back out to the waiting room, she caught him with her watchful eyes. "You're in this, too," she said.

Ushering the couple into a darkened room, which she called the "inner sanctum," the midwife made Daidai comfortable with two sets of pillows on a padded, heated table and laid a thin blanket over her torso. For Hiroshi's comfort, she pointed to a pile of colorful beanbags.

The instructions for that first session were simple. Close your eyes. Breathe. Imagine your breath filling your stomach, then your lungs. In through your nostrils, out through your mouth. That was it. The exercise was clearly designed to be relaxing, yet when Daidai closed her eyelids she kept seeing Satsuki's face hovering over her, so close she could smell the bitterness of her tea breath. Despite her attempt to will her vague image or her distinct smell away, it was no use. She had to keep glancing around the room to reorient herself.

"You should practice the meditation at home," Daidai was told before being cleared to leave that afternoon, meaning, she thought, *You're not very good at this. Can't you even keep your eyes shut for ten minutes?*

The unexpected benefit to that session was the realization of how tense her body was. "Stress is not good for the fetus," the midwife warned. Walking out to the car, Daidai felt guilty for creating an inhospitable growth environment and vowed to do what she could to improve the living conditions.

"That wasn't bad." Hiroshi turned the key in the ignition, apparently having experienced none of his wife's foreboding.

"Really?" His comment served only as an acknowledgment that the divide between his reality and hers was growing larger by the day. "I thought you'd have found it hokey."

"I'm backing you up." He flashed his sideways grin. "Besides, what harm can it do to close your eyes and turn your mind inward. That's all meditation is."

"When have you ever meditated?"

"I used to chant every Sunday at temple. My family attended Nishi Hongwanji for years."

"How come I didn't know that?" Hiroshi had jarred her out of her moment of self-pity by his startling revelation.

"There are still some things you don't know about me," Hiroshi said, deadpan, before breaking into a smile and poking Daidai's biceps. "Hey, lighten up!"

"I don't feel very light. I feel heavy and slightly nauseated all the time and I'm worried about everything."

"I'm sorry. I'm sure sharing your body is no fun, at least in the beginning. Maybe you and I should join a temple. If we want this baby to have some religion, that is."

Hiroshi and her joining a temple might not be a bad idea. Mako had been raised Buddhist and still made an offering of food and said a prayer each morning in front of her small shrine. She'd never included Daidai in this practice, perhaps out of respect for her husband, a Catholic, or a "formerly devout Catholic," he liked to call himself. But Mako would be pleased, and it wasn't too late for this baby. "I wouldn't mind trying," she told him.

"Maybe we can get Satsuki to come with us," he added.

"Why would we take her with us?" Daidai demanded, her good mood turning quickly to anger.

"Most Japanese have some temple affiliation, though I haven't asked about hers. Have you?"

She hadn't, but once the subject of religion had been raised her thoughts wandered back to the monastery where Ritsuko had spent so many years living as a nun. Was it possible through an act of contrition to change? How much chanting or meditating would a person have to do to arrive at a new place?

Of course, she'd already arrived at that place—it just wasn't where she'd hoped for or expected to wind up. Her husband, she'd pretty much decided during the ten-minute car ride home, was not the man she married, the one she'd vowed to love forever. He'd developed a crush on a student, and whatever he had going with her could not be rationalized away as normal. As they drove, Satsuki was likely sitting on Daidai's furniture and handling objects that belonged to her. She'd struggled to understand whether Hiroshi was complicit or oblivious, but decided that the binary had become meaningless. What mattered was that Satsuki be given a deadline for moving out and that Hiroshi know the impact her not abiding by it would have on their marriage.

"You need to give Satsuki an eviction date."

"Pardon?"

"A date by which she agrees to leave our apartment."

"Okay," he said, easy as that.

40

Louise came unannounced the next morning, which also happened to be Hiroshi's last day of spring classes. Daidai could hardly believe her eyes when she spied her friend through the peephole, plugging repeatedly at the doorbell with one hand, holding a bunch of white peonies wrapped in newspaper in the other. "Lou-Lou, really?" Daidai extended her arms in a state of shock.

"Aren't they beautiful?" Louise beamed as if she'd come to receive the bouquet she bore, which reinforced to Daidai, who stood in her nightclothes, just how mixed up everything felt.

The scent of the flowers mingled with perfumed shampoo as Daidai stepped out from behind the door to usher Louise in and shut it. After placing the flowers on the countertop, she ran off to her room to dress while Louise settled herself in the kitchen.

"So what's the occasion?" Daidai asked, returning out of breath, knowing that Louise had never been one to do anything spontaneous.

"I'm happy for you."

Daidai had decided to wait until the fall to announce the news of her pregnancy, but she regretted that she'd not called Louise directly. Satsuki knew, as did her mother. Daidai couldn't blame Louise for feeling left out. Climbing a stepstool in search of a vase, she could hear Louise's nails thrumming against the tabletop.

"Did you know peonies are the national flower of China?" Daidai asked, recalling the patterned textiles she'd once hung in an exhibit, full of blossoms.

"I grew them in my garden."

"Are they a peace offering? Because I think peonies are my new favorite flowers." Reaching behind the Ball jar from Satsuki's gerberas last fall, Daidai brought down a tall vase, filled it with tap water, and arranged the heavy blossoms after snipping each stem with exaggerated care.

Louise smiled, but responded instead with "You look good."

Daidai knew she looked horrible. Given her height, her slender frame held the six pounds she'd already gained well enough, but on top of the pregnancy weight, her face had broken out in speckled blemishes, and she'd barely had time to wash up. "You're nice to say that," she said self-consciously, running fingers through her hair.

"Are you okay?" Louise asked, leaning over the tabletop.

Daidai withdrew her arm and folded her hands in her lap. "I'm fine," she said, not understanding what Louise was getting at. "Tell me about you. I want to hear about your new girlfriend."

Louise smiled, but it was tentative. She'd come with something on her mind. Daidai could feel it, and she was bracing herself. Reaching into the vase, she pinched a small green bug that she caught crawling up one of the thick stalks.

"I'm enjoying life," Louise said. "Maybe for the first time in a long while. If you want to meet my girlfriend, we should all have dinner."

It was a good idea; it was what should happen. But the mention of dinner brought back the night she, Hiroshi, and Satsuki had sat uncomfortably around the table, trying to eat after the news that Satsuki's mother had been found dead, and Daidai didn't think she could bear the idea of Louise and her girlfriend, she and Hiroshi, and Satsuki crowded around a table. "That sounds nice," she said.

"Gizo came by with Leonard last weekend." Daidai could feel her friend homing in on something. "Leonard mentioned that Satsuki is living with him. But I thought you said she'd moved in here, with you and Hiroshi."

Daidai frowned. "You must have misunderstood. I wish that were the case. But Hiroshi gave her an eviction date of the end of this month."

A siren wailed, growing louder as it approached the apartment. Knowing that whatever she said wouldn't be heard, Daidai pushed her chair back from the table waiting for the noise to pass. "It's all so complicated." She felt sickened that Satsuki had come to occupy the core of every conversation, first with Hiroshi and now with Louise. Even so, her scant explanation felt wholly inadequate for what she believed was really going on.

"I'm worried about you."

"I'm fine. Don't worry about me."

"I think you're obsessed with Satsuki." Louise was unwilling to relent. "I've hardly heard from you since last fall. I couldn't believe you took off for Japan with her without even telling me. Then you showed up with her at my father's funeral. Now she's living here. What's going on between you two?"

"Satsuki and me? Nothing. But I think Hiroshi and Satsuki might be having an affair."

"Hiroshi?" Louise's eyebrows shot up.

"Please stop!" Daidai reached a hand across the tabletop, undeterred when Louise pulled back as she had done. "I know you're mad at me, but nothing's wrong!"

"I'm not mad at you," Louise said calmly.

"Things are bad." Daidai bit the inside of her cheek, noting that Louise's lips were stained a deceptive shade of pink. "I didn't want to involve you. I don't even want to be involved. I'm sorry, okay? So sorry."

Louise smiled, the stern set of her mouth softening a little.

"Let me make us some tea," Daidai said, her manners finally kicking in.

"Sure," Louise relented. "I took the morning off to come visit. Why not?"

"I have some excellent green tea that Satsuki had sent from Japan." Daidai searched the cupboard, aggravated that Satsuki had once again found her way into conversation. Unable to find the tea, she located instead a small stash of the bitter-smelling stuff Satsuki had left wrapped up in the back of a drawer.

"I think foreign-born Japanese are culturally just so different from Japanese born here," Louise commented.

Daidai shook a small amount of leaves into the pot, glad that Louise seemed to have turned some kind of corner in her thinking. "I think you're right. And Satsuki lost her mother at such a young age."

Louise nodded. "A person who's suffered that kind of trauma probably can't form solid attachments."

"She seems to have glommed on to Hiroshi well enough," Daidai said, somewhat comforted but still feeling stung by Louise's pulling away.

"Maybe she's only using him."

Daidai poured water over the tea leaves, turning away from the pungent smell that wafted up from the teapot. "What do you think she wants from Hiroshi?"

"Maybe she wants you."

"Me?"

"I don't know. Just a thought."

Two things happened at once then: Louise's tea, which she'd been carrying to the table, sloshed over the rim of the teacup, scalding Daidai's wrist before shattering on the floor. But instead of cleaning it up, Daidai ran to the bathroom and threw up.

By the time she returned to the kitchen, Louise had swept up the shards and wet tea leaves. Having found the good tea, she'd set a fresh pot brewing on the table. "Do you do that often?"

"That's the first time, actually."

"Hope it stays that way."

Perhaps deciding to avoid topics that might cause another bout of sickness in her friend, Louise didn't bring Satsuki up again until she was on her way out the door. "You're too stressed out," she told Daidai. "I'm going to talk with Gizo. He needs to talk with Leonard, get Satsuki to move back in with him."

41

Less than an hour after Louise had gone, Satsuki arrived back at the apartment looking worse than when Daidai had seen her the day before. Her skin seemed to sag on her bones, and she had the beaten-down look of someone who'd given up on appearances. It was hard not to feel pity for her on a basic human level. A few months ago, she'd been so robust; now her lack of vitality was worrisome, though Daidai's concern was tinged with contempt. "Are you losing weight?" she asked.

Satsuki laughed. "Oh, Daidai, what if for every pound that you were to gain in pregnancy, I were to lose one? Maybe then we'd both be the weight that best suits us."

"I don't think so." Daidai frowned, calculating the twenty-five to thirty pounds she was expected to gain by the end of the year and trying to imagine what Satsuki would look like were she to lose that much weight. Was it even possible?

"I'm just wondering how we can achieve a balance, an equitable distribution."

Daidai had no idea what Satsuki was talking about, and perhaps she knew it.

"I'm afraid it's been a long morning," she explained, and stared languidly at the backs of her hands.

"Finals?" Daidai had planned to follow up on whatever ultimatum Hiroshi had given her about moving out, but, given her disordered state of mind, decided it wasn't the right time. "Are you done with the semester?"

"Yes, thank you for asking."

"What are your plans for the summer?"

"My father's lawyer wants me to return to Japan to close up the house in Mito so that it can be sold."

Mito was a hundred miles away from Fukushima, more than fifty miles outside the zone deemed uninhabitable because of life-threatening radiation levels. Whether it was safe enough was another question. Food grown in the nearby soil had already been found to be contaminated, as had fish harvested from the sea; it would likely be determined later that the airborne radiation in Ibaraki Prefecture was higher than was being reported. Still, Daidai felt uplifted by the news that Satsuki would be leaving soon, even if it meant her going back to Mito. When she returned she could get her own place.

Daidai was fantasizing about Satsuki's departure to Mito when she heard her cell phone ringing. Out of the corner of her eye she noticed Satsuki still staring down at her hands as she ran off, tracing the bleeping to her nightstand. Pleased to see Hiroshi's number lighting up the display, she answered the call. But it wasn't Hiroshi.

"Mrs. Hamada?" The male caller, whose voice she couldn't quite place, sounded tense and official.

"Yes, this is she," she said, already irritated. She hated being called Hamada instead of Suzuki, minded less the title "Mrs." being substituted for "Dr.," though when the caller introduced himself as Martin, she wondered why he hadn't simply called her Daidai.

"I'm with Dr. Hamada at Northridge Hospital. He's been brought here by ambulance. He's being treated in the emergency room."

"What's happened?" she asked, sitting on the bed.

"Well, I'm not sure exactly—"

"I'm on my way." Standing back up again, not waiting for Martin to find the words to continue, Daidai shoved her phone into the pocket of her jeans and went in search of her car keys and wallet.

"What's wrong?" Satsuki looked up dully when she rushed out of the bedroom.

"Hiroshi's been taken to the hospital."

"Do you want me to come with you?"

At the news, Satsuki's pensive face seemed to open in the morning sunlight. It was an image Daidai would carry with her. About to say yes, she surprised herself with the words that came out of her mouth. "Wait here."

The last time she'd been to the level I trauma unit of a big hospital had been when her father collapsed from dehydration during his cancer treatment. In the months that led from his diagnosis to his death, the hospital had become familiar—that forever unpleasant territory delineated by sickness and treachery. The wide glass doors clamped shut behind her like jaws, and standing under the fluorescent white lighting, she experienced an unexpected burst of clarity. The pace inside and acrid accompanying odors alerted her that the margin of error that had for so long cushioned her thinking had ceased to exist. No more room for conjecture, no testing hunches to see how they'd play out. She was pregnant. Her baby was going to be born to a mother who could perceive and meet the demands placed upon her, not one who suffered from careless lapses in perception. Of course, in reality, Daidai had little control over her husband's medical condition, but the reminder of life's temporal nature would clarify the decisions she'd need to make in the days to come.

Hiroshi had been moved out of the ER, and it wasn't that easy to follow the directions she'd been given to the ICU, less so to find him connected by tubing to machines, his nose and mouth covered by an oxygen mask. Though he lay unconscious, his expression was serious, as if he'd closed his eyes to concentrate on something inside his head.

Standing at the bed railing, Daidai bent at the waist, hoping to send the blood flowing back up to her head. His hand lacked the warmth she associated with his body, though she could swear he gripped her fingers to pull her closer.

"Mrs. Hamada?" Daidai hadn't noticed Martin standing at the foot of the bed. "I'm sorry I couldn't be clearer on the phone, but I'm afraid I really don't know what happened. I found Dr. Hamada in the men's room, passed out."

Bringing Hiroshi's free hand to her cheek, she caught a whiff of an antiseptic smell and bitterness unlike Hiroshi's normally musky body scent.

"The paramedic said he was lucky he didn't asphyxiate on his vomit."

Daidai imagined Hiroshi hunched over the toilet bowl. Poor Martin was probably in shock. "Thank you for taking care of him. I'm sure you're busy—it being finals week."

"I was glad to have been there to help."

His tone was stoical, but Daidai pitied him all over again, his youth and the strain caused by the day obvious in the way he slouched, weak-kneed, against the wall. "You can leave if you need to."

"Are you sure? Will you be okay?"

"Yes, Martin, I'm sure." She turned back to Hiroshi. Stretching her hands across the metal bed railing as she straightened out of a crouch, Daidai listened for the cadence of his breathing beneath the oxygen mask and was surprised by the searing pain that shot from her right hip down her thigh. Once again Martin came through, rushing across the room with the offer of a hand. Despite his soft, fleshy face, he had an unusually strong grip.

Less than a minute after Martin had left, Hiroshi opened one eye, then the other. "Daidai?" He murmured her name from under the mask and seemed to be trying to smile, his effort causing her heart to skip a beat.

"Hi, Hiroshi." She stroked the hair away from his brow. "I'm right here."

"Is Martin gone?" he whispered, forcing her to bring her ear down close to his mouth.

"He just left."

"Good."

She smiled, reassured by his voice. "What happened, Hiroshi?"

"What are they saying?" he asked, his interrogative nature apparently still with him.

She smoothed her hand over his forehead, overtaken by a wave of fondness for him. "I haven't seen the doctor yet. I just got here."

"I got really sick."

"Yes, sweetheart." His forehead felt smooth and parched beneath her fingertips. "I can tell that. What happened?" she tried again.

Hiroshi grimaced and smacked his lips together weakly. "I don't know. All I had was Starbucks."

"Did you see Satsuki?" she asked, trying to sound casual, even though her heart was racing out of control.

"She brought it to me . . ."

Daidai dropped his hand after giving it a squeeze. "I need to find your doctor." After adjusting the mask, which she'd displaced in order to hear him, she ran the short distance from his room to the nurses' station to have the attending physician paged.

Dr. Goldblatt introduced himself in the hallway. His dirty spectacles made him seem untrustworthy, or maybe it was his perfunctory responses. Hiroshi had already been at the hospital for nearly two hours. He'd been found unconscious surrounded by his own vomit, which she already knew, and incoherent when the ambulance brought him in. A CT scan ruled out stroke or seizure, and blood had been drawn and sent down to the lab. A preliminary toxicology report was expected back in a couple of hours. Hiroshi's heart was beating at an accelerated rate, but he didn't appear to have had a heart attack.

"Will the tests indicate if he was poisoned?" Daidai asked.

She'd not anticipated what such a question might imply to the doctor, but was not displeased that the obscure litany came to a halt. Dr. Goldblatt peered over the rims of his glasses, seeming to regard her for the first time. "Why do you ask?"

Not wanting to implicate herself in whatever had gone wrong for Hiroshi, Daidai knew she'd need to let the questioning go. "I was thinking food poisoning."

"The patterns thus far aren't consistent with food poisoning," the doctor said, giving nothing away.

Daidai followed Dr. Goldblatt back down the hall, listening in while he asked Hiroshi how he was feeling. When her husband complained of abdominal cramping and numbness in his legs and feet, the doctor asked him if he could remember in detail what he'd done and eaten that morning and the night before. "Sometimes we're not able to identify the reason that a person loses consciousness," he told Daidai after Hiroshi responded that he'd had coffee and nothing more.

"Not very encouraging." Daidai smiled grimly, undeterred from her initial hunch.

"It's good that he's regained consciousness, but after what his body has been through you can expect him to be fairly out of it for a while," he added, not about to be one-upped. "We'll keep monitoring him, but we might not know anything more until the lab results come back."

Having placed too many expectations on her brief exchange with the doctor, Daidai scooted a chair over to the hospital bed and sat beside Hiroshi, alone in the parallel world she occupied beside him. With the rush of adrenaline gone, she didn't have the energy to question the nurse who came to check his vitals, and moved only once, to reposition the blanket when her husband complained that his feet were cold.

Sometime soon she'd call her mother, but at the moment she needed to figure things out on her own. Propped up next to the hospital bed, she recalled her visit with Louise. *I'm worried about you,* she'd said. Louise was right that her thoughts had become disordered. It had been a mistake to quit her job at the museum, to take time off from the work she loved doing. Neither she nor Hiroshi had intended for her life to become less important than his, but it had happened, and along the way his feelings for her had diminished. But perhaps it was not that. Perhaps what had happened instead was that in the time she'd had to figure things out she had changed. With their work and aspirations wedged solidly between them, they'd been safe. She could appreciate the zeal with which he approached his work, but seeing him fawn over his student, she'd lost respect for him.

She observed him as he lay drifting in and out of consciousness, too sick to do anything, and brushing her hand over her belly, attempted to feel something, if not for him then for the baby they'd made together. It was only then that she let herself cry, for what she couldn't feel, had maybe never felt. She'd have to deal later with whatever that meant, but first she needed to find

Satsuki. Recalling how she'd looked when Daidai delivered the news that Hiroshi had been taken to the hospital, she thought of the morning the two had spent in Kairakuen in the dappled shade of the plum tree. Her face had been open with the same expectancy then, when she'd been trying to tell Daidai about events that had taken place half a lifetime ago, when she was a teenager, and earlier still a child.

She knew Hiroshi was surfacing from wherever he'd gone when the ends of his lips curled up. Not long after that, he began shifting restlessly under his gown. "When can I go home?" he asked out of nowhere.

"Not until the doctor clears you." She tried to sound firm but upbeat and reassuring. "You need to relax. If you're thinking of your students, I can assure you that they're not going to be crestfallen if you delay their finishing up for a few days."

"I hate falling behind."

"Better a few days than permanently."

"Don't be so dramatic."

"I'm not the one lying in a hospital bed."

Even without being able to see himself the way she saw him, he had to admit she was right. "Louise came to see me," she said, trying to lighten the mood. "She'd left just before Martin called to tell me you were here."

"Isn't that unusual," he commented, becoming thoughtful. "A visit from Louise on a weekday?"

"She found out I was pregnant."

"I don't think I slipped with the news. If I did I'm sorry," he said, after thinking for a while.

"Don't worry about it," she told him, guessing Satsuki had told Leonard who'd told Gizo.

"I'm excited about the baby."

"I'm glad."

Hiroshi shifted in his bed, apparently realizing that his wife did not share his enthusiasm. "When you come back, can you bring my briefcase? It has a stack of student papers I need to grade. And bring some clothes," he said, shifting beneath his hospital gown. "Apparently mine were ruined."

Daidai rolled her eyes, reaching behind her for the plastic bag left by the nurses. On top, a Ziploc bag with his wallet and keys. Jiggling it to get a better look, she found that it also contained a perfectly round, dime-sized stone, which she held up for Hiroshi to inspect. "What's this?"

"No idea," he said.

"Strange," she said, remembering how the paramedic from Mito had found a similar round stone in the breast pocket of Ichiro's suit jacket. It didn't matter that the preliminary toxicology results came back negative. After kissing Hiroshi on the cheek, Daidai slipped out of his hospital room into the night with a promise to return with the things he'd asked for in the morning.

PART SIX

|

TOO LATE
TO LOOK BACK

42

Daidai had left Satsuki at the apartment, but when she returned from the hospital, Satsuki, along with her black duffel, was gone. Standing motionless in the doorframe of the office that contained her husband's work life and smelled like Satsuki, soaking in the feeling of being alone for the first time in a long while, Daidai understood that she'd become peripheral to her own life. She was pregnant with a life she knew nothing about; her husband, a stranger to her, was involved in a relationship with a woman who'd poisoned him. If Satsuki intended to harm Hiroshi, it was likely that Daidai was in danger as well. Her life might depend on finding Satsuki. But first she needed to eat.

Having had nothing since breakfast, she sliced a banana over a cup of yogurt and ate it in front of her computer screen. The boy Satsuki had spoken about, the one who, according to Matsumoto, had drowned while a sophomore at Shodai, turned out to be Kenji Takahashi, born in 1980, which would have made him the same age as Satsuki. His body had washed up on the shore of a nearby lake. According to that first article, there'd been no signs of foul play. When she added "poison" to the list of key words, however, a new list of articles appeared. One from the *Japan Times* mentioned a police investigation, but nothing more. His parents owned a small cherry orchard in Yamagata Prefecture where he'd worked as a child. As a teenager he'd helped his father run the packing and shipping operation and had shown business acumen and a willingness to work hard. It was not difficult to imagine the mother Satsuki had spoken of, the one who'd risen early each morning of Satsuki's stay in Atami to pack a bento box. A good mother, she'd put her time into raising her son. Believing he lacked the advantages of children who grew up in more cosmopolitan settings, she'd sent him away to Shodai as a high school sophomore, wanting him to have the edge he needed to enter a public university. Of course, the ultimate plan was for him to be in a position to expand the family's small business after receiving his college degree, to return home. But, as Matsumoto's letter indicated, Kenji had not made it to the end of his junior year of high school.

At half past eleven, alone in the apartment, Daidai fought to keep her fear and anxiety from spiraling out of control. Wiping her sweaty fingertips on her pant legs, she listened for footfalls in the stairwell that would signal Satsuki's return. She'd need to think carefully about what to do next. She guessed Satsuki wouldn't answer her cell phone, but she tried it anyway, listening for clues in the greeting message Satsuki had recorded when the call went to voice mail. "It's Daidai, could you give me a call?" she said, even knowing her call wouldn't be returned.

Leaving with her duffel meant Satsuki hadn't intended to return to the apartment, at least not that night, and wherever she'd gone, she didn't want to be reached. Leonard's was the only place she could think to try. When she couldn't find his phone number in Hiroshi's contacts she called Louise.

"Hiroshi's in the hospital," she began, guessing that since she hadn't called her mother, news of Hiroshi hadn't yet reached Louise. "They're not sure what's wrong with him. Evidently, he started vomiting this morning and Martin found him passed out. They've run a bunch of tests, which have so far come back negative," she added, not wanting Louise to be any more alarmed than she knew she would be.

"So was it just the flu? Or food poisoning?"

Daidai wanted to say what she believed, that Satsuki had poisoned Hiroshi. But she cautioned herself not to voice a conclusion that might cause Louise to shift her suspicion from Satsuki's sanity to hers. Louise was a lawyer. Like Hiroshi, she'd need evidence. "They don't know yet" was all she said.

"How can I help?" Louise asked the question Daidai had been waiting to hear, but there was hesitancy in her voice.

"Do you have Leonard's number?" Daidai asked.

"I thought you said Martin found him," Louise said, signaling with a yawn that she'd been asleep.

"He did. But I'm trying to track Satsuki down. I was hoping she might be with Leonard."

Louise didn't answer right away. Daidai fixed her gaze on the vase of peonies she'd brought over earlier that day, noting the evaporation line. The water would need to be changed soon. It was the middle of the night, and she hadn't been available when Louise needed her. She could think of a dozen reasons she might need to sort things out on her own. "I'm sorry to call so late," she added.

"Do you want me to come over?" Louise finally asked, causing a smile to break from Daidai's lips.

"You wouldn't mind?"

"I just need to get dressed. I'll call Gizo for Leonard's number when I get there."

Daidai was glad to know Louise was on her way, but too frustrated to wait.

"You're good, even after business hours," she said, pleased when Gizo picked up on the first ring.

"What's up, Daidai?"

What a relief to hear Gizo's calm, chipper tone. Smiling to herself, she let her mouth fall open and shook her jaw out, deciding what to tell him. Hiroshi was sick, was what she decided on, and she needed Leonard's number.

Daidai felt an overwhelming rush of love when she opened the door to the apartment to find Louise standing under the hall light, a thin jacket thrown on over her pajama top. Leaning in for a hug, her hand felt strong and steady on Daidai's back.

Shutting the door behind her, Louise led Daidai by the hand back into the kitchen. "You've gotten too skinny. I can count your ribs! You need to eat."

Ignoring Daidai's claim that she'd already eaten, Louise sliced an apple while she heated the boxed soup she found in the cupboard. "So what part of this has to do with Satsuki? And why isn't she here?"

Not yet knowing how the facts fit together, Daidai used Louise's questions to talk her way through from the beginning.

"Okay," Louise said when she'd finished, not rendering an interpretation of the information she'd been given.

"I called Leonard. Satsuki isn't with him," Daidai continued. "But he said I could stop by. I told him you were on your way over."

Louise smirked. Opening the refrigerator to examine its contents, she pulled out a partial six-pack of Corona, then checked the fruit bin and filled an empty slot with a couple of limes. "Let's bring him a few beers."

When Louise offered to drive, Daidai didn't argue. Overcome by fatigue, she opened the passenger window and hung her head out, letting the night air rush against her face.

43

Leonard's house looked like a flat Daidai had once shared with roommates and, maybe because the visit took place at a time of night when she was normally asleep, felt like a throwback to college. "Hey, Mrs. Hamada!" Leonard nodded in Daidai's direction by way of a greeting, causing her to recall that earlier in the day Martin had also used Hiroshi's last name in place of hers. But aside from that detail, there appeared to be little to connect the two. While Martin was shaped like a linebacker, Leonard reminded Daidai of a younger Hiroshi—lanky, handsome, and seeming to want to hide behind his build rather than flaunt his height. Hiroshi hadn't learned to stand up straight until he started as a lecturer.

The room behind him was lit by a standing lamp and smelled vaguely of cat urine. The culprit, a wide-eyed tabby, jumped down from the windowsill and stood beside Daidai meowing like a petulant child. When she didn't respond, it strode over to the guitar leaned up against the wall and struck a muted note with its tail. Her ear attuned to the note, Daidai caught the lonely bellow of a trombone coming from another room, a plaintive sound turned low but perfectly registered. Louise had referred to the house as Leonard's, but clearly he had roommates. Daidai was about to ask who else lived with him when Leonard began gesticulating. "Would you like something to drink?" His elegant, tapered fingers shot out behind him in a dance. Daidai wondered whether he'd heard that Hiroshi had been rushed to the hospital earlier that day. Trying to smile while declining his polite offer, she decided to take his laid-back demeanor—so incongruous to the purpose of their late-night visit—as a good sign.

"Come." He sauntered to the couch carrying his cat. "Sit."

"I'm fine standing, really," Daidai said, realizing Louise had been about to speak for her. Not catching on to the hint that business awaited, Leonard sat back on the couch as if to demonstrate relaxedness.

"Did you hear about Hiroshi?" Louise asked, seeming to read Daidai's mind.

"I didn't see him on campus today." Leonard frowned.

"That's because he's in the hospital," Louise informed him. "What's the deal with you and Satsuki?"

Leave it to Louise to deliver sensitive news with almost offensive bluntness. Her role as Gizo's older sister clearly gave her liberty to ask questions Daidai couldn't.

"She rents the room, but she hasn't been around much since she returned from Japan," Leonard explained, apparently used to Louise's style of questioning.

Louise raised an eyebrow at Daidai, confirming that she'd heard right the first time; Leonard had no idea that Satsuki had been living with her and Hiroshi. "Did you two have a falling out?" Louise continued.

"What?" Leonard sounded nonplussed. "We barely know each other."

"So you two weren't dating?" Louise used her older sister authority to rib Gizo's friend.

"No." He held his hands in the air, the humor eluding him, releasing the cat from his lap. Strutting into the kitchen, it leaped to the windowsill and brushed against a row of SAVE JAPAN flags taped above the sink, as if to call attention to Satsuki's presence in the house. Leonard rose from the couch, made uncomfortable by Louise's questioning of him, and lifted the cat back into his arms when it rushed to his side.

Turning over his shoulder, he signaled for Louise and Daidai to follow him. Down the long hall past three doors: the first shut; the second—the one with music playing inside—slightly ajar; the third, at the end of the hall, also shut.

"This one's Satsuki's?" Daidai asked without touching the knob.

"Hers through the end of June." Leonard folded his arms across his chest, seeming confused.

"She just needs a couple books." Louise spoke for Daidai, steering Leonard back down the hall.

Standing at the closed door, Daidai waited to enter the room until after Louise and Leonard had disappeared, listening for Leonard's laughter, pleased when it was followed by the spray of beer, compliments of Louise. Her first thought was that the decor didn't match the rest of the house. Against the far wall, a futon mattress atop a wooden frame had been made up with a pretty yellow quilt and decorative pillows. A shiny walnut chest of drawers stood next to it, and beneath a high window a secretary's desk and hardback chair. The remaining wall space was taken up by a long closet with a sliding door; inside, filing boxes stacked five high, along with jeans, an assortment of dresses, and coats hung neatly in a row. Daidai worked her way through the dresser drawers first, riffling through stacks of bras and panties, then shirts sorted by color and season. The bottom drawer contained shorts and leggings. The desk was also neat, pens and paper clips in the top drawer, a row of hanging folders containing research materials and dissertation work. Nothing more. Moving back to the closet, she began making her way through the boxes, aware of time passing as she worked, not wanting to keep Louise waiting. In the last box, two black fabric-bound ledger books filled with writing and rows of numbers printed in neat Japanese script. Recalling Satsuki's mention of her father's ledgers, Daidai transferred them to her bag, intending to have her mother translate them into English.

Satisfied that there was nothing more to see, Daidai sat back on the bed, imagining what it would be like to occupy the room. It was a stage set, really, used to create the semblance of life, but unlived in. She felt betrayed to know that Satsuki had rented a room at Leonard's this entire time, but who was deceiving whom? She'd entered in the middle of the night to search for evidence, but what had Satsuki come looking for? What was *she* looking for? Arching her back, elbows straightened, palms downturned on the bedspread, she craned her neck and felt the blood flow to the back of her head. There'd been so many things never intended for her viewing: Ritsuko's painting, locked in the room Satsuki had described as Ichiro's inner sanctum; Hattie Fujioka's collection of shell corsages; Satsuki's early life in Japan. Was it as simple as passing the closed doors, the way she'd done when she walked down the hall just now? Her mother had warned her to stay away from things not meant for her to see. Certain things remained hidden precisely because you weren't supposed to look at them. Was one supposed to go through life averting one's eyes as a matter of course?

But where protocol was concerned, even Mako would be able to see that right or wrong no longer mattered. The error was in the past. A serious crime had been committed, likely more than one. Even if she didn't yet understand what motivated Satsuki, she was aware that she was seated in the locus. She felt it not in Satsuki's belongings, but in the careful placement of each object, laid out for show. Nothing of personal value had been invested so that the space called no attention to itself, just like Satsuki herself.

Rising from the bed, Daidai turned reflexively to smooth the single ripple she'd left in the quilt before restacking the boxes and sliding the closet door shut. She hoped that Leonard would keep the middle-of-the-night visit a secret, but unable to think of a way to caution him without implicating him in her actions, she said nothing, following Louise out the door with only a wave in Leonard's direction.

44

By the time Daidai arrived back at the apartment it was nearly two in the morning. Despite how tired her body felt, her mind remained alert. Retreating to the bed, she thought about sleep, but imagined Hiroshi lying awake in his hospital bed. They'd so rarely spent the night apart. Now he lay surrounded by a staff of nurses rotating in and out to check on him, undoubtedly wishing for solitude while she craved his company to comfort her. Her happy times with Hiroshi had come to an end. Furthermore, she still had no idea where Satsuki had gone or what she was planning next.

Surprised to be able to sleep, she woke just before dawn and placed a call to the hospital, relieved to hear that Hiroshi had been moved out of the ICU. With plenty of time before visiting hours, she gathered the items he'd asked for and headed to her mother's. She hadn't told Mako about Hiroshi, and now that he appeared to be recovering she might not have told her at all had she not needed Mako's help translating the ledgers.

Surrounded by so many other solo drivers making their way over the hill, she recalled her morning commute, the drive she'd made every day for six years. Flipping through news stations, she listened for an update on TEPCO's containment process at the Daiichi nuclear plant. Two months into the all-out nuclear disaster, and workers still hadn't been able to get the cooling systems to function properly, yet the news coverage had ended. Life would not be returning to normal. Not with Hiroshi in the hospital and a baby on the way. Recovery would not be possible in this lifetime. Yet the world seemed to have given up.

Not wanting to startle Mako by ringing the doorbell so early in the morning, she picked up her cell and called from her driveway. Claiming to have been up for hours, Mako set to work preparing breakfast, pouring Daidai a glass of milk as she explained the events that had taken place in the last twenty-four hours.

"Why did you wait to tell me all this?" she asked once Daidai had caught up to the present.

"I didn't want you to worry," Daidai said, still trying to cover the gaps.

"That's my job—to worry," Mako scolded, her eyebrows twisted into a stern expression. "Why would you want to take that away from me?"

It seemed more likely that she was just trying to be nice, rewarding Daidai for giving her the news that she was finally pregnant. No one in her right mind would take anything away from the old woman if she could help it. Still, Daidai regretted the half-truths and gaps in the information she'd shared with her mother in the last months. Until Satsuki, there had been no space between them, no reason to withhold information, no reason to lie.

"Is Hiroshi going to be okay?" Mako asked, having gotten no response.

"Yes." Daidai mustered a wan smile. "I think so."

"After your father's death I had to recalibrate," Mako said, seeming to take pity on her daughter. "There's no point in dreading something that may or may not happen. You can't move on unless you can accept the facts, and as long as you're alive you have no choice but to move on."

"I need to take care of Hiroshi," Daidai said, not understanding.

"Right now you need to rest."

Why was Mako always right? Daidai let herself be led down the hall to the room she'd slept in as a child, the bed cluttered with theme pillows muted from too many washings. Closing her eyes dutifully, she held her nose against the strong smell of her mother's laundry soap and counted down from a thousand before returning to the kitchen, where she found the contents of her favorite cloth shoulder bag emptied onto the tabletop.

"What are you doing going through my things?" Daidai demanded, staring down at the set of keys, pocket toothbrush, pair of portable chopsticks, lipstick, pen bearing the museum logo, and cell phone, all piled neatly on top of the ledgers.

"Your bag had a stain. I threw it in the wash."

Realizing the pointlessness of trying to stop her, Daidai cleared away her belongings and cracked open the first ledger for Mako to see. Even without being able to read the pages, she could see the care that had been taken to produce such even rows and columns of fine script. Each lined sheet appeared like a work of art.

"This doesn't belong to you. Whose is it?" Mako peered down over Daidai's shoulder.

"It belonged to Satsuki's father. Can you tell me what it says?"

"Didn't you mention that her father was an art dealer? On the left are descriptions, and on the right charges, both billed and paid."

"An ordinary ledger, then?"

"Except for the notations written in the margins." Mako flipped through a couple of pages. "These notes weren't included in the original accounting."

"Satsuki took these ledgers from her father."

Daidai was glad Mako didn't say the obvious, that she'd then taken them from Satsuki. "Most of these names aren't Japanese. See here?" She pointed to entries written in Romaji, which designated the names as foreign. Still, aside from verifying the details of Ichiro's business that Daidai had already researched, the listings provided nothing new.

Daidai shut the first ledger and opened the second. "How about this one?"

Mako flipped through the pages, working in silence long enough for Daidai's attention to be drawn away by the patterns of light on the tabletop. The sun having just risen, the natural light from the window had begun to bleach the yellow haze cast by the overhead lamp, which hadn't yet been turned off. Next she expected her father to walk down the hall, kiss her on the top of the head, and take his seat across from her, the way he'd done every morning before eating his breakfast, eager to start each day. Now his place lay empty as Mako stood behind her, scrutinizing the pages of the ledger. "This one is personal. These must be Satsuki's expenses."

"What does it say?"

"He kept track of everything." Starting with the most current entry, she moved backward through the earlier ones, giving Daidai time to grow impatient. "Each page covers one month." She pointed at the date printed on the top right corner. "Everything is itemized: rent, food, gas, car insurance, clothing, makeup—everything."

"Huh, so Ichiro kept close tabs on his daughter."

"I'd say this is much more than that." She began reading down a list of expenses so long it made Daidai dizzy. "He was very generous. Why do you have this?"

Daidai stood accused, the recognition of having intruded on something private greater than it had been when she'd wandered into Ichiro's studio. "I took it when I was looking through Satsuki's things. I thought it might contain information that could help me figure things out."

Mako regarded her with the same disapproval Daidai had seen in Hiroshi's eyes. Turning back to the ledger, Daidai snapped the cover shut, ready to pack it away. The old binding crackled under her fingertips, sending up the musty smells of dried glue and parchment. "How old do you think this ledger is?" she asked, opening the cover back up to reexamine the first entry.

Japanese referenced the era according to the reigning emperor. She could never remember exactly how those dates translated to the Western calendar. Bending over her, Mako squinted at the numbers. "The first recorded date is S61 April 4," she said. "You were born in Showa 54, so that would make it twenty-three years old."

If Mako had calculated correctly, Ichiro had been keeping the ledger since Satsuki was seven. No wonder the binding had come loose. The fabric covering had buckled where the glue had dried. Daidai ran her finger along the crease where the pages attached to the spine, her eye catching on the furled edge of something hidden under the backing. Careful not to rip the fabric, she lifted a corner, surprised to find an old, pocket-sized photo that was unmistakably

Satsuki with a man behind her, whom Daidai guessed to be Ichiro. Satsuki couldn't have been older than five, her lips pressed closed over protruding   teeth, the gleam in her eyes promising untold mischief. Daidai had assumed the image to be a photo, but on closer inspection realized that what she held was a copy of a painting, worn around the edges from age and handling. Sliding her things off the table into one of the recyclable grocery bags Mako kept on hand, Daidai attempted an apology for not being able to wait for her bag to come out of the wash. "I'll come back tomorrow," she said, expecting Mako would need to be placated.

"Why tomorrow?"

"Maybe Hiroshi will be discharged by then. He and I can drive over together. If not, I can come without him." She had no idea what prompted her to make that promise, only that she no longer felt guilty about leaving.

Back in the car, Daidai noted that the clock on the dash read 8:47. It was still morning and she was headed back to the 405 to make her way into the Valley.

45

Back at the hospital Daidai found Hiroshi's bed unmade and empty. After being told at the nurses' station that he'd been taken down to radiology, she did what had become routine in hospitals during her father's prolonged illness: sat in the chair next to the bed to wait. She needed to find Satsuki, but not without first seeing Hiroshi, and maybe the down time was a good thing after little sleep the night before. As keyed up as she'd been leaving her mother's, pregnancy had drained her energy. She had no idea how much time had passed when she woke with a crick in her neck, not immediately recognizing where she was. Hiroshi faced her in a wheelchair, pushed by a male orderly who walked away with the chair even before Daidai had gotten Hiroshi back to his bed. He looked awful, in some ways worse than when she'd seen him the day before, drifting in and out of consciousness. Without his ready stance and self-assured grin, he was a long way from resembling his former self. "I've got no legs," he said by way of greeting as Daidai pulled the blanket up and adjusted the pillows behind his head. She'd never seen him that weak, unable even to stand unassisted.

"The nurse said the antinausea medication affects the balance," he said, downplaying his condition, not wanting his pregnant wife to worry.

"No driving for you," Daidai joked, unnerved, but bent on maintaining the levity he seemed to be searching for.

"Thanks for bringing my things." He was smiling even though she felt close to tears. "How are you holding up?"

"Tired. Fine." Ashamed, she might have added, that he'd felt the need to reassure her. "Don't worry about me. We need to take care of you."

"What time is it?"

The room, though decked out in fancy medical equipment, did not have a clock. Reaching into her back pocket, Daidai pulled out her cell phone, noting that the lunch hour had passed while she slept.

The display screen showed a message from Satsuki. Pressing the play button, she listened to Satsuki hanging up without leaving a message. When she called back, the phone went straight through to voice mail. "It's Daidai again," she said. "Call me back?"

"She came by this morning," Hiroshi said, watching his wife.

"What?" Her temples suddenly throbbing, Daidai put the phone back in her pocket and pressed her forehead against the bedrail.

"She seemed pretty stressed."

"Did she bring you anything?" she asked, focused on Hiroshi's face.

"Just the flowers."

How had she not seen them? Three orange gerberas in a Ball jar. Crossing the room to the nightstand, Daidai lifted the glass to eye level, sniffed the flowers, then turned the glass in a circle looking for clues before setting it down again.

"What are you doing?" Hiroshi tracked his wife's movement with his eyes. "She said she was sorry she missed you. She left a note."

Beneath the Ball jar, a sheet of paper folded over with her name printed in block letters. Inside, it said simply, *Sorry*.

"Why are you acting so strangely?" Hiroshi demanded.

"I think she tried to poison you, Hiroshi." Daidai sat back down, trying to sound calm.

"That's ridiculous, Daidai," Hiroshi said, but she wasn't listening. She had to restrain herself from reaching over to wipe away the bit of spittle that had collected on the side of his mouth. "First you think she has a thing for me, and now you think she's trying to kill me?"

Trying to appear confident, she kept her response short, knowing the last thing she wanted was to be perceived as irrational. "I need to talk with her. Did she say where she was going?"

"No. She didn't stay long. She asked where you were."

"What did you tell her?"

"I didn't know."

"So you're feeling better, then?" She smiled as she rose from the chair, feeling the need to leave the hospital as quickly as possible.

"I'm a lot better than I was yesterday."

Another look at Hiroshi revealed that his face was flushed. She hoped a red face wasn't a sign that his condition was worsening. "Can I bring you anything else?" Packing the note into her makeshift tote bag, she readied herself to leave.

"There are more papers in my office on campus."

Daidai felt sorry for him then, lying flushed in his hospital bed, trying to think how he could get himself back to work. She had no intention of going to his campus office in search of more work to bring him.

By the time she got back in the car the weather had turned. The sun, which had promised summerlike temperatures, lay hidden behind cloud cover bleeding light into the sky in a milky glow. The heat would come soon enough, but for the time being the air was still pleasantly cool. Taking a deep breath, Daidai sat back with her eyes closed, arms perched over the steering wheel, trying to recall the path Louise had taken to get to Leonard's. The interior of his house had planted itself sharply in her memory, but she had no recollection at all of what it looked like from the outside or the route Louise had taken to get there.

46

The black duffel was back in Hiroshi's office. Seeing it from the doorway, Daidai called out to Satsuki before making a sweep of the apartment, not wanting to be caught by surprise. Once she felt certain she was alone, she returned to the duffel.

She half expected to find it empty, flattened as it appeared. Unzipping it, she peered inside. The late-afternoon light streaming through the window exposed the contents against the black interior: a cord of rope wound and tied around the middle; beneath it, a textured metal gun with a rectangular barrel. Dropping the bag, Daidai reached for her phone, changing her mind once it was in her hand about whom she needed to call. The police would require more evidence than she could give them, but she still had Leonard's number, written on a scrap of paper, which she pulled from her front pocket. Punching it into the phone she shifted the contents of the duffel with her free hand, craning her neck to get a better look inside. At the bottom, pushed into the corner, a finger-sized flask of clear liquid.

"Hello?"

She recognized the muffled sound of Leonard's voice. "It's Daidai," she said, and before he could respond, "Is Satsuki there?"

"She's not here," he said, matching her brusqueness. "I honestly don't know where she is."

Still worried about wasting critical time, she ventured a more serious question. "Do you have any idea why she would have a gun in the bag she left here?"

"What type of gun is it?"

"The kind you shoot people with." Annoyed, she shifted the bag once again to get a better look, not having any idea about guns.

"Hold on," she heard him say. A series of footfalls trailed away from the phone, and Leonard returned moments later. "It might be my .22. I didn't give it to her, but it's missing."

Why did Leonard own a gun? Daidai thought to ask, but there wasn't time. "You can't think of where she might have gone?"

"No, I have no idea."

"Do you have my number on your phone?"

"Yes."

"Will you call me back if you see Satsuki or think of anything that might help me find her?"

"Of course."

Her next call would have been to the police had Satsuki not appeared in the doorframe just then. Hearing the deadbolt click into place, Daidai turned to look over her shoulder. She knew it was Satsuki, though her thoughts flashed to the reception where they'd met, dressed as she was in Daidai's orange-sherbet sundress. Daidai had worried about the suggestiveness of the dress's snug fit, but it practically hung off Satsuki, who appeared frailer than she'd been even two days earlier, shrunken into a child's body. Even stranger was her hair, which had lately looked so unkempt; but now its unnatural fullness suggesting a wig. Her eyes had been outlined with thick black liner, her lips accentuated in a bright shade of orange to match the dress. Tiptoeing into Hiroshi's study, she looked like someone playing dress-up in her mother's clothing, and Daidai recalled the afternoon she'd walked in to find Satsuki wearing her favorite cardigan.

Her benign smile called attention to her overlapping teeth. "Did I scare you?"

"Well, yes." Daidai focused her gaze on the costume and overdone makeup.

"Who were you talking to?"

"I was trying to find you." Aware that Satsuki was staring at the duffel, unzipped at her feet, Daidai slowed her breathing, grasping for the connection that Satsuki seemed to desire.

"You're angry with me."

"I'm a bit annoyed," Daidai said, attempting irony.

Walking closer to stand over her shoulder, Satsuki gazed down at the items on Hiroshi's desktop. "What are you doing with Leonard's phone number?" she demanded, startling Daidai with the directness of her question, and making it clear with her accusatory tone that Daidai was not the only angry one. After giving Daidai ample time to respond, she prompted her with an answer. "You've been to Leonard's."

"Yes," Daidai said, relieved that her revelation came from seeing Leonard's number rather than seeing Leonard.

"You know it was wrong to go through my personal things."

"I know," Daidai said, realizing that she'd guessed wrong. Her body was giving off a worrisome odor, and she hoped the nervous sweat beading along her hairline wouldn't be noticeable.

"You lied to Leonard," Satsuki said, lowering her voice so that it sounded like her father's. A man devoid of emotion, wasn't that what she'd called him? "You violated my trust in you, Daidai."

"I'm sorry." Daidai averted her eyes so as not to gawk. Satsuki's features had become exaggerated with excess makeup. But there was something else as well that Daidai didn't recognize.

"If you have more questions can you just ask me?" Her tone shifted once more, this time to remonstrance.

"I said I was sorry." Understanding that further apologies might only compromise her position, Daidai swiveled in her chair to face Satsuki.

"You still don't understand, do you?" Satsuki shot back, contempt creeping into her tone.

"That's not true. I think I do understand," Daidai lied, in an attempt to reassure Satsuki, to make her believe once more in their connection. "I'm sorry for what you've had to go through."

Satsuki squeezed her eyelids shut and pursed her lips. A tear leaked out of the corner of her eye and made a wet black trail down her cheek. "Don't think you can understand so easily!"

It had been a mistake to express her sympathy. Satsuki had created a facade because she needed it, and Daidai would have to put it back together. "You're right. I don't understand," she conceded, determined to sound confident. "But you must see that I've been trying."

Satsuki swiped her forearms across her cheekbones, streaking them with black, and closed her eyes. Seeing her chance, Daidai rose for the gun, but Satsuki pushed her over the desk chair and, before Daidai could regain her footing, grabbed the duffel and turned it upside down, leaving the rope, vial, and gun exposed on the carpet.

47

"Don't!" Satsuki warned Daidai, clutching the gun with an out-stretched hand as she righted herself. "It's loaded, and the stuff in the vial can kill you."

The objects laid out on the floor spoke plainly enough, but seeing them side by side, Daidai was less frightened by the rope, which looked similar to the one Ichiro had used to hang the painting, than the clear liquid, proof as to how Hiroshi had wound up in the hospital. "What are you doing?" she asked calmly, refusing to show how afraid she was of the gun. Able to see that the barrel wasn't pointed at her, she noted instead Satsuki's movement between her and the items she'd emptied from the duffel.

"I'm disappointed in you, Daidai." Satsuki's castigating tone amplified Daidai's fear. A sting radiated out from the backs of her eye sockets as if she'd been hit from inside. "You let me beat you to the gun." Seeming to sense her victory, Satsuki sat back on the couch with the barrel clamped between her knees.

"What would I do with a gun?" Daidai asked, believing that Satsuki didn't intend to use it—at least not yet. Anyone who'd take the trouble to buy a wig, line her eyes, and color her lips wanted an audience; and she hadn't yet made her point. But what point did she wanted to make? "I like your hair," she said, hoping

Satsuki would be flattered into believing she hadn't noticed the wig.

"Really?" Satsuki stroked a strand with her fingertips, letting Daidai know she was on the right track.

"Yes. And your makeup. It's very pretty. You should wear makeup more often."

Satsuki reached a trembling hand to her brow in a gesture that let Daidai know she wanted to be seen as attractive.

"Orange suits you," Daidai remarked, not sure how she was supposed to respond to seeing Satsuki in her favorite dress. "It looks better on you than it did on me."

"Do you think so?" Flattered to have the details of her appearance so closely observed, Satsuki had apparently forgotten the gun pointing down at the ground from her right hand.

"I do," Daidai said wryly. "Less so the accessory."

A chill flashed the length of Daidai's body, following the barrel's trajectory as Satsuki lifted her arm to emphasize that she was still the one in control.

Daidai prompted her to tell her story. "So why would you want to poison Hiroshi?"

Satsuki merely laughed. "Don't worry about Hiroshi. He'll be okay. The effects are readily counteracted. I can assure you that one more day without the antidote won't make a substantial difference in his prognosis. I expect that he'll make a full recovery."

Her fitful gestures were worrisome. She had laid the gun on her lap and was clenching her hands into tight fists then releasing them. Daidai wondered what could be the cause of such violent bodily tremors. The computer keyboard and Daidai's cell phone both lay inches from her fingertips, but it'd take only a second for Satsuki to engage the gun and shoot her. Aware that Daidai's gaze still rested on the gun balanced on her lap, Satsuki picked it up again.

"*Ano ne,*" Daidai said, noting that their breathing had synchronized. "There's something I've been needing to tell you."

"What?"

Daidai wanted to find out the name of the poison, but she focused her attention on Satsuki, knowing that the contents of the vial could easily be analyzed. "I think I know why you had to use poison on Hiroshi, and I don't blame you. I know you're fond of Hiroshi and me. Why else would you move in here and take such good care of us? I don't think we've expressed how grateful we are—how grateful I am—for all you've done for us."

"Really?"

"Yes. I mean that."

"Thank you," Satsuki said, and her shoulders relaxed.

"I don't think you wanted to harm Hiroshi. After all, we're in this thing together. The baby—you, me, Hiroshi. But it was too complicated, and you wanted to keep things simple. It's really much simpler with just you and me. You could see that Hiroshi was the odd man out, and you didn't want that for him."

Satsuki's lips curved slightly up, and Daidai tried to smile.

"I know you respect Hiroshi and wouldn't harm him unless you found it absolutely necessary to do so."

Satsuki nodded. Another tear leaked down her cheek and Daidai began to understand: Satsuki had curated her life into this moment, staged the emotions she wanted to feel.

"Don't cry." She crossed the room to sit beside Satsuki on the couch. "You'll ruin your makeup." She believed she'd gained the upper hand, but her confidence vanished as the gun rose quickly from Satsuki's lap.

"No! You sit there," she commanded, pointing to the desk chair.

Backing herself into the chair, Daidai tried to match her expression to Satsuki's. "I'm fine to sit," she said, needing to shake off her mounting fear. "But there's still something I don't understand." She was taking a risk, but felt she had to. Because while she'd guessed correctly about the twisted impulse that had led Satsuki to poison Hiroshi, she still didn't understand how she factored into Satsuki's plan. "Why would you want to harm me?" she asked, trying to modulate her pitch to sound both direct and polite. "I thought we were friends."

Satsuki nodded. "You stopped trusting me. I didn't know how to get you to trust me again," she murmured under her breath.

She was right. Daidai hadn't trusted her, but surely she could see the irony of their present situation. "I wanted to trust you, Satsuki." She watched Satsuki's face for her response while biting the inside of her cheek, wanting not to make a mistake. "Tell me why I should trust you."

"You betrayed me!"

Her heartbeat quickening, Daidai needed to find a way to reassure her. "I never betrayed you. You know that's untrue."

"You drove out to Holy Heart Monastery," she clarified. "You talked with the nuns there to find out about my mother's relationship with them. You believed I killed her."

Daidai nodded to show that she understood. The gun still lay barrel up in Satsuki's lap, but the fear she'd struck when she picked it up had abated and left in its place a strange pang of sympathy. "I don't think you meant to harm your mother," Daidai said gently. "I was trying to put together a story about her because I care about you. Of course I was curious to know what happened to her because her disappearance had such an impact on you. Tell me what happened."

Satsuki sighed. "I came to Los Angeles with the plan of going to the monastery, but something else happened instead that fall. I was very happy studying with Hiroshi, and I believed that you liked me, too. I should never have gone."

Daidai thought of Hiroshi then, and of the warm afternoon in December when Satsuki had come to the apartment and they'd all done their part to prepare a celebratory feast. The food set out on the table when the phone rang; the stockpot simmering on the stove. Hiroshi had admonished her not to press Satsuki for details. He'd said outright that she might not want to know.

"Japanese say that truth will eventually rise to the surface. I drove out to the monastery because I could," Satsuki told her, and Daidai began to see as she spoke, her own story unfolding alongside Satsuki's. "At first I told myself, *If I can't rent a car, I won't go*. Later I said the same thing about buying a gun. But it seems there's no end to what can be accomplished. Matters are rarely as complicated as they are made to seem."

It sounded simple, yet Daidai strained to understand what she was saying.

"In the end, we are not so different, my Daidai friend. In the end I went to Holy Heart because curiosity got the best of me."

Daidai nodded, needing her to continue.

"What is the other thing they say? *Minu ga hana:* things will never be as you imagine, so you're better off not seeing them. It's true, I think."

Was it true? What would Daidai have been better off not seeing?

"I went on a Friday," Satsuki said. "You were with Hiroshi that afternoon, trying to get pregnant. My mother happened to be working in the little shop—the one where they sell the big *ahn-pans*. She greeted me as a stranger, but I recognized her at once.

"When I told her who I was she refused to give me the explanation I'd come for. She was distracted, needing to get the shop cleaned up and closed promptly. But she agreed to see me again if I'd return in two weeks.

"What right did she have to put me off after what she'd done to me? I regretted having promised her I'd come back, because over the next week I couldn't concentrate on my studies. You were sweet to notice, saying I looked unwell."

Reaching both hands to the crown of her head, Satsuki shifted beneath the wig, causing it to become lopsided. It was difficult to look at her this way. "I cried when I imagined telling you about my wish to see my own mother dead. After thinking about it, I realized that the only way I could free myself from the horrible thoughts I'd been having was to shoot her. That's when I got the gun. I planned how it would happen. It would have been easy, really.

"But I should never have gone back. The next time I saw her she was more emotional. She cried and begged me to forgive her. I should have expected as much. She seemed so pathetic. Watching her break down, I thought about you and Hiroshi, and how things had just started to look up for me. I didn't want to spend my life in prison. Then the idea came to me that maybe I didn't have to shoot her."

A gasp rose from Daidai's throat, a deep sadness that escaped from her lungs as if her body already understood the scenario her mind couldn't yet fathom.

"I had no trouble with the gun, but I left it in my bag on the passenger seat, figuring I'd tell her what I'd come to say before deciding what to do. When I went back to the car, I took it out and held it on my lap. I even turned the safety off and ran my finger over the trigger. Believe me, the thought crossed my mind to use it on myself. But as I contemplated ending my own life, I noticed a white box lying empty on the floorboard. I'd eaten the candies, and the gun fit perfectly inside. So I carried it back into the shop that way."

Recalling the chocolates she'd bought and shared with Satsuki, Daidai visualized the empty box used to house the gun.

"She claimed to know nothing of what had happened to me after she left. I believed she was feigning ignorance. She could have found me at any time. Then it occurred to me that she'd simply not bothered to keep track. I'd ceased to exist for her in the years after she left Japan."

"I'm sorry." Daidai tried again to convey her sympathy, touched by Satsuki's words and her pained expression. "What she did to you wasn't right."

"I told her about—" Satsuki fell silent.

"Did you tell her about Shodai?" Daidai prompted her.

Satsuki held her fingers cupped over her mouth and nodded. "I had never spoken of my childhood to anyone. But I told her what it was like. I felt that she had to know."

Satsuki winced, her shoulders breaking as she bent her head, yet she still fingered the gun.

"Did you tell her about the business your father was running, and the paintings?" Daidai asked.

Satsuki smiled without looking up. "Before I left I handed my mother the box. The right object will always become an obsession. My father's dealings in the art world illustrated that. You should know that, too," she scolded, giving Daidai a sideways glance before continuing. "I knew as well as she that once the gun had been placed in her hands she would have no choice but to use it. The seed had been planted; it was only a matter of time before it would grow."

A spasm contorted Satsuki's expression, indicating she was in considerable pain. Her hands twitched, and she placed them on her lap, palms down over the gun, to steady them. Her pallor, along with the ruts and deep striations in her nails, shifted Daidai's concern from what had happened to Satsuki's mother to what was happening to her, and in that moment Daidai could see how Satsuki intended the scenario to play out. "You're a very powerful person, I see that now." She needed to do what she could to reorient Satsuki's thinking.

Satsuki stared back at her blankly. "Why would you say that?"

"You're more powerful than I am. You were always the one in control." Satsuki smiled, ready to deny it was true, but Daidai cut her off before she could respond. "Do you remember telling me about your theory, that people are born into boxes?"

Satsuki nodded.

"You can't bear the guilt, can you?"

She winced again and averted her eyes.

"You wanted your parents dead because your life had been ruined. But you couldn't see that when their lives were over yours would be, too."

"He didn't deserve to live!" Satsuki said.

"I saw his ledgers," Daidai interrupted. "I know he kept track of every yen you spent."

"He was a monster."

"I understand." Daidai still hoped to project an alternate version of the relationship Ichiro had with his daughter. "But do you think he kept track to spite you?"

Black patches appeared above her cheekbones where she rubbed her eyes. "Keeping track was his obsession."

"I think he loved you." Relieved to have voiced her conclusion, Daidai continued. "I went to Leonard's. And I took the ledgers to my mother to translate because I couldn't read them myself. I saw the accounting he kept. If your father didn't care about you, why would he have kept such detailed records?"

A gurgling noise came up from Satsuki's throat. Daidai couldn't tell if she was laughing or choking. "My father didn't love me."

"Why would he spend so much money on you, then?" Daidai asked flatly, knowing Satsuki's monthly allowance amounted to far more than Hiroshi's and her expenditures combined.

"It was his way of controlling me."

"I don't think that's all of it," Daidai said, trying to string her along, to figure out what she knew.

"What are you talking about?"

It was as she'd thought. Satsuki had taken the ledger her father had used for her expenses, but shame had prevented her from looking inside to examine the contents. "Let me show you something." Moving slowly, not wanting to scare her, Daidai removed Ichiro's ledgers from her makeshift tote bag and placed them on her lap, opening the front cover of the one he'd kept on her. Gently lifting the inside fabric, she pulled the faded photograph out by its frayed edge, holding it by one corner, and extended her arm toward Satsuki.

"What is this?" Satsuki's hand trembled as she reached for the photo.

"Isn't that you?"

Holding the photo close to her chin to examine it, she began to sob. "It's of a painting my mother made."

Daidai watched recognition unfold in Satsuki's hands. The image Ichiro had kept with him all those years: her in a schoolgirl uniform with him standing in shadow behind her; the gleeful child's innocence that had inspired her father's dealings in the art world and led to the dissolution of his marriage; his wife, unable to take part in her husband's corruption, running off, leaving Satsuki. Her hands, which had gone still, started up their trembling again. "It's too late." She held the frayed paper image out so that Daidai could take it back.

"What do you mean?" Daidai returned the photo to the hiding place where it had been kept so many years.

"A girl in Numazu used thallium to poison her mother. I learned the technique from her. It has the advantage of being odorless and tasteless, so I mixed it into my tea. Taken in small doses, it causes excruciating symptoms, but small doses are not lethal. I could have stopped, but not now. It's too late now."

"So you've poisoned yourself, too?" Daidai asked, stunned by this disclosure: Satsuki had nothing to lose by killing her. The tremor that had started at the back of Daidai's neck now caused her teeth to chatter. Clenching her jaw, she willed her body not to betray her. "Why would you want to hurt yourself?"

"That's right." Satsuki looked like someone Daidai didn't recognize. "You understand what's happening now, don't you?"

Daidai forced her jaw to relax, her thoughts traveling backward for answers. The night the call came with the news that Satsuki's mother had been found dead. She'd replayed that scene again and again, and now looked past the doorway, through the white peonies standing tall in their glass vase, to the spot where Satsuki had sat with Hiroshi bent over her. "The night the police called. Hiroshi rushed over to you. I can still see him hunched over you, trying to comfort you."

Satsuki smiled. "I had a glimpse of the future that night. Have you ever glimpsed the future, known for certain something you couldn't have known?"

Daidai didn't respond, but she nodded, understanding Satsuki's reference to the part of them that was the same.

"I knew the moment you stopped trusting me." Her voice grew soft. "I didn't blame you, but I doubted you'd ever trust me again." She pulled the gun up from between her knees, and Daidai felt her face blanch as Satsuki pointed the barrel at her head.

"You were suspicious of me because of Hiroshi, worried that your marriage might be wrecked because of me. It never occurred to you to think of the effect your marriage had on me."

A shudder ran the length of Daidai's spine. She cleared her throat to stifle the sound of something broken escaping from between her teeth.

"I tried to show you a good time in Japan, but the earthquake and visit with my father changed everything. After Japan, you were determined to return to your life with Hiroshi, without me."

Through the doorframe the white peonies caught the last of the afternoon sunlight. "I'm sorry, Satsuki," she said, knowing her apology was not enough. Aware of her own shuddering, Daidai drew in a deep breath, letting the air out of her lungs through pursed lips before attempting to respond. But instead of speaking, she watched the tears drain down Satsuki's cheeks, falling from her chin into her own lap. In a provocative gesture, still holding the gun in one hand, she pulled off the wig. Large patches of baldness streaked her scalp where before her long hair had merely appeared to be thinning.

Daidai's fear returned with a gasp. Satsuki pressed her knuckles into her eye sockets as if to stanch her tears, causing blackness from her mascara to flow in rivulets down her cheeks as she steadied the gun with her free hand. "You could have prevented all this."

Daidai knew even before Satsuki had spoken that she was right. She saw through the tears. It was not abject misery itself, but the wretchedness of what she needed Daidai to see: tears blackening the orange fabric of her dress, lipstick smears and streaks of baldness that caused her to avert her eyes. Daidai looked Satsuki in the eye, the way she sensed Satsuki needed her to do. But then she turned away, and glancing up then, and seeing Satsuki's gaze fixed on her, she knew she'd made a mistake.

48

The sun was setting quickly, a beam of light through the high window casting a glow like embers over the gun. "I was the one keeping your marriage together," she said. "What did you think Hiroshi and I were doing together all those afternoons we stayed late on campus?"

Afraid to hear the answer, Daidai put her hands over her ears. But her response only proved Satsuki's point. "I was giving him what he needed," she said, and smiled.

"What were you doing?" Daidai spoke through clenched teeth, attempting to slow her breathing.

"You could never be the Japanese woman he needed in a wife. He needed something more than you could give him. But I took care of that."

"You didn't do it for me." Daidai launched herself from Hiroshi's desk chair, bringing Satsuki down beneath her weight. Inches away, the whites of Satsuki's eyes contrasted against her dark pupils like an absurdist painting, and Daidai felt herself being drawn in. She could feel the gun barrel against her skull as Satsuki pressed her mouth against hers.

"That's right." Satsuki pulled her back by the hair, her teeth gritted. "You're finally free to do what you want."

Daidai wiped her mouth across Satsuki's shoulder, and Satsuki pushed her away, backing herself onto the couch, breathing hard, the gun barrel pointed squarely at Daidai's forehead.

"It's just as your mother said," she spat through the strands of hair that clung to her cheek, hiding her face. "You are so naive."

"Shut up!" Daidai demanded, curling her thighs against her chest.

"You're the one who couldn't see. You believed there was something between Hiroshi and me because I look the way you wanted to see yourself."

"I don't know what you're talking about."

"So naive! Hiroshi loves Hiroshi. He isn't capable of loving you or me."

But Daidai's thoughts were no longer focused on Hiroshi. "You're hardly one to talk. What about Kenji? Was it satisfying to get away with that?"

"Kenji drowned," she said in a monotone, the fading sunlight replacing her distorted features with a blackened shadow image on the couch. "Read the reports."

"I did."

"Spoiled, so selfish," Satsuki hissed. A chill ran up Daidai's spine and through her limbs in a twinge of lightness that threatened to overtake her, and Satsuki's whisper filled the available air space. "The school hosted a memorial for him. His parents came. It hurt me to see his mother. Her son never appreciated how much she loved him."

"You killed him," Daidai said.

"All this, it's your fault. Can't you see?" Satsuki thrust the gun out accusingly, like a pointed finger. "She loved him."

She loved him. Instead of Kenji, Daidai saw Hiroshi, lying prone in his hospital bed, the slow, even cadence of his breath. Hiroshi, wobbling as she moved him from the wheelchair back to his bed. "You didn't feel bad for Kenji's mother," she told Satsuki, "and your feelings for Kenji were misplaced. You envied him, and you hated his mother. That's why you killed him, isn't it? You don't know the difference between love and envy. You wanted to be me. You wanted my life."

"You used me," Satsuki said accusingly, the strength gone from her voice.

"How could you say that?"

"You only saw what you wanted to see. My father never loved me. He only kept track of what he owed me. My relationship with him was a business transaction. You took the ledgers. Couldn't you see that? My expenses weighed against what he considered my share of the profit he made from the sittings."

An image took shape deep inside Daidai's head: a child's face and body juxtaposed beside the paintings she'd seen in Ichiro's studio. Seated across from her, Satsuki lowered the barrel, aiming for Daidai's chest with both hands, her eyes locked on the middle distance between them.

"I wanted to be with you. Why couldn't you see that?"

Daidai could see Satsuki's hands trembling the way her own hand had when she'd forced Satsuki to the ground. She hadn't seen, but she saw it then, with the last of the sunlight casting its pulse across everything touched by light. She'd pulled away from the life that had been set in place before Satsuki, and all the while Satsuki's life had been slipping away bit by bit. She'd seen the effects of thallium poisoning. She'd been right there as Satsuki had ingested the poison. She saw the years she'd spent curating, assembling experiences that were not her own into story, trying to fit herself into a frame where her image didn't exist.

"That's right." Satsuki steadied the barrel, her eyes locked on Daidai's. A loud thump turned Daidai's attention to the front door. From the other side her name being called, muffled at first, then Gizo standing in the light cascading through the doorframe, having managed somehow to force his way through the locked door. Turning from him, Daidai saw Satsuki's teeth gleaming in the darkness. She pointed the gun at herself. Her head jumped loudly, and her body thudded to the ground.

Falling to her knees, Daidai took her in her arms, the length of Satsuki's arm and neck pressed against her chest. The bullet had entered through her face, leaving a hole where the blood drained into Daidai's hand as she tried to stanch it. The damage was barely visible from the outside. She rubbed her finger along the stubborn set of Satsuki's jaw until it relaxed. Her mouth dropped open to expose her bloodied teeth, and the bitter smell of her final exhale brushed against Daidai's cheek. She looked like a child waiting to be fed.

49

From her spot on the beige carpet, her hands suffused in Satsuki's blood, Daidai waited for what she imagined was inevitable. Her teeth were chattering so violently that Gizo didn't seem to understand when she asked where he'd come from. She still didn't understand when he said that Leonard had called him. Turning to the couch, Gizo reached for the blanket Satsuki had used to sleep and draped it over Daidai's shoulders. He'd called the police, he said. They'd want to question her, but he'd take care of it.

Daidai would not have resisted had the police tried to arrest her on the spot. She was surprised to hear Gizo tell them she was pregnant. She knew he was using whatever he could to keep them away, his tone familiar and confident. When their conversation ended, with Daidai mute on the floor, the uniformed officer asked her, very gently and politely, if she'd be able to return with her to the station to make a statement, which, of course, she did.

The police had surprisingly few questions. It was not difficult to answer them, nor for them to accept a version of reality that would stand on the official document she signed: Satsuki Suzuki, same last name but no relation to Daidai, had come to Los Angeles to study in the graduate program directed by Daidai's husband, Hiroshi Hamada. Ichiro Suzuki, her father, had died in the aftermath of the Tohoku earthquake, and Satsuki was staying in the apartment with

Hiroshi and Daidai until her father's estate could be settled. During that time, Satsuki developed a crush on Hiroshi, but when Daidai became pregnant and Satsuki realized the futility of her future, she poisoned Hiroshi and threatened Daidai with the gun she'd used to kill herself.

As Daidai made her statement, she kept seeing Satsuki. She was standing under the gnarled bough of a plum tree laden with blossoms and she was smiling.

Gizo waited at the police precinct for her. She was released to his care.

"Thank you," she told him once they were in the car, having no words to further express her gratitude to him for arriving when he did.

"You don't need to thank me, Daidai." He didn't take his eyes off the road as he pulled into traffic, but he took his hand from the steering wheel and brushed it along the outside of her thigh. "You're a smart woman. I don't need to tell you that. But I can tell you one thing: don't let yourself feel too guilty. She forced you into a position. She did it to herself. You're pregnant. That's all you have to think about now."

Staring ahead at the lit up road, Daidai wondered about the lives of all the people whose paths would never cross hers, out on the street so late at night. She hadn't told the police what more she knew: that Satsuki had poisoned Kenji; that she'd staged her parents' deaths as well. As the car made its way along the familiar streets, Daidai had a sense that she was glimpsing Satsuki in a way that wouldn't be possible the next day or in the daylight; Satsuki's life opened as she made her way from the world of the living to the world of the dead, and Daidai saw the dark impulse that had acted upon her.

"It's my fault, Gizo."

Observing the road ahead as he waited for the light to turn, Daidai noted the absence of emotion in her voice. "I know what you're thinking," he said softly.

"I don't think—"

Gizo put his finger over her lips. "You're gonna go over this in your head for a long time. There's no way around that. It just means you're human. I'm here for you, Daidai, and I'm not going to tell you what to think, but in the end, the only way to live with yourself is if you agree with me."

He turned to look at her in a way that made her think he could be believed, causing Daidai to wonder if maybe people weren't all just mirrors, holding reflections up for each other. Cars began passing to the left, but Gizo kept his eyes fixed on Daidai until he was done talking. Then he took his foot off the brake and the car eased its way back into the flow of traffic that led to the freeway.

With the police still at the apartment conducting their part of the investigation, he drove her to her mother's, where the night would finally end.

EPILOGUE
THINK OF ME

The vial in Satsuki's duffel was used to verify thallium poisoning; it was just as she'd said. The antidote was administered that same night. Hiroshi, who lay in the hospital oblivious to all that had gone on, was ready to be discharged the next day. After picking him up, Daidai drove with him back to her mother's, remembering the promise she'd made Mako to bring him for dinner as soon as he was out. Seated next to her mother and across from her husband, Daidai tried to explain what had happened in a way that would make sense to them both. Hiroshi's stint in the hospital had left him pale, but what little color there was drained out of his face when he heard that Satsuki was dead. His eyes teared up, and Daidai felt sorry for him, for his loss. He would recover without permanent damage to his nervous system, though weeks later clumps of his hair began to fall out in yet another assault on his vanity.

Louise called later that month to say she'd heard that the investigation into Ritsuko Suzuki's death had officially been closed: the record would stand as suicide. Apparently, Ritsuko had never changed her citizenship and the LAPD wasn't anxious to get involved in a death involving a Japanese national.

With a little research, Daidai was able to track down the executor of Ichiro's estate, an elderly man by the name of Yuichi Hirano.

For several months she'd worried that without the appropriate gesture Satsuki would just disappear. Where immediately after her death Daidai thought she might be forever haunted by what had happened, Satsuki's presence had slowly begun to dissipate, and somehow that felt worse than not being able to stop thinking about her. Daidai got in touch with a California-based agency that coordinated relief efforts in Japan, wanting to make a donation in Satsuki's name, only to discover that a legacy fund had already been established. When she told Hirano she'd stayed with Satsuki at her father's home, just prior to his death, he explained how the proceeds from Ichiro's estate had been divided. At Satsuki's request, a sum had been set aside as aid for victims needing to move away from the area contaminated by nuclear fallout. The remaining amount had been distributed in generous checks to the women whose names appeared on her father's payroll.

For Daidai, there was no turning back from what she'd seen, but she also felt that she'd never really seen herself. As Satsuki put it, no one really knows what her own box looks like. Satsuki had understood her need to contain things. She put things in boxes, on display, narrated stories the way she wanted them understood. But Hattie Fujioka had been right, too. Daidai finally understood what she was saying when she destroyed the shell brooches: the boxes are made, not given, and they can be refused.

Daidai's baby was born nearly two weeks late, the Friday before Christmas. She worried that his life had gotten off to a bad start—how could he not have been affected by all that had gone wrong when she was pregnant with him? Mako warned her not to worry about the past, urging her instead to plan for the future, though Daidai didn't yet know what that meant.

She'd given up her work life for a baby who fussed most nights. What she offered him, he didn't want; he wanted something, just not what she had to offer. In those early days of motherhood, she recalled Satsuki when he shook his fists at her, his constant unspoken demands, and all that she'd never thought of, insisting, *Think of me.*

ACKNOWLEDGMENTS

Many thanks to Julie Mars, Nikki Nojima Louis, Virginia Nicholson, Carmela Starace, Michael Noltemeyer, Felipe Gonzales, Mark Peceny, Gail Houston, and the students in the University of New Mexico's MFA program who worked alongside me through the writing of this novel. As well, I am grateful to my daughter Kiyomi whose contribution to early drafts made me a better writer, my agent, Laurie Liss, without whose patience and extraordinary dedication this work would not have found a home, and to my editor, Olivia Taylor Smith, who honed my vision with her fresh perspective and incisive eye.

ABOUT THE AUTHOR

Julie Shigekuni is the author of four novels. Shigekuni was a finalist for the Barnes and Noble Discover Great New Writers Award and the recipient of the PEN Oakland Josephine Miles Award for Excellence in Literature. She teaches in the creative writing program at the University of New Mexico.

ALSO BY JULIE SHIGEKUNI:

A Bridge Between Us

Invisible Gardens

Unending Nora